Catch a Fallen Angel

KATHLEEN KANE

St. Martin's Paperbacks

Acclaimed, award-winning author of
Wish Upon a Cowboy and *Simply Magic*

KATHLEEN KANE

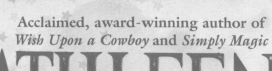

Catch a Fallen Angel

Would he be
her destiny—or
her downfall?

ST. MARTIN'S
PAPERBACKS

U.S. $5.99
CAN. $7.99

READ THESE OTHER DELIGHTFUL
NOVELS BY KATHLEEN KANE

WISH UPON A COWBOY

SIMPLY MAGIC

DREAMWEAVER

THIS TIME FOR KEEPS

STILL CLOSE TO HEAVEN

THE SOUL COLLECTOR

AVAILABLE FROM ST. MARTIN'S
PAPERBACKS

ISBN 0-312-97575-9

9 780312 975753

50599

EAN

"Ms. Kane tickles your funny bone and waves her magic wand to ensure a good time is had by all. Missed spells and thunderstorms whet your imagination. As Ms. Kane reminds us, 'Witchcraft is not important . . . Love is the greatest power in the universe.' Bravo!" —*Rendezvous*

"Kane blends folk legend and magic into a charming . . . plot."
—*Publishers Weekly*

SIMPLY MAGIC

"This historical romance by Ms. Kane is magic itself, with a wonderful blend of danger, love and otherworldly magic. It is simply a must-read!" —*Old Book Barn Gazette*

"If you want to feel that tingle down to your toes, then rush out to get yourself a copy of *Simply Magic*."
—*Romantic Times*

"Have you ever wanted to hug a book just because it made you feel good? *Simply Magic* is simply wonderful. Kane gifts her readers with stories that live long in the memory, and uplift the heart." —*Affaire de Coeur*

"Anyone who's read a Kathleen Kane novel knows that they are in for a thoroughly entertaining experience. *Simply Magic* employs the trademark blend of the supernatural with a western romance in a humorous but poignant storyline. As with all her superb novels, Kane has succeeded once again with creating a necessary read for romance fans." —*Painted Rock Reviews*

DREAMWEAVER

"Kane incorporates tender and fantastic touches . . . true to her talent, Kane keeps the conflicts lively to the end and fills the plot with many surprises." —*Publishers Weekly*

"The innovative Kathleen Kane gifts readers, once again, with a beautiful paranormal love story. *Dreamweaver* will warm your heart and leave you with a smile."

—*Romantic Times*

"Ms. Kane just gets better and better with each one of her books."

—*Interludes*

THIS TIME FOR KEEPS

"If you like your heroes tall, dark and sexy, and if laughter is your aphrodisiac, then rush to your nearest bookstore."

—*Telegraph Herald*

"Wondrous romance that will leave you longing for more. Ms. Kane's extraordinary talents shine." —*Romantic Times*

"A lively plot of all-out seduction with Kane's witty dialogue and fine portrayal of the headstrong, hot-to-trot heroine and the equally stubborn cowboy." —*Publishers Weekly*

"Peppered liberally with intrigue and humor . . . A wonderful story that everyone is sure to enjoy!"

—*Old Book Barn Gazette*

"Ms. Kane takes you on a fun-filled merry chase through history, bringing this reader to laughter and tears. Don't miss this one!" —*Bell, Book and Candle* (five bells)

"Kane has fashioned a likable heroine . . . and a fast-paced plot . . . all with a gently humorous touch."

—*Library Journal*

To my niece, Maegan Carberry. From Papa Smurf and "Worry, worry, worry," straight up through U.C.L.A., you've been a great kid. Keep it up, Mae. The best is still out there, just waiting for you.

Catch a Fallen Angel

CHAPTER ONE

Gabe Donovan felt the noose tightening around his neck and he swallowed hard in reflex.

"String 'im up!" An upright, respectable townsman had a wild look in his eyes that offered no comfort to the subject of his brief speech.

"Hell, a bullet's cheaper'n a rope!" another voice called out from somewhere in the back of the small group of outraged citizens.

Gabe didn't know whether to be admiring of the man's thriftiness or insulted to think he wasn't worth the cost of a mangy rope.

But when it came right down to it, he supposed it didn't matter. Hell, he'd always expected to end up this way . . . surrounded by God-fearing Christians with a thirst for quick justice. He just hadn't expected the day to arrive so quickly.

He was only thirty-two. There were plenty of poker hands to be dealt and miles of country still to be seen. Yet here he was, about to breathe his last, at the hands of a bunch of yokels. A cold autumn wind shot down from the mountains and shook loose a handful of coppery-colored leaves from the ancient cottonwood they were gathered beneath. And it suddenly hit him how much he'd like to see another winter.

Hell. Another *day*.

Someone slugged him upside the head and Gabe staggered before falling to his knees. Since his hands were tied behind his back, he guessed he was lucky he hadn't landed on his face.

A sharp-edged rock lying hidden in the tall, dry grasses stabbed at his right knee and had Gabe telling himself there was no reason to go adding insult to injury. If they were going to kill him, then by God, be done with it.

But wasn't that just the way with townsmen? Always yammering on about one thing or another when they should be doing something. The ropes around Gabe's wrists chafed at his skin and the urge to jump on his horse and beat a hasty retreat chafed at his soul. But there was no chance of that. This little posse had him good and cornered. The fact that for the first time in his life, he was innocent of the crime charged, held small consolation, considering his predicament.

"A rope is what's fittin'," the first man bellowed, grabbing Gabe's attention. "And we're here to do what's fittin'."

Of course. Wouldn't want to go home with tales of a simple shooting when your audience was expecting ghoulish stories about a man slowly strangling to death. Gabe just managed to suppress a shudder at the mental image of himself swaying at the end of a too short rope.

Damn, but hanging was no way for any man—let alone *him*—to end his days.

"Toss that hemp across the branch yonder," the first man shouted to someone Gabe didn't bother to glance at. "Then we'll pull him up and tie it off around the trunk."

He groaned quietly. A hanging it was, then, Gabe thought. And not a nice, quick, neat one, either, where he was dropped from the saddle of a spooked horse. There'd be no chance of a broken neck hurrying his death. Nope, he'd be pulled up by hand and left to linger and gasp frantically—futilely—for air.

Biting back the sharp, acrid taste of fear, he struggled awkwardly to his feet. If he was going to hang, then he'd by damn meet it standing up. He wouldn't give these righteous citizens the satisfaction of dragging him off his knees.

He shook a hank of dark brown hair out of his eyes as one of the men slipped the noose around his neck. The rough, prickly feel of the rope against his skin sent a surge of panic through him that Gabe had to battle down. Every nerve in his body was alert. Every muscle screamed at him to run. All he needed was a second or two to climb into the saddle and that horse of his could outpace any other. He'd always insisted on a fast mount. In his business, it paid to take care of your horse.

But there was nowhere to go now and he knew it.

Shifting his gaze from one face to the next, he looked in turn at each of his executioners. Not a remarkable one in the bunch. Every last one of them had the unmistakable look of a "mark." Easy targets for a bottom deal or a fast-talking con, they were the stuff that made men like him. After all, professional thieves, card sharps, and cons needed victims. He'd made his living for years by being able to read just such faces as these. What he read in the eyes glaring at him now, though, was enough to give him another chill.

And he was somehow sure that hanging a man on a Friday wouldn't keep any of them out of church come Sunday. In fact, they'd probably congratulate each other all the way home for sending a sinner on toward judgment.

Well, that was fine for them, but Gabe didn't fancy himself their kind of hypocrite. He didn't figure on standing before some gray-bearded Saint Peter trying to con his way through the Pearly Gates. Actually, he was pretty confident that Heaven didn't exist. But he knew for damn sure that Hell did. Living his too short life as a gambler, Gabe had seen way more evidence of the Devil than he had of some benevolent God.

And once his actual *dying* was finished, he had no doubt at all that he'd be running into old friends and enemies dealing games in the flames of Hell.

"It's only proper," the leader was saying, "that we give the condemned a chance to speak his piece." As the other men quieted and turned to look at Gabe, the man asked, "So? You got somethin' to say before we get on with this?"

Oh, Gabe thought, he had plenty to say, but none of it to these men. He wanted to whisper pretty words in the ears of a willing woman again. He wanted to sing along to a well-played piano. He wanted to utter the magic words "full house, aces high" one more time, as he dragged a pile of chips toward him. Yep. There was lots he had to say, now that he'd run out of time.

But what he settled for was, "Mister, get on with it. If I've got some dying to do, I don't fancy standing around here talking about it with you."

The big, balding man half sneered at him. "I reckon

you won't be talkin' so high-and-mighty once that rope tightens up some."

Another chill rippled through him, but Gabe wouldn't let them know it. "I'm hoping I won't be able to hear, either."

Someone laughed and the big man puffed up like an overfed rooster. "You talk smart-mouthed enough, but it's clear you ain't as smart as you think, else you wouldn't have got caught, huh?"

Caught? Hell, he'd been escaping posses for years. Would have this one too, if he'd been expecting it. Not hard at all to catch a man when he doesn't know he should be running. He would have said so too, except that he took a step toward the big man and his words were choked off by the tightening of the noose around his neck.

In the sudden silence that followed, the townsman said flatly, "You come into town, lookin' for the man what took our money in the first place . . ."

Henry.

A cold, hard knot of anger wormed its way past the panic swirling in his stomach. This was all Henry Whittaker's fault. The old fool had run a con and hadn't bothered to let Gabe in on it. Then when Gabe had shown up to meet Henry, the whole damned town had jumped on him, demanding to know where their money—or the contract they'd tried to buy with the railroad—was.

Of course, Henry'd taken the money. He had no connections with the railroad. But over the years, he'd sold countless phony contracts to towns eager to grow by becoming railheads. Then Henry would disappear with the cash and the town would settle down with the shame of knowing they'd been hoodwinked. Naturally, when

Gabe had shown up in Red Dog, asking about Henry, the townsfolk had assumed that he was Henry's partner.

Now, Gabe would be wearing the rope meant for Henry.

"Since we can't hang him, we'll settle for his partner," the man was saying.

By damn, when Henry finally did earn his way into Hell, Gabe was going to have plenty to say to the old liar.

"All right," the big man snapped suddenly. "Enough talkin'. Let's get this done. Esther's got pot roast cookin' and I don't want to be late for supper."

Gabe's stomach growled and he cursed silently. Not only was he dying, he was dying hungry.

"I don't know . . ." a lone, dissenting voice whined from off to one side and Gabe felt a flicker of hope before it was doused by the man in charge.

"You hush up, George, and do what you're told."

A couple of the others nodded, and when the big man gave a nod, Gabe braced himself for what was to come.

"All right, boys, pull 'im up."

They did and as the rope tightened, tearing into his flesh with tiny, aggressive bites, Gabe went up on his toes, even knowing it was hopeless. He moved with the rope, and wished he could grab at it. But his hands were still tied and all he could do was whisper goodbye to the ground as the rope steadily pulled him off his feet.

A roaring in his ears muffled the sounds made by his executioners. His throat tightened and his chest felt as though it were being squeezed by iron bands. The last breath he'd drawn was trapped in his lungs and Gabe half expected his chest to explode with the building pressure. His vision clouded, gray creeping in at the edges. His head fell forward and he watched the well-polished toes of his boots swivel slowly in the wind. Only inches from the ground. A few miserable inches and he would die.

From the corner of his narrowing vision, he saw the group of men mount and ride away. Apparently, church-goers had a hard time actually *witnessing* the executions they performed. Something inside him laughed at the absurdity of it all.

Gabriel Donovan bested by a handful of sodbusters and merchants.

He'd probably be laughed out of Hell.

Flashes of memory crossed his mind in a frenzied blur. Images, pictures of his life rose up and fell away in rapid succession. His mother. His father. The river-boat aboard which the elder Mr. Donovan had plied his trade and taught his son the intricacies of separating a mark from his money. Faces of people came and went. Acquaintances, enemies, no real friends. No real lovers either. Just a parade of temporary, willing women with whom Gabe had whiled away countless hours.

Not much to show for thirty-two years, he thought as the world grayed, muddied, and went black. And still he struggled to breathe, tears leaping to his eyes as pain gathered deep within him. Head pounding, heartbeat staggering, he felt a sudden hard, sharp wind buffet his body, slamming him into the trunk of the cottonwood. Every blood vessel in his head felt as if it were explod-ing. Over the roaring in his ears, he thought he heard a loud snap, but then his heart stopped and his world ended.

ONE HUNDRED MILES AWAY IN REGRET, NEVADA . . .

Maggie Benson clutched the battered tin coffeepot and chased after her last customer as he dashed from the restaurant.

But she couldn't catch him. He hit the edge of the boardwalk and sailed off as though a host of demons were hot on his heels. When he landed on Main Street, he kept running, gaining speed with every step.

"Well, beans and biscuits," she muttered as she watched him round the corner of the livery stable and duck out of sight. That was the fourth customer she'd lost that week. And all of them had gotten away without paying for their meals.

"He runs lots faster than the last fella."

"Yep," she said and turned to glance down at her son, Jake. At only six years old, he didn't miss much. "Yes, he does," she said and set the coffeepot down onto the porch railing.

"Did he forget to pay too?"

"I'm afraid so," she said and mentally counted up the money she'd actually managed to take in in the past week. It wasn't much. In fact, if her restaurant wasn't a scheduled stop on the stage route, she doubted she'd be able to stay in business at all. And she had to make this place a success. Jake needed—*deserved*—security. Just as he deserved the kind of mother who could manage to cook a meal without burning down the house. The kind of mother who didn't inspire gossip just because she was a little . . . different.

"You want me to try to catch him?" Jake asked, clearly wanting to help.

Maggie smiled and ruffled her son's hair. "No, but thanks for offering."

She looked down into his big brown eyes and told herself again that this move to town had been worth it. She wanted Jake to have a normal life . . . the kind she'd never had. All that was necessary to accomplish that was for her to fit in. Especially now that Jake was old enough to understand the talk about her, she had to silence the gossips by being an ordinary mother.

She sighed inwardly. But who would have guessed that being ordinary would be so difficult?

Her gaze slid slowly across the dusty main street of the town she'd known most of her life. Merchants sat in armchairs that blocked half of the boardwalk in front of their stores. Piano music drifted out of the nearby saloon and she absently noted the darn thing needed tuning again. A few horses were tied to the meandering line of hitching rails. From the end of the street came the sound of children playing.

She *would* fit in, she told herself firmly. She would become a part of this town if it killed her.

A heavy dray wagon rolled past her and sent dust flying into the air. Warm autumn sunshine fought against the chill wind blowing down from the mountains and lost.

Maggie shivered slightly and picked up the coffeepot again. Her gaze drifted to the shadowy purple mountains ringing the town. Gray clouds hovered at the peaks and looked as though they were gearing up to charge.

Storm coming, she thought and a ripple of unease rolled along her spine. But it wasn't the probable storm making the small hairs at the back of her neck stand straight up. It was something else. Something she couldn't quite put her finger on. It was almost as though she could *feel* change in the air.

"What's burning?" Jake asked suddenly.

Frowning slightly, Maggie dismissed the odd feelings, sniffed the air and half turned toward the restaurant. A telltale wisp of black smoke snaked out of the open kitchen doorway reaching for the dining room.

Gasping, "Beans and biscuits, the bread!" Maggie rushed toward her latest disaster, her son's laughter following after her.

When he opened his eyes, Gabe looked up and saw the jagged, broken edge of the cottonwood branch his killers had looped the rope across. He shook his head despite the pain and drew a long, deep breath into lungs that felt starved for nourishment. It was only then he noticed the noose was no longer around his neck and his wrists had been untied.

"What in the hell . . ."

"Exactly," a voice from close by said.

Gabe glanced to his right. A tall, shadowy column twisted in the wind and writhed like a drunk trying to get dressed in the dark. As he watched, the shadows thickened and gained shape. Slowly, that shape took the form of a tall man with black hair and eyes the color of an iced-over lake. Dressed like a gunfighter, the man wore black broadcloth pants, a dark blue shirt, and a tied-down Colt on his hip. His dust-colored hat was settled low on his forehead as if drawing attention to those icy eyes.

Now, a normal gunfighter didn't just appear out of shadows, so Gabe asked the only question that made sense. "Am I dead?"

The other man gave him a brief smile that would have looked more at home on a circling vulture. "Now what do you think?"

The fella expected him to *think*? After just being hanged? Gabe rubbed his aching throat and shifted his gaze to the countryside surrounding him. It was the same, and yet it was . . . different. It looked darker somehow, although the sun was still shining.

Frowning, he tried to put his finger on what had changed and he finally decided it looked as though he was staring at things through a filthy pane of glass—and, he thought uneasily, there seemed to be a sort of reddish tint. To everything. This didn't look good.

He turned to look at the gunfighter again. "So that damned posse actually killed me, huh?"

The man smiled again, and Gabe just managed not to wince. "Bound to happen sooner or later, don't you think?"

Hmm. Glancing at the broken branch lying beside him on the ground, Gabe said, "Y'know, I seem to remember hearing that branch snap. You sure I'm dead? That didn't break off in time to save me?"

"That sort of lucky thing only happens in books," the man told him. "And this is no book. I broke it when I got here."

Now that was too bad.

"Gabriel Donovan," the man went on and Gabe got a cold chill when he realized the stranger knew his name. "Named for an archangel," the man was saying with some amusement, "and yet you meet *me* when you die."

He chuckled and it sounded like flints scraped against each other. "Ironic, eh?"

Narrowing his eyes as he studied the fellow, Gabe muttered, "I guess that would depend on who you are, exactly."

The gunfighter gave him a slow, self-satisfied smile and asked, "Why don't you figure that out? You've already discovered that you're dead." He glanced around him at the emptiness. "And you don't see a band of angels anywhere, do you?"

No, he sure didn't. In fact, he'd never in his life felt more alone than he did at that moment.

"So if you're dead and you're not in Heaven . . ." He let his voice trail off and privately Gabe thought that was best. He didn't think he was ready just yet to hear the words spoken out loud.

After all, it wasn't every day a man met up with the Devil, face-to-face.

Not a breath of wind moved. The birds quieted and it was as if the whole world had been caught and gripped hard by a bloody fist. The shadows loomed closer, darker. The hair at the back of his neck stood straight up.

Gabe felt like that noose was back around his neck. His throat closed up and all the air left his body. Staring into those cold blue eyes could freeze a man's soul, he thought, just before he said, "You don't look like I expected you to."

The man gave him a half-bow in silent thanks. "I do try to move with the times."

"I'll bet."

"As a gambler, you probably would."

This was too strange. A minute or two ago, he'd been

strangling, filled with pain and regret. Now, there wasn't an ache in his body and he was apparently having a private conversation with Satan himself.

That shook him right down to his bones. It was one thing to go through life not really expecting Heaven. It was another entirely to actually die and meet up with Old Scratch. And damned if the demon didn't look like any other man. But then, evil'd be a lot easier to avoid if it came with horns and the smell of sulphur, wouldn't it?

"What were you hoping to see?" the Devil asked. "Horns? Tail? Hooves?"

He didn't think "hope" was the right word but, "Well, yeah."

"I can move among people more easily like this."

"Uh-huh." Pushing himself to his feet, Gabe stared at the other man for a long minute before asking, "So. Now what happens?"

"Now you listen to something I've got to say."

Gabe shook his head. "No preaching, thanks. I may have earned my way into Hell, but that doesn't mean I want to hear a list of my sins read back to me."

The Devil laughed. "Your list is fairly unremarkable and not very interesting reading."

"No call to be insulting," Gabe muttered.

"I'm here to offer you a deal," the gunfighter said, ignoring his comment entirely.

Gabe's ear perked right up. A deal? Well, why not? When you actually got around to thinking about it, the Devil had to be the father of *all* gambling. Still, it paid to be wary. "What kind of deal?"

"I'm willing to offer you two extra months of life."

He inhaled sharply. Life. Lord, that sounded good.

Especially to a man who'd just found himself with a one-way ticket to Hell.

But he wasn't fool enough to believe the Devil would go out of his way to do a good deed. There had to be a few strings attached to this proposition. "In exchange for what?"

"Simple, really." He shrugged. "Another soul."

Gabe sucked in a gulp of air and felt the mountain wind chill his insides. He reached up and rubbed one hand across his mouth, relishing the sting of his whiskers against his palm. The sensation reminded him of all things living. And suddenly, alive seemed more important than ever.

The Devil's eyebrows arched. "Is there a problem?"

If he said yes, that would be it. He'd be turning down this deal and he'd find himself in Hell faster than he could blink and it would all be over. There'd be no chance to say a decent goodbye to all the things he'd never really appreciated until now. When it was too late. But if he said no, then he'd have to agree with the Devil's plan and take someone with him when he went to Hell. It was one thing to take yourself off to the flames, but quite another to haul some other poor fool along with you. He might be a sinner in the eyes of anyone who mattered, but damn it, even he had some lines he wouldn't cross.

So rather than answering the question directly, he stalled. "Who is it you're sending me after?"

The Devil paused and Gabe held his breath.

"I want the man I was supposed to get today. Henry Whittaker."

Henry. Gabe's breath left him in a rush of pure anger. Back teeth grinding together, he clenched his hands into tight fists. Oh, the Devil knew just what he was about, all right. To get two extra months of life, all he had to do was hunt down the one man he dearly wanted to see burning in a pit of sulphur and brimstone.

And Gabe wanted those two months. Not just to hunt Henry down like the dog he was, but to enjoy breathing for just a bit longer. To look up at the mountains and feel the wind on his face. To lift a glass of good brandy. To bed a woman and feel the soft, sweet release sweep through him. To feel all the wonderful, irritating things he'd taken for granted for too many years.

"If your conscience"—the Devil said the word in a smirking tone—"is bothering you, you should know that Henry will be coming to me sooner or later, anyway."

"Oh, he's coming all right," Gabe assured him. "That old man has fleeced more sheep than a shepherd."

A fleeting smile curved the Devil's lips. "Then you accept my offer? Two months in exchange for your shall we say, *hurrying* Henry's soul to me?"

"I don't have to kill him myself, do I?" Sneaky bastard or not, Henry'd been a friend and Gabe didn't want to be the one to actually do him in.

"No. Just make sure he's where he's supposed to be at the agreed-on time."

"And where's that?"

The gunfighter smirked. "I'll let you know."

Sounded easy enough, Gabe thought. A tiny flicker of something . . . compassion, regret, pity . . . rose up inside him and was gone again in an instant. Henry'd made his choices. Just as Gabe had. It didn't really matter if the man met eternity in two months or twenty years.

Besides, Gabe reminded himself, Henry owed him at least this much for leaving him to the hangman.

"Your decision," the gunfighter snapped and Gabe felt the lash of his words slap at him.

Something his mother used to say suddenly leaped into his brain and he could almost hear her voice whispering, "If you lie down with dogs, sooner or later, you'll get fleas."

Well, he'd spent his life with the dogs. Some more flea bitten than others. For years, he'd told himself that he wasn't as bad as the rest of them and was much better than most. Yet here he stood on the brink of eternity and it seemed that, at last, the fleas had caught up to him.

"All right, Devil," Gabe said, lifting his chin slightly to meet the other man's gaze. "You've got yourself a deal."

Icy blue eyes stared at him for a long moment and Gabe wasn't sure if the Devil looked pleased . . . or disappointed, somehow.

"In two months' time then," the Devil said softly. "I'll have your soul and one other."

"Deal," Gabe said and reached out one hand to shake on it.

But the gunfighter had already begun to fade, twisting again into a writhing black column of shadows. And as the last of him dissolved into the wind, the barrier between Gabe and the world disappeared, as well. And everything was as it should be.

Except that he was a walking dead man.

CHAPTER TWO

FOUR DAYS LATER . . .

Gabe passed a small, tidy church and glanced at the group of kids playing in the sparse grass out front. Apparently, the church doubled as a school and he'd hit town just as they'd been let out for the day. Their whoops and hollers filled the air and he grinned at their excitement. It had been a lot of years since he'd been that happy about anything.

He rode slowly on, down the center of the pitifully short main street of Regret, Nevada. A tiny town crouched at the base of the mountains, it had a tired, weather-beaten look about it. False-fronted buildings leaned against each other like drunken cowboys and shingles rattled in the wind coming down off the mountain. Not exactly the kind of town he would have picked to spend his last days in, but it was just the sort of place he'd expect Henry to call home.

His sharp gaze swept back and forth, taking in everything, before settling on a man crossing the street in front of him. "Say," Gabe called out, "where can a man get a meal and a bath?"

The tall, lean man paused, then came closer. His face deeply tanned from years of working in the sun, he had squint lines etched into his brow between a pair of sharp blue eyes. "New in town?" he asked.

Gabe nodded. "Just rode in."

"Come far?"

He smiled inwardly. Every place was the same. Strangers always prompted curiosity. And, having lived a life skirting the edges of the law, Gabe well knew how to dodge questions. "Far enough to warrant a bath, that's for damn sure."

He said it with a friendly smile and immediately the man's features relaxed. Pointing off down the street, the fella said, "You'll find the bathhouse yonder, just past the livery on the right."

Good news. He hadn't figured on finding a real bathhouse in a small place like this. But apparently, enough cowboys came into town on a Saturday night to make it a worthwhile business. Lord, Gabe could almost feel hot water sluicing over him already.

"And the meal?" the man was saying.

"Yeah?" Food was his first priority. At the moment he was so hungry he could probably eat a bathtub, soap and all.

"There's only the one restaurant . . ."

"And?" Gabe had definitely heard an implied "but" in there.

The man shook his head and shrugged. "If you ain't too picky, it'll do ya."

"Hell, mister," he said on a chuckle, "if they served me a stack of shingles and called them flapjacks, I'd eat 'em right up and call them tasty."

His new friend laughed shortly. "Then you'll like this place. Shingles are the specialty."

Still laughing to himself, the man moved off and Gabe frowned after him. Hell, if it was that bad, how'd they stay in business? Then he answered his own question. If they had enough randy cowboys coming in on Saturday nights to warrant a bathhouse, then there were enough of them to keep even a bad restaurant open. Lord knew, those cowhands were used to eating mighty poor food.

He rode on, studying the town as he went. There was a mercantile, a millinery, land office, and gunsmith. The livery was at the end of the street, and just beyond it, lay the bathhouse, as promised. There was the restaurant, across the street from the saloon. Gabe stared thoughtfully at the batwing doors and he felt the old familiar pull tug at his soul.

If there was one thing Gabe knew, it was saloons. He'd sure as hell spent enough time over the years huddled over a poker table. His fingers itched to be holding a deck again, feeling the slide of the cards as he shuffled a new deal. But he'd already decided that if he was going to leave this world in two months' time, he wanted to see more of it than dark, smoky card parlors.

With a sigh, he shifted his gaze again and spotted another place he hoped to avoid. The sheriff's office and jailhouse, which was bordered on one side by an alleyway and on the other by a bank.

Gabe shivered reflexively and deliberately looked away from it as if staring too hard at the place would be enough to draw the sheriff's attention. Over the years, he'd seen the inside of too many cells and the view from behind bars wasn't one he was eager to see again.

Nope. What he had to do was find a place to hole up and wait for Henry. He'd known the old man long enough to know that every other month, Henry Whittaker headed to this town. Why, he'd never said. But Gabe had always assumed it was simply the man's home base.

Most men who danced back and forth over the lines of the law had a place they could retreat to. A place where they could lie down and rest without worrying about a posse chasing after them.

And this time, when Henry showed up, Gabe was going to be waiting for him.

But right now, after a long, hard four-day ride, all Gabe wanted was some food and then a bath. Soon enough he'd have to find himself a place to stay and a way to earn some money. Still, first things first.

He climbed down from the saddle in front of the restaurant, tied his horse to the hitching post, and stepped up onto the boardwalk. Taking off his black flat-brimmed hat, he smacked it against his jacket and then his thighs, trying to rid himself of most of the trail dust clinging to him. Then he resettled his hat and paused under the overhang to look up and down the length of the boardwalk.

Women in hats and shawls hurried along the wooden walkway, ignoring the occasional comment from a lounging cowboy. Children scampered in the street, and an old dog stretched lazily in a puddle of afternoon sunshine. From somewhere down the street, a door slammed and then the blacksmith's hammer rang out on an anvil. An ordinary day in an ordinary town. And he couldn't help wondering what these folks would say if they knew that he was a walking dead man.

Then his stomach grumbled and he remembered that even dead men had to eat.

He grabbed the latch and turned it, opening the door. The bell attached to its top clanged out and Gabe winced as he stepped into the restaurant. Once inside, though, he stopped dead. Even the air smelled scorched. Apparently, that fella hadn't been exaggerating about the restaurant.

Glancing around the empty room, he noted six tables, all set with plates and utensils, ready for customers who weren't there. Reaching up, he scrubbed one hand across his jaw and had to ask himself if he really wanted to do this.

"Help yourself to coffee," a woman's voice called out from what he guessed was the kitchen. "It's on the stove. I'll be there directly."

He had two choices, here. Leave now and starve. Or eat and risk God knew what. Then he smiled to himself. Hell. Even if the food was downright poisonous, it wouldn't do him any harm. He was already dead. His smile faded. Things were bad when being dead was the bright side. Slowly, he walked across the room to the potbellied stove in the far corner.

He poured himself a cup of coffee, took a sniff and felt his eyebrows curl. Strong stuff, he thought and doubted whether he really needed a cup to hold it. The coffee smelled like it was old enough and tough enough to stand on its own. Just the way he liked it.

From the other room came the distinct sound of a hammer striking metal. A couple of pans rattled and the woman said, "Beans and biscuits," loud enough for Gabe to hear the disgust in her tone.

He shook his head. Why people didn't just say "damn" when they meant "damn" was beyond him. "Is everything all right in there?" he asked loudly.

"Fine, fine," she yelled back. "Drink your coffee."

Gabe did just that and told himself that maybe it wasn't just her cooking keeping the restaurant empty.

She didn't exactly shine at making customers feel welcomed.

Another slam of a hammer followed by a grunt of disgust and Gabe took a step toward the closed door leading to the kitchen. He stared at it, as if he could see through the panel into the room beyond. What in the hell was she up to in there?

"Lady?" he called.

She grunted something he didn't catch.

Frowning, he yelled, "You need some help in there?"

"No!" she shouted, then after a long pause, added, "Thank you."

He took another sip and shook his head. Nothing worse than a hardheaded woman.

"Oh, for pity's sake," she said plainly, then, "Oooohhhh . . ."

A crash of sound reverberated through the building and even the plank walls seemed to tremble.

"Jesus!" Startled, Gabe jumped, sloshing hot coffee over his hand. It sounded as though the roof had caved in. He cast one quick, wary glance at the ceiling, then, skin still sizzling, he hissed in a breath, dropped the cup, and rushed across the room. He slammed the door open, ran into the kitchen and skidded to a stop.

His heartbeat slowed and a smile struggled on his mouth. "Are you all right?"

"Blast it, go away!"

He didn't move.

She sat in the middle of the floor, surrounded by fallen pots and pans. A thick layer of soot covered everything. Including her. The stove chimney had split apart. Half of it lay on the floor beside her and the other half hung weirdly from the ceiling, still sifting soot into the air. As he watched, a skillet lid trembled at the lip of the stove, then crashed down onto the floor.

"What are you looking at?" she grumbled and glared up at him.

He chuckled. "I'm not sure," he admitted.

"Well, stop looking," she muttered and wiped one hand across her mouth, leaving behind a clean streak in the charcoal mask she wore.

Gabe laughed and she shot him a look that convinced him to swallow the rest of the laughter building inside him.

Sniffing, she lifted her chin and said, "I thought I told you to drink your coffee."

"So you did," he agreed and went down on one knee to look directly into her eyes. She looked like a raccoon in reverse. She must have closed her eyes just before the soot flew because two paler circles surrounded the eyes staring at him.

"So why aren't you?" She blew out a breath that shot a few loose tendrils of hair off her forehead and a spray of soot into the air.

He shook his head, reached out to brush a big clump of dirt from the top of her head, and when she smacked his hand aside, said, "I dropped my cup when I heard your kitchen blow up."

"It didn't blow up."

He let his gaze drift around the filthy room before looking back at her. "You sure?"

"Yes," she muttered, pushing herself to her feet. He reached out to give her a hand up, but she ignored him. "Why don't you go away?"

Gabe shrugged. "I'm still waiting to eat."

She grimaced tightly. "Perhaps you've noticed?" She

waved one hand and frowned when dirt dropped from her sleeve to the floor. "My stove—"

"Blew up?" he suggested.

"Broke," she corrected.

He laughed again until she glared at him. "Look, I'm sorry for laughing, but you have to admit . . ."

She tapped her toe against the floor, tilted her head to one side, and folded her arms over her chest. "Admit what?"

"Nothing," he finished, as he realized she wasn't finding this the slightest bit funny. Changing the subject, he looked her up and down and asked, "Are you all right?"

Frowning again, she reached up and pushed both hands along the side of her head, smashing the grime into her hair. "I'm not hurt, just. . . ." She paused and looked herself over.

"Filthy?" he offered, his gaze running across what had once been a white apron tied atop a flower-sprigged dress.

"Dirty," she said and lifted her chin, hoping for dignity.

But that was hopeless under the circumstances. "Lady, I've seen coal miners cleaner than you."

She brushed dirt off her lips again and looked at him. "Who *are* you, anyway?"

He shrugged. "A customer." Then he added, "In fact, your *only* customer." His gaze shifted to the broken chimney and the soot-covered stove. "And it looks as though I'm going to stay hungry."

Maggie shook her head and saw clouds of soot fly free of her hair. Wouldn't you just know something like this would happen when she had an actual customer? And a stranger to boot? A man who didn't know that she was the worst cook in Nevada? Oh, beans and biscuits. "If you're not choosy, I can let you have some cold meat and bread."

Lord knew, with the way business had been lately, she couldn't afford to lose a customer. Any customer. Even one who laughed at her in the middle of a disaster.

"I'll take it," he said and stepped aside as she walked toward the sink and pump.

"You'll find the bread in that box there," she said and pointed to a wide pine box on the counter. "And the meat's in the cold larder on the porch."

She worked the pump handle and sent a stream of water rushing into the sink. Cupping her hands, she washed the soot from her face, groped blindly for a towel, then turned to face the stranger in her kitchen.

He already had bread sliced and was carrying a shank of ham to the table when he said, "Exactly what were you trying to do?"

Maggie sent a withering look at her enemy, the stove, before glancing back to him. "I was trying to tighten that stupid chimney."

One corner of his mouth quirked. "By tearing it apart?"

"That was an accident." If she hadn't lost her balance on the stool, she wouldn't have grabbed at the chimney, and she wouldn't now be covered in grime, staring at a too handsome man who was still laughing at her.

He nodded, carved a chunk of ham from the bone, and set the knife down. Taking a quick bite, he chewed and said, "I noticed you didn't have many customers."

"It's been a slow day," Maggie said and figured it was none of his business that every day was a slow day. For the first time, she took a good look at him. Tall, well built, he had dark hair that curled at his shirt collar and his green eyes were shadowed by the brim of his hat. He wore a jacket and pants that had miles' worth of trail dust covering them, a white shirt buttoned all the way to the neck, and no gun on his hip. Fairly unusual for this part of the country. "Are you passing through?"

"Actually," he said after he'd swallowed, "I was thinking of staying around town for a while."

"Why?"

His eyebrows lifted slightly at the question and she realized she'd done it again. People were always saying that Maggie Benson asked too many questions. But she'd always figured it was the only way to find out a darn thing. And it was a reasonable question. Regret was far too small to induce anyone passing through it to put down roots. Still, she reminded herself, for Jake's sake, she was trying to learn to curb her curiosity.

"Never mind," she said and walked past him to get the broom out of the pantry. If she didn't get busy cleaning this up, she'd be at it all night. "It's none of my business, really."

His gaze followed her as she worked, dragging the broom around the floor, sweeping up what looked like an ocean of soot. Several minutes passed with the only sound in the room that of the straw bristles scraping against the wood floor. Then the stranger spoke up again and Maggie turned to face him.

"You run this place all alone?"

"Yes," she said and couldn't quite contain the sigh that slipped out.

"A lot of work for one person."

"My son helps me," she said and a smile curved her mouth just thinking about Jake.

"And your husband?"

The smile disappeared and Maggie looked at the stranger. "I'm a widow."

"I'm sorry." Sympathy shone in his eyes and Maggie flinched from it.

"Don't be. It was a long time ago."

Six years to be exact. Her late unlamented husband had taken off right after Jake was born. She'd learned months later that he'd been shot in a card game in Abilene. Apparently, he'd tried to cheat the wrong man.

But, she told herself firmly, that was in the past. Old hurts faded, if you gave them enough time. Kersey Benson had been a sore disappointment as a husband, but he'd given her Jake and for that she'd always be grateful.

"Must get lonesome," he said quietly.

Maggie looked at him. "Are you?"

"What?"

"Lonesome."

He laughed shortly. "Me? No."

"Then why do you assume I am?"

"Well"—he waved a slice of ham at her—"because . . ."

"I'm a woman?"

His smile broadened a bit. "You are that."

Maggie flushed. It wasn't often a man took notice of her. Now, for this man to say something despite the layer of soot covering her was enough to fluster her momentarily. But the feeling passed just as quickly. Flattery came as easy to some men as breathing did to others.

"Look, Mr. . . ."

"Donovan," he supplied. "Gabe Donovan."

Gabe. Gabriel. Someone had named him well. He did have the face of an angel. A fallen one.

"Fine. Mr. Donovan, I appreciate your interest but—"

"Mind my own business?" he asked, giving her a smile that Maggie was sure he'd used often to his benefit. Why, if she hadn't sworn off men years ago, even she might have been affected.

"Actually," she said, "yes."

"Fair enough," the man said and took another bite of ham. Really, he was concentrating so on that makeshift meal, Maggie guessed he hadn't been eating regularly. "But . . ."

"What?"

"If you don't mind my saying so," he said, clearly determined to say it whether she minded or not, "it looks like you could use some help around here."

"Help?"

"As it happens, I'm looking for temporary work and—"

She almost laughed. "You want a job?"

There was that smile again.

"Now wanting a job and needing one are two different things, I'd say."

"Not five minutes ago, you pointed out that I didn't have any customers."

He grinned at her and helped himself to another slice of bread.

"And now you want a job? Doing what?"

Pointing to the stove, he said, "I could fix that for you for starters."

Well, she hadn't expected this. She'd seen plenty of men drifting through town looking for work. And Gabe Donovan looked like none of them. Most often, the drifters were cowhands hoping to sign on with a big ranch to sit out the winter. But Maggie would eat that stove pipe if this man had ever spent time riding herd on cattle. His suit coat might be dirty, but it had been excellently tailored. In fact, he looked more like a gambler than a hired hand . . . and Maggie didn't need another gambler in her life.

She shook her head slowly. "What do you know about fixing stoves or repairing roofs?"

"Not much," he admitted then shrugged. "But I learn fast."

She studied him for a long minute, then said, "You look like a man more accustomed to dealing cards than swinging a hammer."

Eyes wide and deliberately innocent, he asked, "Would you hold a man's past against him?"

"Easier than holding his future against him," she pointed out. Although, even as she said it, she realized that she was trying to live down her own past here in town. So who was she to say a person couldn't change?

"What have you got to lose?" he asked, interrupting her thoughts. "I need a job, you need the help. And it's only temporary in any case. I'll be leaving town in two months."

"What if you end up wanting to stay?" She had to ask, though she couldn't imagine him fitting in around Regret any better than she did.

"I can't stay."

"Can't?"

Gabe took a breath and said simply, "I have an . . . appointment I have to keep."

He watched her, waiting. She was thinking about it, he knew. Just from studying her expression, he could tell she was leaning toward hiring him.

"There are some things that I could use some help

with," she admitted slowly, "but I don't know anything about you."

"What's to know?" he asked. "I'm a man who needs a job and you're a woman who needs the help. A match made in Heaven." Or rather, he reminded himself, Hell.

Before he could say more in an effort to convince her, the back door flew open, slamming into the wall behind it. A small boy raced into the room and right through the freshly swept pile of soot, scattering it up into the air where it hung like a black cloud before settling down again.

"Jake—" she started, then caught herself as she realized it was far too late to slow the kid down any.

"What happened?" he asked, shoving a hank of dark brown hair out of his eyes as he tossed a stack of belted schoolbooks onto the table.

"The chimney broke." She went to her son and scooped his hair back from his forehead. "About time for a haircut, don't you think?"

"Aw, ma . . ." He ducked out from under her touch. Apparently, he was getting just old enough that caresses from his mother were more embarrassing than comforting.

She smiled and turned the boy around to face Gabe. "This is my son, Jake. Jake, this is Mr. Donovan." She paused, then added, "He's going to be working here for a while."

He smiled at the boy. "Call me Gabe."

"You're gonna work for my mom?" the boy asked.

"Looks that way," he said, relieved. At least now, he'd have room and board for the next couple of months.

"That's good," Jake said solemnly. "She works too hard sometimes and I don't get to see her much."

"Well, we'll fix that then, all right?" Gabe said and looked down into brown eyes much like the woman's.

"If you two are finished talking about me," she said lightly, "why don't you go on into the dining room, Jake, and start on your homework?"

The boy scuffed his shoe against the floor, drawing lines in the soot. "I could do it later," he said hopefully. "Some of the other kids are going over to the stables to watch 'em break horses."

"Homework first," she said, shaking her head.

Gabe sympathized. He could still remember the thrill of being turned loose at the end of a school day. The last thing any kid wanted was to spend another hour or two doing more work. But apparently, the boy knew when he was beaten because he turned and, shoulders slumped, head bowed, started for the dining room.

"Nice kid," he commented when they were alone again.

"Yes," she said and a shine lit her eyes briefly. "He is."

"Thanks for the job," he said.

"You're welcome. Now as to your pay, Mr. Donovoan . . ."

"Gabe."

She nodded. "Gabe. My name's Maggie Benson."

"Nice to meet you, Maggie." He paused then said, "Don't worry about the pay. I don't need much. Just enough to pay for a room somewhere."

"Well, you're not hard to please, I'll say that for you," she said on a chuckle. "As to a room . . ." She pointed off toward the pantry and the closed door beside it. "That's a storage room. There's a cot you can use if you don't mind small spaces. We don't have a hotel in town."

He smiled. This was working out fine. He had a job, a place to stay, and a good spot in town from which to keep an eye out for Henry.

But she was still talking. "Jake and I live right upstairs, if you need anything else."

"I won't, but thanks."

She nodded and glanced behind her at the fallen chimney. "You'd best get that fixed as soon as you can, Gabe. The restaurant is a stage stop and we'll need to be able to cook for the passengers tomorrow."

"We'll be ready."

"We, huh?" She shook her head slightly as if she could hardly believe it herself.

Gabe couldn't help wondering why this woman was alone. There just weren't that many good-looking single women in the West. Some man should have scooped her up long before now. Hell, even covered in soot and dirt, she looked pretty damned good. He could only imagine how well she'd clean up.

And yet, here she was alone, but for a too small boy.

But even as he wondered, he reminded himself that he was in no position to tell someone else how to live their life. Hadn't he made a big enough mess of his own to end up in Hell? So she was alone. At least she was alive.

At that thought, he reached out and took the broom from her. His fingers brushed against hers and he felt her warmth stagger through him as though he'd been stranded in a blizzard and had just found a fire. She seemed to notice the sensation too, because she stepped carefully back and said, "Well, I'll leave you to it. I think

I'll go upstairs and have a bath before helping Jake with his schoolwork."

"One more thing," he said, and she stopped to look back at him over her shoulder.

"What?"

"Why'd you hire me?" He would have bet good money she wouldn't, and yet, she had.

She smiled ruefully and shrugged. "I'm not sure," she told him. "Let's just say that stove pipe must've hit me on the head."

He nodded. "Guess that's as good a reason as any."

She looked at him for a long minute before saying, "Good luck with the chimney."

Gabe nodded stiffly, his fingers curling tightly around the broomstick. One thing he didn't need in his last two months of life was the complication of finding himself attracted to a "good" woman. Nope. If he felt the need for a little companionship, he'd take himself down to the saloon and rent affection by the hour.

Maggie Benson was his boss, nothing more.

And it'd be best all the way around if he remembered that.

CHAPTER THREE

Bright and early the next morning, Maggie walked into the kitchen and her gaze went directly to the stove pipe. She'd heard Gabe working on it half the night. The clang of metal pieces slapping together had been so rhythmic for a while, it had sounded as though the building itself had a heartbeat.

And for most of the night, she'd tried to figure out exactly why she had hired a perfect stranger. Not only hired him, she reminded herself, but actually allowed him to move into the home she shared with her son. She'd slept only in fits and starts, with her splinters of dreams filled with the face of Gabe Donovan.

What was it about him that had convinced her to let him into their lives, however temporarily?

The small hairs at the back of her neck stood up, sending a chill along her spine, and Maggie shivered. There it was again. That feeling of . . . *change* coming. Was it Gabe? Was he the reason for the vague sense of unease in the air? Or was the lack of sleep making her silly?

"That's probably it," she told herself firmly. After all, it wasn't as if she was worried about her new employee. In a town the size of Regret, all a woman had to do if she was feeling the slightest bit threatened was to scream. Within seconds, there would be dozens of townsfolk, most of them armed, surrounding her. Besides, Gabe didn't *feel* threatening.

And that had to be the most illogical statement of all time. But illogical or not, Maggie wasn't one to disregard her feelings. Not anymore anyway. The one time she hadn't listened to her instincts, she'd paid a heavy price. And she wasn't a woman who made the same mistake twice.

Opening the door wider, she let the dawn light drift into the room, chasing away the last of the shadows. A soft, chill breeze swept through the room, bringing the scent of the mountains with it.

The stove was in one piece again and Maggie was glad to see all of his banging in the night hadn't been wasted.

She walked across the room to inspect his work close up and had to admit she was impressed. He hadn't seemed the type to be so good with his hands. But the pipe was back in place, the break fixed. Looked near seamless, too. Smiling to herself, she bent down and stoked the smoldering coals in the firebox. Feeding slivers of pitch pine and a bit of kindling into the still warm fire bed, she waited for the flames to catch before adding larger pieces of wood. Then she closed the iron door and turned around to get busy. It was only then she noticed that not only had her newly hired man fixed the stove pipe, he'd actually mopped up the last of the soot from the floor.

"Well," she muttered thoughtfully, "maybe hiring him was a better idea than I knew." Any man who actually knew how to use a mop was one worth keeping around.

"I'm glad you're pleased," he said and Maggie

whirled around to face him, one hand clutching at her chest.

"You shouldn't sneak up on people that way."

"I didn't sneak. I'm just standing here."

"Well," she said as her heartbeat slowed down to its normal rhythm, "you could have said something."

"I did," he said with a short laugh. "That's what scared you."

Maggie laughed too, and tried to remember when the last time was that she'd laughed with a man. "True enough," she said. "I guess I'm just not used to having someone besides me and Jake here."

He tilted his head to one side. "Does it bother you having me around?"

Maybe it should have, but it didn't.

"If it bothered me, I wouldn't have hired you."

"I just thought . . . some women might have hired me and then regretted it." He looked at her for a long minute. "But I don't guess you're one of those."

Their eyes met and Maggie nodded, acknowledging the compliment. "Once I make a decision, it stays made," she said. "Regrets are pretty much a waste of time, don't you think?"

"I suppose," he said, and for a moment his features tightened and his green eyes darkened. "But most people have a few, anyway."

She wondered then what it was he was regretting. Because plainly, his mind was no longer on their conversation, but turned inward to thoughts that didn't appear to be at all pleasant.

Standing in the open doorway to the storage room, he leaned against the doorjamb, arms folded across his chest, booted feet crossed at the ankle. Like her kitchen,

Gabe Donovan looked better than he had the day before. Freshly shaven, he wore a white long-sleeved shirt, open at the collar, black pants, boots shined to a mirror gloss and strangely enough, a red bandana tied around the base of his neck.

Ordinarily, you'd only see an outlaw or a cowboy wearing the scarves. Outlaws used them to hide their identity and cowboys wore them to keep from breathing in miles of trail dust. And he surely didn't look like a cowboy.

Pointing to it, she asked, "Planning on leaving me for a trail-riding job? Or are you thinking to rob the bank after breakfast?"

"Hmm? Oh." He smiled and reached up to finger the bandana. "I wear it for luck."

Maggie frowned slightly. If that were true, why hadn't he been wearing it the day before? But even as she wondered, she told herself it didn't really matter. If the man wanted to pretend to himself he was a cowhand, what difference did it make to her? And if he was an outlaw? Well . . . he'd have to be a pretty stupid one to take a job with her only to rob someone in the same town. Somehow, Gabe Donovan didn't strike her as a stupid man. So, as long as he behaved himself around her and Jake, she wouldn't question him.

He was watching her, as if waiting for her to ask him more questions. She surprised him by changing the subject.

"You did nice work on the stove pipe."

His features relaxed a bit, and if she hadn't been watching him so closely, she might not have noticed. Again she wondered what he was hiding, even while telling herself to stay out of it.

"Thanks," he said and looked pretty darned pleased with himself. "It's been some time since I did work like that. Took me longer than I thought it would."

"I know," she said, nodding. "I heard you. You must have been up all night."

"I didn't mean to make that much noise," he said, straightening up from the doorjamb. "I'm sorry, I didn't even think about what it must sound like upstairs."

"Don't be. I'm awake late most nights." That was the truth. Although most of her thoughts last night had been centered on him, Maggie didn't get much sleep as a rule anyway. She had too many thoughts whirling around in her mind. It seemed that as soon as she laid her head down onto a pillow, her brain started running at a gallop. She'd come up with some of her best ideas while lying in the darkness, listening to the workings of her own mind. She even kept a pad of paper and a pencil on the table beside her bed so she could write out plans that might otherwise be lost. One day, Maggie fully intended to bring all of her inventive notions to life.

But it wasn't time now to be entertaining those plans. Now, she had to get breakfast started and Jake off to school.

Ordinary, she reminded herself.

She would be an ordinary mother if the attempt killed her.

Lord knew, it surely might. Taking a deep breath, she said, "The important thing here is it's fixed."

He nodded and stepped into the kitchen.

Glancing past him at the bare-looking storage room, Maggie asked, "How did the cot work out for you? Will the room be all right?"

"I've slept on worse," Gabe told her with a wry grin.

In fact, he hated to think of some of the places he'd called home, however temporarily. "And the room's fine," he added.

She frowned, still looking into the tiny storage area. "If you like, you could empty some of that stuff out and put it in the shed out back."

He could. If he was planning on staying. But the reality of his situation was, there was no point in getting too cozy. Better he get used to being uncomfortable now. It might help him adjust to Hell all that much faster.

"Thanks, but it's fine," he said.

"Up to you," she said with a shrug and turned toward the counter and the coffee grinder. "I'll start breakfast. Why don't you go into the dining room and fire up that stove? I like to keep a pot of coffee going out there too."

"Yes, ma'am," he said.

But before he could take a step, the back door opened and a woman stepped inside.

Maggie took one look at that familiar face and felt her insides tighten up until it was a chore to draw breath. She curled her fingers over the edge of the counter and squeezed hard but it didn't help. Nothing would.

The woman stared at her for a long heartbeat and Maggie knew exactly what she was thinking. What she'd *been* thinking for years. That Maggie was the daughter of a no-account, no better than she should be. All her life, Maggie had heard whispers about her family. Lies and half-truths designed to wound. And maybe that was why she'd rushed into a marriage with a man who had turned out to be a bitter disappointment, both as a man and as a husband. She'd been looking for respectability.

A choked laugh was born and then quickly died in the knot in her chest. She certainly hadn't found it. But she was bound and determined to give Jake the kind of life she'd always longed for. She would see to it that he was raised properly. That no one would be able to gossip about him or his mother. She was going to ensure happiness for Jake, no matter what it cost her.

And right now, the price was being polite to the harpy who'd just walked in her door.

From the corner of his eye, Gabe saw Maggie stiffen slightly and he looked at the stranger with interested eyes. About forty, the woman was tall and skinny to the point of being rawboned. Her hair was pulled back from her face into a knot so tight it was a wonder her eyes didn't slant from the pressure at the sides of her head. Small blue eyes narrowed as her gaze swept the room and landed on him. Her nose twitched like a hound on the scent. Her lips were pinched and even when she tried a smile, it didn't ring true.

"Maggie," she said, with barely a glance at the woman she was talking to. "I simply *had* to come see how you'd survived your latest disaster."

"Disaster?" Maggie asked, and to Gabe her voice sounded strained, tight.

"Why, dear," she said, waving one hand in the air, "these old walls are so thin, everyone can hear what goes on. And Bass Stevens said he heard what sounded like an explosion in here yesterday afternoon."

"Bass should spend more time cutting his customer's hair and less on gossiping," Maggie said.

"But honey, it isn't gossiping if it's true." The woman eyed Gabe up and down and he felt like a horse being appraised at an auction. He wouldn't have been surprised if she'd asked to inspect his teeth. "I just had to come see for myself that you hadn't been injured with one or other of your silly notions."

Gabe shot a curious glance Maggie's way. What kind of silly notions?

Maggie spoke through gritted teeth and a person would have had to be blind not to notice how much it was costing her to be civil. "You were so concerned you waited until the next day to come check on me," she said.

The woman absently waved a hand at her. "Oh, I was sure enough you weren't badly hurt or dead or something. Jake would have come for help if he'd found your body."

Maggie slammed the flat of her hand onto the countertop.

The other woman remained blithely unaware.

"And who might this be?" she asked, a speculative gleam shining in her eyes as she stared at Gabe.

Sighing, Maggie turned from the coffee grinder and said, "This is Gabe Donovan, he works for me. Gabe, this is Sugar Harmon."

Sugar, a woman so wrongly named it boggled the mind, sailed across the room, extending one hand toward Gabe as if she was a queen bestowing favors on a peasant.

"A pleasure," she said, though judging from the tight expression on her face, she wouldn't have known true pleasure if it had sneaked up and bit her on the—

"Ma'am," Gabe said and shook the hand she'd obviously expected him to kiss.

She bore her disappointment bravely, though. "My husband's the mayor of Regret," she said as if that explained what she was doing intruding on people just after the crack of dawn.

"How nice for him," Gabe said dutifully and shot another look at Maggie.

She rolled her eyes and bit down hard on her bottom lip.

Why wasn't she tossing this nosy busybody out the door?

"And how do you come to be working for our Maggie?" Sugar asked.

Gabe faced his inquisitor and slapped a polite smile on his face. He didn't want to cause Maggie any trouble, and if she was being so blasted cordial to this biddy, he figured she must have a reason. So he bit back what he wanted to say and answered simply, "I needed a job, she needed the help."

"Uh-huh," Sugar mused and again looked him up and down. "Well now, Maggie, if you needed help, you should have asked for it. You know my Redmond would have been only too happy to lend a hand."

"Speaking of Redmond, won't he be expecting breakfast about now?" Maggie forced a smile.

"Very shortly," Sugar said and kept her gaze steadily on Gabe. "Mr. Donovan, wasn't it? If you're looking for extra work, I could certainly use someone to replace a stair tread."

"Why didn't you ask Redmond?" Maggie muttered and reached for the coffee grinder again. "I'm sure he'd be happy to help."

Gabe smiled to himself.

Sugar ignored her. "Where did you say you were from, Mr. Donovan?"

"I didn't," he said, and looked into the woman's eyes

and felt like a rabbit facing down a snake. There wasn't a doubt in his mind that one day he'd be running into Sugar Harmon somewhere in Hell. He'd come across women like her many times in his life. They carried righteousness like shields before them and stomped all over anyone who might happen to be different. They'd been known to close down saloons and run dance-hall girls out of town on rails. They mouthed gossip as readily as good folks said their prayers and he was willing to bet there was a whole section of Hell staked out just for them.

Gabe let go of that pleasant image when Jake came running down the stairs and entered the kitchen in a clatter of sound only six-year-old boys were capable of. The kid stopped short, though, when he saw Sugar, and Gabe watched as the boy looked from the woman to his mother and back again.

"Morning, honey," Maggie said in a too light tone.

"Morning," Jake echoed, and took a step toward her, almost as if he was getting ready to defend her.

Gabe frowned to himself and wondered just what in the heck was going on here besides a nosy, mean-spirited neighbor ruining a perfectly good morning.

"My," Sugar said, letting her gaze slip from the boy to Maggie. "He looks more like his father every day, doesn't he? Guess that apple didn't fall far from the tree."

Maggie's jaw clenched, and even from a few feet away, Gabe saw the muscle in her cheek twitch. She laid one hand on Jake's shoulder and said, "Honey, you go on out into the dining room. I'll be there in a minute." She waited until her son had gone through the swinging door into the other room before addressing the woman again. "Thanks for stopping by, Sugar, but I have to get Jake's breakfast started, so . . ."

But Sugar ignored her and turned back to Gabe. Before she could get going again, though, Maggie turned the crank of the grinder and just for good measure, threw another handful of coffee beans into the mix.

Loud, continuous noise rose up, nearly deafening in the otherwise still morning air. Gabe had to hand it to her. She'd found a way to shut up her neighbor without being out-and-out rude to her.

For a moment or two, it looked like Sugar might just shout to be heard over the noise rather than concede defeat. But the moment passed and the woman, after giving Maggie a look that should have singed the hem of her dress, turned for the door.

"I'm sorry I can't stay longer," she yelled while sending Gabe what he guessed she assumed to be a flirtatious smile.

He nodded and glanced at Maggie. She was turning that crank with enough elbow grease to spin straw into gold.

"Perhaps later," Sugar shouted, then swept out the door.

The grinding continued relentlessly until Gabe walked over to Maggie, laid one hand on her shoulder, and shouted, "She's gone!"

Instantly, silence crashed down on them.

Gabe watched her lean both hands on the counter and hang her head low over the grinder. She took several long, deep breaths before speaking.

"I can't help it," she muttered, "that woman is enough to drive a body to drink."

"I'll buy," he offered in an effort to cheer her up some.

A heartbeat later, Maggie chuckled, lifted her head and looked at him. It pleased him, seeing her shake off Sugar Harmon's visit so quickly.

"It's a little early," she joked. "But thanks for the offer."

Maybe to keep her smiling a bit longer, he asked, "How could anyone have named her 'Sugar'?"

Maggie shook her head, turned around and leaned back against the counter. "She is a little sour."

"Sour? That woman gives lemons a whole new meaning."

Laughing softly, she said, "And she doesn't even know you yet. Wait until she's comfortable enough around you to tell you what she really thinks."

"She thinks?" he asked, with a laugh.

Maggie grinned at him conspiratorially. "That's the rumor."

Gabe felt a flash of something he couldn't quite describe shoot through him. It was warm and comforting and yet somehow unsettling. And she was at the heart of it. Damn, he should have gone to work for a man. Or at the very least, a woman who didn't look quite so good first thing in the morning.

She had an unconventional kind of beauty that appealed to him more than he cared to admit. Without a layer of soot covering her skin, he could see that her complexion was a pale peach color, telling him she didn't bother wearing hats in the sun. Big brown eyes dominated her features and her short nose had a few golden freckles dotting its surface. Then he looked closer and frowned inwardly. Oh, there were freckles there all right, but there were also small dots of what looked like *actual* gold paint. Now why in the hell would she have gold paint on her face? Interesting, he thought as he noted that her mouth was too wide, but when she smiled, it lit up her entire face.

Her soft brown hair hung in a long, single braid, the end of which landed at the small of her back. Loose, curly tendrils lay against cheeks still flushed from her encounter with Sugar and the plain apron she'd tied over her blue and white striped dress was tight enough to draw attention to what looked like a remarkable figure.

Apparently, she had the ability to stir even a dead man. Real depressing how he kept remembering the fact that he was no longer alive. Briefly, he recalled their conversation about regrets. He'd had quite a few before he'd ever come to the aptly named town of Regret. And now, on this beautiful morning, standing beside a woman who looked both fierce and vulnerable . . . he had one more.

He couldn't help wondering what it might have been like between them if they'd met when he was still alive. But then he admitted that when he was alive, he hadn't been interested in her kind of woman. They were from two different sides of town, he and Maggie. She was picket fences and lemonade after church on Sunday. He was poker hands and bad whiskey on Saturday nights.

Maybe he'd made a mistake by coming to work for Maggie. But it was too late now. He wouldn't quit on her and add one more regret to an already growing list.

She was watching him curiously and he realized that he'd drifted too far from their conversation. Smiling, he said, "From what I've just seen, I'd advise you not to bet on the rumor about that woman actually thinking."

Her smile faded as abruptly as it had been born. "I don't listen to rumors. Or gossip."

He'd hit a nerve there, he thought and found himself wondering what lay behind the sudden shadows in her eyes. The way she'd stiffened up told him that maybe she'd been the subject of gossip herself once or twice.

Was it her late husband folks had talked about . . . or, remembering what else Sugar'd had to say, he asked quietly, "What did she mean about your notions?"

She flushed and shifted her gaze from his. A short, harsh chuckle shot from her throat as she answered his question with a question. "Who knows what she means? I don't even listen to her half the time."

He had a feeling she listened more than she claimed and was hurt deeper than she pretended. The fact that she clearly didn't want to talk about it told him that the pain still lingered. That bothered him more than he would have thought.

"I would imagine not many do," he said, trying to help somehow.

"You'd be wrong," Maggie said under her breath.

"I suppose," he said. "Folks tend to enjoy chewing over someone else's troubles."

"Why is that, do you think?" She dumped the ground beans into the pot and then filled it with water. Setting it on the stove, she turned and grabbed a skillet and a some eggs.

Gabe watched her go about the homey ritual of making breakfast. Strange, he hadn't watched a woman performing this simple act since he was a boy. Odd how comforting it was. He shook the feeling off and answered the question as best he could. "I don't know really. Guess it seems to some that if they stay busy enough with other people's problems, they won't have time to worry about their own."

"Maybe," she said, but didn't sound convinced.

"Or"—he offered another explanation—"could be they just like causing misery."

The aroma of sizzling butter and frying eggs filled the room and Gabe's stomach grumbled.

"That's probably closer to the truth," she muttered, more to herself than to him.

"You could've thrown her out," he said, noting the tension still evident in the way she held herself.

"You know," she snapped, tapping her spatula against the rim of the skillet, "I didn't hire you for your assistance with my neighbors."

He held up both hands in mock surrender though she couldn't even see him. "Sorry, lady, just my opinion."

"Then since it's yours, why don't you keep it to yourself."

Man, she had a hell of a temper when she got going.

"It's not me you're mad at, remember?"

"It's easy for you to show up and hand out advice like it's nothing, isn't it?" Maggie spun around to look at him, turning her back on the eggs. Twin spots of color filled her cheeks and her eyes fairly snapped with emotion. "You've been here one day. You're only staying here two months. I have to live here. My *son* has to live here."

Long-buried pain shimmered in her brown eyes and Gabe wanted to kick himself. She was absolutely right. Who the hell did he think he was, sliding in here and questioning how she handled something that must happen to her on a regular basis? Wasn't it enough that she had to put up with that female? Did he have to make it worse by adding insult to injury?

"You're right," he said, then tried to make her smile again by adding, "Still, I've got to say, I admire your restraint."

A small smile tugged at one corner of her mouth and he felt rewarded. Ridiculous. But damn she was fascinating. A woman who got mad at the drop of a hat and then smiled again almost instantly.

"Sometimes, it's not easy," she admitted. "Once, I came so close to dumping a five-pound sack of flour over her head, I could actually *see* her strolling down the street like some skinny snowwoman come to life."

He grinned at the image, then frowned as he caught a whiff of something burning. Looking past her, he said, "Maggie? The eggs?"

"What?"

"The eggs're burning."

"Oh!" She spun around, snatched at the handle of the skillet and yelped at her singed palm. Using her spatula, she pushed the cast-iron pan off the fire. "Beans and biscuits!"

Shaking his head as she muttered more ridiculous curses under her breath, Gabe asked, "If you mean 'damn,' why don't you just say 'damn'?"

"Because ladies don't say 'damn,' damn it."

He grinned at her and told himself this was going to be an interesting two months.

CHAPTER FOUR

Once she got Jake off to school and Gabe busy fixing the loose step out front, Maggie headed off to the mercantile. Still fuming inside, she needed someone to talk to. Someone to be herself with. Before she exploded as completely as her stove had.

Clutching fistfuls of her skirt, she held the hem off the ground so the uncomfortable pointed toes of her shoes wouldn't catch on the fabric and send her sprawling facedown in the dust. Oh, that's all she would need to put the final touches on an already superb morning.

"Watch it, lady," someone yelled and Maggie came out of her furious thoughts in time to step wide around an approaching cowboy as he reined in sharply. He was still scowling at her as he spurred his horse into a wide arc around her.

"Sorry," she called, but then wondered why she should apologize. *She* was the one who'd almost been run down like a dog. Because, she told herself, it was what a "lady" would do. "Oh, beans and biscuits, pots and pans, and . . ." Her voice faded off because she couldn't come up with any other silly curses.

Remembering Gabe's admonition to simply say "damn" when she needed to rose up in her mind and she wished it were that simple. Of course, not so very long ago, it *had* been that simple. Back when she and Jake had lived alone on their little farm.

Lord, how the memories of those times shone in her mind. But, she reminded herself as she pushed aside happier memories, she'd made her decision. It was for Jake's sake she was here. And for Jake's sake, she would make it work.

At the opposite side of the street, she took the steps at a run, forgetting momentarily that a "lady" would walk slowly, sedately. She nodded at a man who tipped his hat as she passed, then walked down the boardwalk to the general store. Her heels tapped out angrily against the wood and she hardly slowed down as she grasped the brass latch and threw the door wide.

The string of bells over the door jounced and clanged as the door slammed into the wall. Sound echoed in the big store, and from the back of the mercantile, a woman's voice called out, "I recognized that slam, Maggie. I'll be right there!"

"It's all right, Dolly," Maggie answered loudly as she checked to make sure she hadn't done any damage to the door or the glass panel in the middle of it. Thankfully, this time she was safe. The last time Sugar'd made her mad, Dolly had had to order a new glass pane in from Reno. "Nothing's broken."

"Well, good!" The laughter in the other woman's voice warmed Maggie's heart and the fury inside her dissipated just a bit. "Glass is getting to be as dear as gold."

Taking a deep, hopefully calming breath, Maggie inhaled the familiar scents of the general store and tried to block Sugar Harmon and other women like her from her mind. Slowly, old memories of good times and happier days drifted through her, pushing the fury within her aside.

The mercantile had had this effect on her since she was a child. The mingled scents of hard candy and coffee and leather goods and exotic cooking spices all came together to blend into an aroma that smelled of home and safety and acceptance.

The sound of high heels clicking against the shining wood floor drew Maggie out of her pleasant memories.

"Lordy, girl, you come over this early in the morning just to break another door for me?" Dolly Trent walked along the length of her counter and came to a stop beside an ornate brass and silver cash register that glimmered and shone in the morning sunlight.

The older woman's graying blond hair was piled into a loose knot high on her head and two pencils jutted up from the bun like wooden horns. In her youth, she'd had an hourglass figure, but now, she liked to say, "The sands had stuck in the middle," leaving her more round than well rounded. But she had kind gray eyes, a sweet smile, and a nurturing heart.

Maggie crossed the floor to the counter and, as she had ever since she was tall enough to reach, took the lid off a candy jar and pulled out a licorice whip. She took a healthy bite, chewed for a minute, then said, "I had to come and see you, Dolly."

"What's wrong, child?"

The concern etched into her features warmed Maggie's heart. No matter what else happened in her life, she knew she'd always have at least one good friend to count on.

"Sugar Harmon," she said and then added what she'd wanted to say earlier. "Damn her hide."

The other woman frowned and shook her head. "For

pity's sake, what'd she do now? And why in God's name do you listen to that female?"

"Oh, the sun was hardly up before she was at my back door, sticking her nose into the kitchen and my life."

"About what?" Dolly leaned both forearms on the counter and looked at her.

"She said Bass Stevens told her he'd heard an explosion at my place and—"

"Hmph!" Dolly snorted and shook her head. "Bass wouldn't hear an explosion if a stick of dynamite went off under his barber chair. The man's deaf as a post and dumber than two bricks."

A short but apt description of the town barber. "True, but he heard enough to start talking."

"More likely, Sugar was snooping around and heard it herself." Then what she was saying dawned on her and she paused before asking, "What explosion? You didn't . . . ?"

Maggie held up one hand to stop the flow of questions. "I didn't do anything except have an accident."

"An accident? Are you all right?" Dolly looked her up and down as if checking for any blood that might have been overlooked yesterday.

"I'm fine," Maggie said shortly and took another bite of licorice. "I fell is all, and then I knocked the stove chimney off and *it* fell and threw soot all over me and the kitchen."

Dolly's lips twitched.

It did sound funny. Now that it was over. Smiling herself, she said, "Go ahead and laugh, Gabe did."

"Gabe?"

To quell the interest in the other woman's eyes, Maggie quickly explained about the man who'd come to the restaurant as a customer and ended up staying on as a hired hand.

"Interesting," Dolly mused. "A stranger walks in off the street and you hire him."

Frowning slightly, Maggie reached for another piece of licorice.

"Is he handsome?"

"I suppose," Maggie said.

"Well, now," Dolly said softly, "this is interesting news indeed."

"No it's not," Maggie told her, refusing to let her old friend start building up a romance where none existed.

"So you say now."

"So I'll *always* say."

Dolly scowled. "You're too young a woman to lock yourself up inside, girl."

"Dolly," she said on a sigh, "I'm a widow and a mother. I've been married and I've been alone. I like alone better."

"Pshaw," the other woman said. "You haven't been married. Kersey Benson don't count at all."

Oh, they'd had this conversation too many times. Dolly was bound and determined to help Maggie find another man . . . whether she wanted one or not. And she definitely didn't want one.

The only decent thing Kersey had ever done in his life was make Jake. And though she might secretly yearn for more children . . . actually a houseful of them . . . Maggie wasn't willing to tie herself to another man to get them.

"And you say Sugar got a look at him too?"

"A look at him?" Maggie said on a laugh, grateful

for the slight change of subject. "She never took her eyes off him." Then she shook her head and continued. "But I didn't come to see you about Gabe. It's Sugar. I swear, I don't know how much longer I can put up with her and not say something."

"Who said you have to?" Dolly demanded hotly.

"Oh, I don't really mind when she starts in on me," Maggie told her. "Lord knows I'm used to being talked about and whispered over."

"You're exaggeratin'," Dolly said.

"No I'm not," she said flatly. "You know as well as I do that folks in this town have been talking about me for years. First they talked about my father and then when he married Mama it was her they started in on."

"Now, Maggie . . ."

"It's true and you know it, Dolly," Maggie said. "They picked on Mama until she died and then they turned their claws and teeth on me." Her fingernails drummed on the counter.

The other woman's mouth snapped shut. She could hardly argue the point when she knew it to be gospel. Still, she had to say, "Maybe it's time you started talking back, then."

"I can't . . . *won't*," Maggie said. Shaking her head, she took another bite of licorice and briefly savored the sweet taste in her mouth that went a long way toward ridding her of Sugar's aftertaste. "The only thing that will shut folks up is if they don't have anything to talk about. I'm going to be so damned proper, I'll make myself sick."

"Oh, now that sounds nice."

"And Jake won't be running around getting into any mischief." Nodding to herself, she went on. "Folks are not going to throw his father in his face. They're not going to look at him and see Kersey." When Dolly opened her mouth to argue, Maggie cut her off. "I want Jake to be accepted here. I want him to feel like he's a part of this town."

"Honey," she said and laid one hand on Maggie's forearm, "as long as that child has you, he'll be happy as two fleas on a shaggy dog."

Maggie smiled softly. Jake did love her, she knew. And she loved him right back. Enough to change herself, make herself over in an attempt to give her son a happier life. Wasn't that the main reason she'd moved to town in the first place? And by God, she'd do whatever she had to, even put up with Sugar, to make sure her plans and hopes for her son came true.

"Jake *is* a part of this town, honey. Same as you."

"No." She shook her head. "Not yet." Oh, Jake had friends his own age, but she'd seen the adults in town watching him. Watching her. They were all waiting for her to fail. To do something . . . *odd* again so they could talk and laugh about her. But that would change with time. All she had to do was be patient and keep remembering to behave like a "lady."

Which she could do as long as people didn't pick on her son.

"Just a while ago, Sugar started in on Jake. Right in front of me." She remembered the look on the woman's face and Maggie felt the urge to smack something. But ladies didn't show their tempers, unfortunately. She had to wonder who'd made up all the rules about ladylike behavior and, privately, she decided that it must have been a man.

Instantly, her friend stiffened in outrage. "What'd that viperous female say?"

"Oh," Maggie said, remembering and feeling a fresh rush of anger fill her. "It doesn't really matter. All that matters is that I barely kept myself from slapping her face so hard she'd have to look over her shoulder to see straight ahead."

"That's just what she needs," Dolly muttered.

Maggie couldn't have agreed more. But that wasn't the point. If she was going to give Jake the kind of life he deserved, then she needed to win over the townspeople like Sugar who made enough noise that folks listened. She shouldn't have to worry about her son having to listen to old gossip about his no-good father *and* new gossip about his mother.

For pity's sake, why couldn't they just leave the memories of Kersey where they belonged? In the past.

The more she thought about it, the more furious she got.

"I'm just so mad I could spit," she muttered and started pacing, relishing the sound of her quick steps on the floor. One corner of her mind pretended she was walking back and forth across Sugar's prone body and she smiled darkly at the thought.

"Go ahead and spit if it'll make you feel better," Dolly offered. "Just aim for one of the spittoons if you don't mind."

Maggie laughed and stopped dead. "You know darn well, ladies don't spit."

"Ladies aren't supposed to gossip either, but that don't stop Sugar any."

"True."

"I swear, the worst thing we ever did was elect poor

Redmond mayor." Dolly reached up and smoothed her hair unnecessarily. "As soon as we did, Sugar figured she was in charge around here and she sharpened her tongue on a razor strop."

"But what can *I* do about her?"

"You? Nothing," Dolly said, adding, "that is, if you're still determined to be Miss Almighty Prim and Proper."

"You know I am."

"I still say it's a mistake to be anything but what you are."

"Dolly . . ."

She snorted again. "Fine, fine. Don't listen to me. But you can let me handle Sugar."

It was the right thing to do, she knew. Though it grated on her to back away from a fight, Maggie was in no position to challenge Sugar openly. Not when she'd spent the last two years trying to convince everyone that she'd outgrown her . . . *outlandishness*. Sighing, she walked back to the counter. "I don't envy you the task."

"Pshaw," the woman said with a wave of her pudgy hand. "The day I can't handle the Sugar Harmons of this world is the day the good Lord can call me home."

If she was a more generous soul, Maggie might even feel sorry for Sugar. But she didn't. Smiling, she said, "I don't know what I'd do without you, Dolly."

"I expect you'd get along much better than you think you would."

Maybe. But she was glad she didn't have to find out.

"Now," Dolly said, being deliberately hearty, "I've got something that I *know* will cheer you right up."

"Really?" Maggie leaned on the counter, studied her friend's sly expression, and knew exactly what she was talking about. "What color this time?"

"Sunset-gold."

Even the name was inspiring. Uplifting. And oh, how she needed uplifting at the moment.

"I'll take it."

"I thought you would."

Truth be told, Gabe still wasn't used to having bright sunlight dazzle his eyes. He was a moonlight man. Always had been. And this business of starting his days at the crack of dawn seemed oddly . . . *wrong*. Still, it had its own kind of beauty. It even managed to make a spit-in-the-road kind of town like this one look somehow golden. He squinted into the sunshine pouring down atop Regret and let his gaze drift across the town that would be the last place he ever lived.

But even as that thought entered his mind, he had to correct it. He wasn't really living at all, was he? He was a dead man that hadn't laid down yet. Gabe frowned to himself and shifted position on the porch, leaning his shoulder against a post. Briefly, he remembered those pale icy blue eyes of the Devil he'd met and, despite the soft yellow warmth of the sun, felt a chill sweep along his spine.

Damned disconcerting, this kind of existence.

Dead, but not completely. Alive, but not living. Just what the hell was he, anyway? A gambler who no longer gambled? A handyman for a restaurant that had no customers? One condemned soul sent to capture the soul of a man he'd once called a friend?

Oh, he didn't care for the sound of *that,* Gabe realized and mentally shied away from the thought. But it was Henry's own fault, right? The old thief had earned his way into Hell, same as him. It wasn't as though the Devil had sent Gabe to fetch some sterling character with high moral qualities. To trick some poor unsuspecting soul out of his rightful place in Heaven.

But that fact didn't make him feel any less the traitor. Damn it.

Why he should feel sympathy for a man who'd let him be hanged, he didn't know. But there it was.

Still, when a man was on a slick slope with a slide straight into Hell, he didn't have the option of granting mercy to anyone.

He let his gaze sweep across the shop fronts lining Main Street, and as he did, he wondered who in this town knew the most about Henry Whittaker. Who was waiting for the man's next visit? It stood to reason that the old thief had friends, probably family in or around Regret. Otherwise, why choose it as a home base?

Henry had to have people in town he could count on. People he trusted. And who would a man trust more than family? So who might it be? There was no way of telling. He couldn't rightly ask around without arousing suspicions. And he surely couldn't risk someone warning Henry off.

So he would have to content himself with waiting. And listening. He'd keep his ears open for talk of Henry and hope that the man showed up on time to keep the appointment he didn't know he had.

In the meantime, Gabe told himself as he noticed Maggie step out of the mercantile, there were *other* things to think about.

He watched her as she hitched a wooden crate higher in her arms and noted that it was heavy enough to make her stagger slightly. She blew a lock of hair out of her eyes and smiled to herself. Maybe Maggie Benson wasn't so different after all, he thought. Like every other woman he'd ever known, she had cured her troubles with a shopping trip.

She started for the steps and Gabe moved too. His mother hadn't raised a man who could sit still while a woman needed help. He jumped off the top step, landing in the street. Glancing first one way, then the next, he walked toward her. Stepping quickly around a buckboard, he headed for the steps that Maggie was just trying to negotiate.

"Need some help with that?" he asked, giving her a smile even as he reached for the crate.

"No, thanks," she said and moved to keep her treasure out of his grasp.

Surprised, he just stared at her. "But it looks heavy."

"It is," she agreed, and started past him down the steps. "So don't stop me now or I'll never make it."

"Maggie . . ." He frowned at her back as she walked away from him, headed toward the restaurant. Stubborn woman. It had been a long time since a woman had refused him anything and Gabe wasn't at all sure he liked it.

How was he supposed to do the gentlemanly thing if she didn't let him?

He stared after her for a long minute and caught himself admiring the sway of her hips as she moved. Something inside him shifted and a low purr of simple male pleasure rolled through him. Yet, as soon as he realized what he was doing, he shook his head and forced his gaze away from the lure of her hips and behind. He started moving, catching up to her in three easy, long-legged strides.

"Why not let me carry it for you?"

She hardly glanced at him as she shook her head. "No need. Remember, I've been taking care of myself for a long time and will again after you've gone."

"Yes, but while I'm here—" he started to say.

"While you're here," Maggie interrupted him with a smile, "there are plenty of other things for you to do."

She climbed the steps slowly, awkwardly, and Gabe fell in behind, just in case she toppled over backward. He should have known better. She was up the steps, across the boardwalk, and back in the restaurant in a flash.

She made a man feel damned unnecessary.

Right behind her, he followed her across the dining room and into the kitchen. She paused briefly and turned around to look at him. "I've got a few things to do upstairs."

And she looked like she was damn anxious to get started. Now what could put a flush of color in her cheeks and a sparkle like that back in her eyes? After Sugar had left, Maggie had been plainly furious. Now, she looked happy and excited. Just what kind of shopping had she been doing? He waited, hoping for some kind of hint, and was sorely disappointed.

Maggie took a deep breath and said, "While I'm busy, maybe you could fill the oil lamps in the dining room and then fix that loose step out front?"

"I can," he said as his gaze dropped to the crate she held clutched to her chest. Damned if he wasn't curious as to what was inside it.

As if she knew what he was thinking, she tightened her grip on the box and took a backward step closer to the staircase that led to her second-story living quarters.

"Well, that's good, then." Another step backward. "I'll uh . . . see you later this afternoon, all right?"

And before he could say anything or ask any questions, she turned and headed up the stairs without looking back. He walked to the base of the stairs and watched her go, his gaze once again dropping to the swing of her hips and the tip of her long braid that swung back and forth like a clock's pendulum.

She entered her room and closed the door firmly behind her. He even thought he heard the tumblers of a lock click into place.

What the hell was she up to?

CHAPTER FIVE

Dead men shouldn't have to work this hard.

Grumbling under his breath, Gabe told himself maybe he'd made a mistake in taking the Devil's offer. At the time, two more months of life had sounded like a good idea. Which just served to prove how wrong a man could be.

He set the last of the refilled oil lamps into its slot on the wagon-wheel chandelier then leaned back to look over his handiwork. In the late afternoon sunlight, the brass lamps sparkled and shone like a gold field. Tiny flames flickered and danced beneath the glass globes and wavering shadows played on the unpainted plank walls.

Shaking his head, he pulled the rope that lifted the chandelier into position on the ceiling, then secured it to the brass hook on the wall. Then, tired of his own company, he walked out onto the boardwalk, leaned one shoulder against a porch post, and stared out at the town of Regret.

People walking, hurrying along on their errands, occasionally tossed him a curious glance and he knew they were wondering about him. Strangers in a small town always excited curiosity. But even that curiosity wasn't enough, it seemed, to draw them into the restaurant.

Looking over his shoulder into the empty building, he told himself it was a wonder Maggie was able to keep this place alive. He hadn't seen an actual real customer in the two days he'd been there. Hell, if anything, the citizens of Regret tended to walk an extra wide path around the restaurant, as if afraid that someone might drag them inside and force them to eat. Apparently, Maggie's cooking had a helluva reputation.

And instead of doing something about it, like learning to cook without setting things on fire, what was she doing? Hiding upstairs in her living quarters doing . . . what?

All day, he'd heard the sounds of furniture scraping across the floor, heavy objects being dropped, and once, even snatches of a song Maggie was singing in a completely flat tone. He shook his head again. If she wasn't worried about the damned restaurant, why was he?

Folding his arms across his chest, he told himself that Maggie's business—or lack of it—wasn't his problem. If it was, of course, he'd have one or two ideas on how to draw people in. It took more than good food to make a restaurant popular. It required a little more atmosphere than unpainted plank walls and bare floors and windows.

There were a lot of things that could be done to spruce the place up a bit and make it more welcoming to potential customers.

But . . . he was only here for two months. And he'd be better served to just do the job he'd promised to do and leave the worrying to the living. Besides, Maggie hadn't asked for his help, and remembering how she'd brushed his offer of assistance aside only that morning, he had the distinct feeling his suggestions wouldn't be welcome.

His thoughts were scattered by the sounds of children's laughing shouts. Gabe turned his head to look up the street and found himself smiling. At least twenty kids were running down the street, headed for home.

"Some things never change," he muttered, and remembered how it had felt to be turned loose on a Friday afternoon with nothing to do all weekend.

Then his gaze narrowed on one of the kids. A boy, walking alone, behind everyone else. Head bowed, he still managed to keep a wistful eye on his schoolmates.

"Jake," he said to himself and wondered why the boy wasn't yipping it up with the others. He kept his gaze locked on the child as he walked toward the restaurant. Unexpectedly, something inside him twisted a bit in sympathy for the kid. He looked so small. So alone, in the busy street. No one paid him any attention. No one seemed to notice him at all.

Jake shuffled his feet, the toes of his shoes scuffing at the dirt, sending small clouds of dust up in front of him as he walked. And, since his eyes were downcast, the boy didn't see Gabe until he had climbed the steps.

"Hi."

"Hi, yourself," Gabe said, shifting position so he could watch the boy more closely. "Something wrong?"

"Uh-uh," he said and shook his head.

But the droop of his shoulders and the hangdog look of him belied that denial.

Sighing softly, Gabe took a seat on the top step and motioned for the boy to sit beside him. Hell, he'd never had much experience with kids. Working all night at a poker table pretty much assured a man he wouldn't be running into a lot of children. But there was something about this boy that reached into his untouched heart and made him want to help. Maybe, he thought, it was because the boy had so much of his mother in him.

He looked at him now. Same sparkling brown eyes, alive with interest. Same nose, same wide, smiling mouth, although at the moment, a smile was nowhere to be found on his face. Was that it? he wondered. Was he drawn to this child because he saw Maggie in him? And if that was true, what did it say about his feelings for Maggie?

Oh, better not to think of that right now. Or ever. As a dead man, he really didn't have much of a future.

"So," he said softly, shifting his gaze from the boy to make him more comfortable. "Want to tell me what's wrong?"

"Nothin'." He shrugged narrow shoulders and seemed to shrink in on himself further.

Well, who said talking to a kid would be easy? Together, they stared out at the street and Gabe waited a second or two before asking a different question. "If nothing's wrong, how come you weren't running with the others?"

Jake slanted him a look, then ducked his head again. "I'm too little," he said in a clearly disgusted tone.

Gabe smiled inwardly, but thought it wise to hide it on the outside. "Too little for what?"

"Everything."

"That takes up a lot of territory," Gabe commented.

Jake swung his belted schoolbooks back and forth between his upraised knees. He kept his gaze on those books as if his life depended on it. "They're going down to the creek," he finally said, then turned to look up at Gabe. "And Mom don't allow me to go."

"Ah . . ." He nodded thoughtfully, then pointed out, "it's a little cold to go swimming."

"Oh, they're not swimming," the boy told him, "it's only sometimes they fall in on accident."

"Sure," Gabe said with a smile, imagining just how many "accidents" those kids would manage to have. "Do you know how to swim?"

Disgusted again, Jake said, "No. Mom was gonna teach me last summer but she was too busy, and then she said how swimming ain't as important as schooling so she got hold of some books for me instead."

"And you spent the summer doing schoolwork?"

"Yeah."

"And you still say 'ain't'?" He grinned at the boy conspiratorially.

A like grin spread across the kid's features. "Not when Mom can hear me."

"Smart boy."

"That's what she says," Jake complained. "But I don't want to be smart, Gabe. I want to know how to swim and do the stuff everybody else does."

"What stuff?"

Well, that question set loose a tornado of information. Jake wanted to learn how to ride and how to play baseball and how to hunt and how to do so many other things, they were lost in the torrent of words.

Gabe nodded and listened while the boy talked a blue streak. He felt for the kid. He remembered all too well what it felt like to not really belong. Oh, he'd known how to swim and do the other things that were so important to Jake. But with Gabe it had been different. His father was a professional gambler and the parents of the "nice" children didn't want their kids playing with a gambler's boy. Plus, every couple of years, Eamon Donovan would announce it was time to move again, usually just a step or two ahead of the sheriff, and Gabe would have a new school, with new kids, and he'd have to start trying to belong all over again.

Which probably explained why he'd left school at thirteen never to go back.

He frowned to himself at the memories and pushed them aside. The past didn't matter anymore. It was long gone and impossible to change.

Jake's world, however, was wide open. Anything could happen. And looking down into those brown eyes, shining with hope and anticipation, Gabe decided then and there that as long as he was in Regret, he'd help the kid all he could. After all, what else did he have to do for the next two months? Smiling to himself, he interrupted the still-talking boy.

"So what are you supposed to be doing now?" he asked.

Jake gulped a breath, tossed his hair out of his eyes, and scowled. "Homework."

"How about we put that off for a while?"

A flash of eagerness danced in the boy's eyes briefly. Then it disappeared again. "Where's Mom?"

"Upstairs," Gabe told him, and as if in proof, came the distinct sound of something else being dragged across the floor. "What is she doing up there?" he wondered aloud.

"There's no telling," Jake said solemnly.

Gabe laughed and stood up. Apparently he wasn't alone. Even her son had trouble figuring out Maggie Benson. And for the moment, that was just fine. He had other things in mind, anyway. Brushing off the seat of his pants, he said, "Why don't you go put your books inside and we'll go do some man stuff."

Big brown eyes got wider as Jake leaped to his feet. "Man stuff? What kind of stuff?"

Gabe scraped one hand across his jaw and said, "Well, I could use a shave . . ." He drew his head back, stared at the boy for a long minute, then reached out and touched his jaw. Nodding to himself, he added, "And so could you."

His eyes were surely going to pop out of his head. "Me? A shave?"

"It's time," Gabe said solemnly. "You don't want to be the only kid in school with a beard, do you?"

Jake laughed and the sound was pure pleasure. Gabe had to wonder why it had taken dying for him to notice how much fun a kid could be. While he waited in the shade of the overhang, he told himself that this really meant nothing. He was just being nice to a lonely kid.

It was simply a bonus that being nice to Jake left him feeling better than he had in years.

Dolly Trent hung a Closed sign on the front door of the mercantile then stepped out onto the boardwalk and closed the door behind her firmly. She didn't bother to lock it. What if someone needed something and didn't have the time to wait for her to come back? No. This way, they could just go inside, get what they needed, and leave her a note. In a town the size of Regret, folks learned to take care of each other. To look out for each other. Which was just another reason why one particular female had Dolly mad enough to . . . well, she didn't know what.

But before she faced that female down, she'd try one more time to talk to the woman's husband. If Redmond could only find a little backbone, Dolly wouldn't have to talk to Sugar at all.

Glancing down, she smoothed her palms over the fall of her skirt, tugged at the hem of her waist-length jacket, then set off full steam down the boardwalk.

"Afternoon, Dolly," someone called out and she half turned to smile a greeting. She didn't stop to chat though. Her mind was far too busy with just what she was going to say to Redmond Harmon once she got hold of him.

Her temper had simmered all day until it had finally worked into a boiling stew. Something had to be done about Sugar Harmon and it was time Redmond found a spine and did it.

Kansas Halliday lounged in a chair outside his gunsmith shop, his long legs stretched across the boardwalk. Now Kansas was the laziest man God ever created. It had been said that the last time anyone had seen him move voluntarily was the night four years back when his bed had caught fire. And even then, he'd only moved from his bedroom to his chair on the boardwalk.

If folks wanted to get past him, they either went through him or around him. So it was a measure of just how mad Dolly looked when Kansas sat up straight and yanked his legs back out of her way.

Dolly sailed past him, her skirts flapping in her wake, heels clipping loudly on the wooden walk. She passed the milliner seamstress without so much as a glance at the pretty red hat in the window, then stomped on by the saloon and the jailhouse and everything else that stood between her and her goal, the bank.

Once there, she walked through the open doorway and paused on the threshold to let her eyes get accustomed to the dimmer light. Three people stood in line in front of the teller cage. A wall clock chimed out three bells and she turned her head toward the far corner of the building where she knew she would find Redmond Harmon.

It was as if he sensed her presence, because he lifted his gaze from the stack of papers he'd been studying and looked directly at her. Dolly couldn't be sure from a distance, but she was fairly certain she saw sweat break out on his forehead.

Good.

Marching across the gleaming wood floor, she walked straight to his desk and sat down in the chair opposite him without waiting for an invitation.

Redmond swallowed hard, glanced at his employees long enough to ensure they weren't watching him, then shifted his gaze back to her. "Dolly," he said carefully, "this is an unexpected pleasure."

"Is it?" she asked, keeping her voice low enough that only the two of them would know what was being said.

His mouth flattened out and she watched his Adam's apple bob up and down a couple of times before he spoke again. "What seems to be the problem?"

"The problem is that wife of yours as you damn well know."

"Now, Dolly—"

"Don't you 'now, Dolly' me, Redmond." She leaned one arm across his desk, scattering the papers, and tapped one fingertip against the pile. "I came here to tell you that if you don't take that woman in hand, I intend to."

His pale gray eyes went even paler at the thought.

And Dolly almost felt sorry for him. Almost. Sugar

was a handful, true, but by thunder, someone had to do something. Maggie had enough on her plate that she didn't need that woman's viperous tongue wagging every blasted minute.

"Sugar is a woman of strong opinions," he said, and eased his papers out from under Dolly's fingers.

"Her tongue is sharper than her opinions and that's what's brought me here today." With an effort, she bottled up her temper, reminding herself that it wasn't Redmond she was furious with, but his wife.

He winced slightly. "This is about Maggie again, isn't it?"

"You're darn tootin' it is."

"Dolly . . ."

"That wife of yours has hated Maggie for years."

" 'Hate' is a strong word."

"But appropriate."

"Perhaps," he admitted with a sigh. Leaning back in his chair, he folded his hands across his chest and fiddled nervously with his watch chain.

"I want to know why," she said, though she had an idea or two of her own.

"I'm not sure myself," he said with a shake of his head. "All I know is that while Maggie was living out on that little farm of hers, life was easier. Sugar's only got this bad since Maggie moved to town two years ago." He sat forward in his chair, placed his still-folded hands on the desktop, and looked directly into Dolly's eyes. "And I don't know why. She won't talk about her to me."

"Well, she's talking to everyone else," Dolly snapped.

"I know."

"What are you going to do about it, Redmond?"

"What can I do?" he asked, showing the first signs of irritation.

"You might try looking for your spine," Dolly told him hotly.

He pulled back and gave her a stunned stare. "There's no call to be insulting," he said.

She looked at him for a long minute or two, then nodded slowly. "You're right."

"I am?" Real surprise colored his tone.

"Yep," Dolly said and stood up. "I never should have come here to you, Redmond. This is something I can only settle with Sugar herself."

"Oh, now Dolly," he said, clearly disturbed at the very notion of the two women facing off. "I don't think that's a very good idea."

"That's the difference between you and me, Redmond. I think the only way to solve a problem is to face it head-on and then plow it under."

With that, she turned and swept out of the bank, leaving Redmond Harmon wishing there was a hotel in town, because life at home was going to be pure misery for a while.

"Well now," Bass Stevens asked loudly, "how's that feel?"

Jake reached up and rubbed his right cheek. "Feels smooth," he said and grinned at Gabe.

The fact that his cheeks had been smooth as glass before the shave didn't matter a damn, Gabe told himself. All that mattered now was that Jake felt all grown-up. He'd sat in that barber chair, had his hair cut and a shave just like every other man who walked through the door.

"Smooth, you say?" Bass yelled, "I hope to shout it's smooth. Been doing this for nigh onto forty years. Hope I've got it right by now." He picked up a wooden-handled brush and swept away loose hairs from Jake's neck before tearing the sheet off him and shouting, "You're set, son."

Gabe winced and wondered why it was a deaf man always shouted to everybody else. Maybe to hear himself talk? "How much?" he asked loudly enough, he hoped, to be heard.

"Lunch?" Bass asked and stared at him. "I don't serve no lunch. This here's a barber shop."

Jake chuckled and scampered off the high seat to make room for the next customer.

"Not lunch," Gabe corrected, speaking a bit louder than before. "I said, how much? How much for the haircuts and shaves?"

Bass frowned at him. "Why the hell didn't you say so?"

Jake laughed again and Gabe's lips twitched. "My fault," he yelled.

"Fall? Who fell?" Bass demanded.

Gabe's chin hit his chest as Jake collapsed against his side, laughter shaking his little body until Gabe had to reach down to hold him upright. This might take all night, he told himself and reached into his pocket for some money. Holding it out toward the barber, he tried again. "How much?"

The barber sniffed, scratched his head, and finally said, "Four bits each."

"Done."

"Of course you're done," Bass yelled. "I can't spend all day on you two for four lousy bits, y'know."

"Right you are," Gabe said on a choked-off laugh. He counted out the money, handed it over, then steered Jake out of the shop. Once outside, the two of them stopped to look at each other and the laughter started all over again.

"He can't hear very good," Jake finally managed to say.

"I noticed," Gabe told him, and laid one hand on the boy's shoulder to start him toward home. "So, you think your mother's got some work for us to do?"

Clearly disgusted, the boy kicked at the boardwalk. "I reckon. She's always busy now."

"Now?" Gabe asked, curious in spite of his better judgment.

"She didn't used to be in such a hurry all the time. She used to be different."

"Different how?"

Again, he scuffed his shoe against the boardwalk and tossed a look up at Gabe. "She was more fun than skippin' rocks. We did lots of stuff together. Now all she does is work all the time and makes me, too."

What had changed her? Gabe wondered, even though he knew it was none of his business and that she wouldn't thank him for butting in.

They'd gone only a few more steps when Maggie rushed out of the restaurant, turning her head this way and that. When her nearly frantic gaze landed on Gabe and her son, she seemed to droop with the relief.

But a moment later, she was headed their way and she didn't look any too happy to see them.

"Where have you been?" Hands on her hips, toe tapping against the boardwalk, she stared at her son.

"We were at the barber's," Gabe answered for him.

She shot him a glare. "I'm talking to Jake."

One of Gabe's eyebrows lifted. "Yes, ma'am."

"It's like he said, Mom," Jake told her and took a step closer to his mother. "Feel me. I got a shave, just like Gabe. And Bass put a really hot towel on my face and then lots of lather and everything. And he cut my hair too, just like you wanted."

That last bit, Gabe figured, was a wild shot for mercy. Reminding his mother that she'd wanted him to get a haircut and then hoping she'd see that he'd done her a favor by doing just that.

"I was worried, Jake," she said. "You shouldn't have gone off like that without telling me."

The boy's gaze dropped to his shoes. "I'm sorry, but—"

"No buts." She interrupted the apology and put one finger under his chin to lift his gaze to meet hers. Then she smiled and took the sting out of her words. "Just don't do it again, all right?"

Mother and son stared at each other for a long minute before Jake nodded. "All right."

"Good," she said, still smiling. "Now take that handsome face of yours inside and start your homework."

"Ah, Ma . . ."

"Scoot."

Maggie waited until Jake had gone inside before she turned to face her hired help. He had the nerve to look pleased with himself and somewhat surprised by her attitude.

"Why would you take him somewhere and not even bother to tell me?" she demanded.

Her voice was low and tight and twin spots of color filled her cheeks. Her eyes flashed warningly and if Gabe hadn't already been dead, he figured that gleam in her eyes would have done the trick.

"I didn't take him to San Francisco, Maggie. We were right next door. I meant no harm," he said.

"I don't care what you meant, he's *my* son."

"That's not in dispute."

"Isn't it?" She stepped up close and had to tilt her head back to glare at him. "You decide to take my son off on a little expedition and don't even bother to let me know he's home safe from school?"

"Maggie," he said on a forced laugh, "you're making too much of this."

"No I'm not," she told him. "I hired you to help with the restaurant, *not* to help raise my son."

"That's not what I was doing," he complained and couldn't help remembering one of his father's favorite sayings. *No good deed goes unpunished.*

"When he needs a haircut, I'll get him one."

"It wasn't about the haircut."

"And he had no business getting a shave, for heaven's sake."

"That's what you think."

"That's right," she said. "And it's what I think that counts. He's *my* son."

With that, she spun around on her heel and headed off to the restaurant. Well, Gabe was just a step or two behind her.

He caught up with her in the doorway and grabbed her upper arm to make sure she stopped. She tried to pull away, but he only tightened his grip a bit.

"You had your say, now it's my turn."

"You don't get a turn," she told him.

"Is that right?" He let her go and tried not to think about the tingling in his fingers from where he'd touched her. "Well, lady, I'm taking a turn anyway. That kid of yours is lonely."

"He is not."

"He is too."

She flinched from him as if he had physically struck her. "We have each other. That's enough."

"Not by a damn sight, it's not." For either of you, he thought, but didn't say. Why in the hell was she alone? Why didn't she find herself another husband? A good father for the boy? Couldn't she see what a waste it was for a woman like her to be alone?

"You don't know anything about us," she told him, her voice tight with emotion.

"Maybe not," he conceded. "But I know what it's like to be a boy. Do you?"

She snorted a laugh. "No. I don't."

"That's why you need a man around him occasionally, Maggie."

"What's that supposed to mean?"

"It means," Gabe told her fiercely, "a boy learns to be a man by being with other men. A mother, no matter how well meaning, can't teach him that. He needs a father."

She sucked in a gulp of air. "Fathers aren't always the best teachers, *Mr.* Donovan."

"Maybe not, Mrs. Benson," he said. "But a boy's got to be able to run a little wild from time to time. Go to the creek, play with his friends. He shouldn't have to spend every waking minute with his nose buried in a book."

She was quiet for quite a while and that should have worried him. But the truth was, he was so caught up in the argument now, he wouldn't have stopped anyway.

"Thank you so much for the benefit of your advice," she said softly.

"I only want to—"

"I'm sure." She cut him off and held up one hand to make sure he stayed quiet while she talked. "I'm sure you've learned a lot after having raised—how many children did you say you have?"

All right, fine. Gabe shifted, shoved both hands into his pockets, and met her dark gaze. "None."

"Ah, so in other words, you know nothing about raising children or what they need."

"I know what he *doesn't* need," Gabe told her. "He doesn't need to be mothered to death. He's not a baby, Maggie. You do him a disservice by treating him like one."

She blanched visibly and only then did he notice the spots of yellow paint speckling her face. She had it in her hair, down the front of her dress, and now that he looked, he saw the backs of her hands were covered in the same shade of golden-yellow.

She cleared her throat and he looked into her eyes.

"My son is my business, do you understand?" she asked.

"Yeah," he said softly. "But do you understand, Maggie, that *everybody* needs help sometime?"

"Maybe," she said, "but when I need your help, I'll ask for it."

He nodded. "All right. But don't wait too long, I'll only be here two months."

She smiled a bit at that and assured him, "I'll keep

that in mind." Then she turned and walked into the darkened restaurant.

She stopped, but didn't turn around when he called out after her, "By the way . . . yellow looks good on you."

CHAPTER SIX

Maggie walked into her son's room and stood in the shadows, watching him sleep. The blankets were in a twist around his legs and his left arm was flung across his eyes. Quietly, she moved forward and gently straightened his covers. He flopped over onto his side, but didn't wake and Maggie sat down on the edge of the bed beside him.

Reaching out, she smoothed his hair back from his face and let her fingertips trail across his cheek. So soft, she thought, and smiled at the mental image of her little boy getting a shave. Soon enough, she knew, he really would be shaving. He was growing so fast, the years slipping one into the other that it staggered her to think how quickly he would be grown and gone from her.

Frowning slightly, she folded her hands in her lap and thought about what Gabe had said that afternoon. There'd been some truth in his words, no matter how she tried to deny them. Jake *did* need a man in his life. She remembered then how her son had looked up at Gabe and smiled and she wondered how it was the two of them had become such fast friends.

Still, her new hired hand was wrong about something too. Not just any man would do for her son. His own father had been worse than useless and she shuddered when she thought about the kind of example he would have given had he stayed with them.

Her gaze drifted around the room, touching briefly on the artwork Jake had done and then nailed to his walls. A shaft of moonlight slanted through the window and fell across Jake's desk, illuminating the surface with a soft silver glow. A collection of rocks lay scattered across his desktop and one of his schoolbooks was lying open where he'd left it.

She stood up, walked to the desk, and slowly reached down to close that book, letting her fingers slide across the worn leather cover. Then she reached out and opened the window a bit, to let in the cool night air.

But along with the breeze came the muted sounds of revelry from the saloon. Frowning, Maggie stared at the garishly bright lights pouring from the front windows of the Howling Dog. And as she watched, a man came flying through the batwing doors, stumbled and fell across the boardwalk, then down the steps to land face first in the dirt. Someone inside tossed his hat out after him, and the man didn't stir when it landed in the center of his back.

"Drunk," she muttered, shaking her head. Yet another fine "lesson" her son could learn from the wrong kind of man.

Turning away from the window, she looked at her sleeping son again. In his innocent face, she saw the hope of a better future and silently she renewed her vow to do anything she had to, to see that hope become a reality.

Besides, she thought as she quietly left Jake's room, her son had a grandfather that Gabe didn't know about. And though her father's visits weren't often enough to suit Maggie, Jake loved him as much as she did.

In the dark, she walked from her son's room to her

own, and as she lay down on the feather mattress, letting the warm comfort of it surround her, her mind drifted once again to Gabe. And whether she liked it or not, she fell asleep with the sound of his voice humming in her ears and the remembered warmth of his touch soothing the lonely corners of her heart.

When Maggie's silhouette left the window, Gabe slowly turned and started walking again. He wondered what she'd been thinking as she stood in the darkness staring out at the night. And then, he wondered why he was wondering about her.

She and her son were none of his business, as she'd pointed out just that afternoon. He'd do well to remember that, he told himself and at the same time admitted that he probably wouldn't. The woman and her son touched something in him he hadn't been aware of until coming to Regret. And damned if he didn't find that annoying.

A dead man shouldn't have to put up with all this other nonsense. Why should his body still stir and his hungers quicken when he knew he couldn't do a damn thing about either of them? Was this some sort of special torture devised by a cunning Devil? If it was, it was damned effective.

Scowling, he listened to the rowdy noise filtering from the saloon and felt its old call reach out to him. Scowling more deeply, he ignored it and kept walking. He passed the silent, darkened livery stable and stepped into the bathhouse.

The old man behind the counter, who always looked

as though he could make good use of his own facilities, stared at Gabe in surprise.

"You back again? So soon?"

He smiled. "Back again."

The man stroked one hand down the length of his dirty gray beard and shook his head, dislodging one of the three strands of hair glued to a bald scalp with a healthy dose of witch hazel. "You're gonna wear out your skin, you keep washin' it this much," he warned.

Gabe's gaze swept across his host quickly. From his straggly beard, to the stained underwear peeking out from beneath an equally dirty shirt, the man appeared to be in no danger from suffering a like fate.

"I'll risk it," Gabe said and tossed a fifty-cent piece onto the counter. It rolled across the uneven wooden surface until a grimy hand came down on it.

"Your hide, I reckon," the man said with a shrug and reached beneath the counter for a worn but clean towel. This he tossed to Gabe and, jerking his head toward a door on the right, said, "Go ahead on. You know the way."

Inside the dimly lit back room, Gabe found himself alone and quickly stripped. He helped himself to the pots of hot water kept simmering on a nearby stove, and when he'd filled the tub halfway, eased his tired body down into it.

Letting his head fall against the high back of the tub, he stared at the ceiling and noted, not for the first time, the five or six bullet holes in the roof. Apparently, the bathhouse customers created their own diversions from time to time, he thought, and smiled as he closed his eyes to better enjoy the heat seeping into his bones.

Of course, this was probably a mistake, he thought.

What he needed here, was *cold* water. And lots of it.

"What you need," a voice from close by told him, "is to keep your mind on what you're supposed to be doing."

Gabe's eyes flew open. He knew that voice. But there was no one in the room with him.

"Over here," the voice said and Gabe turned to look at the shadow-filled far corner of the room. As he watched, those shadows thickened, taking on a shape he remembered all too well.

The gunfighter stepped out of those shadows and came within a foot or two of the tub where Gabe sat, feeling at a distinct disadvantage. Cupping his hands, he covered himself as best he could and shot the Devil a glare.

"Can't a man take a bath in peace?"

The Devil laughed shortly. "You want peace?" he asked and shook his head. "Then you shouldn't have made a deal with me."

"You're saying I had a choice?"

"There's always a choice," the Devil said with a shrug and walked slowly around the room.

Gabe followed him with his eyes and tried to slink lower into the water. His knees jutted up from the surface even as his chin came level with the water's edge. "I thought I had two months," he said, then spit out a mouthful of water.

"You do."

"Then why're you here now?"

"Call it . . ." the Devil said and paused before turning to fix an icy stare on him, "a reminder visit about what you're supposed to be doing."

"You really think I'm likely to forget?"

The tall gunfighter lowered himself to sit on the edge of another tub. Setting his palms on his knees, he smiled a slow smile that did nothing to ease the tightness of his features. "Then why aren't you busy getting me what's mine?"

"How'm I supposed to do that?" Gabe asked and noticed the water was cooling off. Goose bumps raced along his flesh and he shivered slightly. At the same time, he couldn't help thinking that in two months' time, he'd never again have to worry about being cold.

"That's not my problem," the Devil said, inclining his head toward Gabe. "But it is definitely yours."

"And I'm taking care of it."

"How? By playing games with a child?"

A mental image of Jake rose up in Gabe's mind and he felt a sudden swirl of anger rush through him. That boy was no business of the Devil's. "Leave him out of this."

A half-smile lifted one corner of the Devil's mouth. "Protective instincts? From the condemned?"

That sneering comment only fed the flames of the anger burning inside. What he did with his last two months of life was up to him. As long as he lived up to his side of the bargain, Hell shouldn't give a damn how his task was accomplished. And he didn't have much to lose by saying so.

"Why don't you back off?" Gabe suggested. "I'll find Henry my way, in my own time."

"Your time? It's time *I* gave you, remember."

"Not likely to forget, am I?" he said, reaching one hand up to finger the rope-burn scar at the base of his neck. He'd been wearing that stupid red bandana for days now to hide the evidence of his hanging.

"Fine," the Devil said after a long, thoughtful moment. "But remember this," he went on and stood up to his full, imposing height. "None of these creatures are of any concern to you. The woman. Her boy. You're no more than a shadow to them. You'll pass through their unimportant lives and then be gone and forgotten almost before the doors of Hell swing shut behind you."

Gabe swallowed hard against a tight knot of regret rising in his throat. He knew the demon opposite him was right. Felt it in his bones. Maggie and Jake would go on with their lives whether he was a part of them or not. And when he was gone, he'd never see either of them again. Since he hoped to high heaven neither one of them would have the misfortune to spend eternity in the flames.

"Heaven?" the Devil said on a laugh, plucking that one word from his mind like taking an egg from beneath a setting hen. He threw his head back and let loose a roar of laughter that shook the tub, making the cooling water tremble around Gabe. "Headed for Hell and hoping to Heaven?"

"A man's got a right to private thoughts," he snapped.

"Not anymore, you don't." The Devil strolled leisurely to the far corner again, dissolving into the shadows as if he'd never been. But as the last of him folded into emptiness, his voice whispered, "The clock is ticking, *Gabriel,* take care that you don't disappoint me."

Then Gabe was alone again and he knew there wasn't enough hot water in the world to ease the chill from his bones.

*   *   *

When dawn broke, Gabe was already awake and working on his second cup of coffee. Late-night chats with the Devil weren't exactly conducive to a sound sleep.

He leaned one elbow on the tabletop and cupped his head in the palm of his hand. His eyeballs felt like two marbles rolling around in sand. Rubbing his eyes with his fingertips, he tried to remind himself that he was dead and shouldn't be crying about a lost night of sleep, for God's sake.

God.

That one word stopped him cold. He hadn't been inside a church since he was a boy and the only time he could remember saying the Lord's name out loud was when he was cussing. Which no doubt helped to explain why he was at the Devil's doorstep. Oh yeah, he was the perfect man to guide a boy like Jake into manhood.

What the hell had he been thinking?

"Oh, my goodness!"

He jerked upright in his chair, startled at the abrupt end to the stillness of the morning. Half turning in his chair, he looked toward the staircase. Maggie came flying down the stairs like a disheveled whirlwind. Barefoot, hair free of her usual braid, her eyes were wide and panic shone clearly from their depths.

"I can't believe this is happening," she muttered darkly as she rushed across the room.

Instantly, Gabe went on the alert. *What* was happening? In the few days he'd known her, he'd seen her happy and furious, but he'd never seen her in such a blind panic before. He stood up so quickly, he tipped his chair over and it clattered on the floor behind him. She barely spared him a glance, while Gabe's gaze darted around the empty room, looking for the source of the danger.

"What is it?" he demanded. "What's wrong?"

She shook her head and ran straight for the pantry. He heard her rummaging through her supplies and winced when something dropped and broke.

"Damn it, Maggie?" He looked toward the stairs again and wondered wildly if he should go up and check on Jake. Maybe she was hysterical. Maybe the place was on fire. Maybe . . . hell. He didn't *know* what.

"What's going on?" he yelled.

Poking her head around the corner, she glared at him. "What're you shouting about? You'll wake up Jake."

"He's all right, then?"

She looked at him like he was out of his mind. Strangely enough, that was just how he felt.

"Of course he's all right, he's sleeping." Ducking back into the pantry, she continued in a furious whisper, "*I'm* the one in trouble."

"What kind of trouble, damn it?"

She stuck her head back out long enough to flash him a look that should have singed the soles of his shoes.

"Are you going to help me or not?"

"Help you *what*?" He came around the corner of the table, walked as far as the pantry, and stopped on the threshold. He watched as she gathered up a basket brimming with fresh eggs and a loaf of bread and then tried to grab the ham.

He saw the basket of eggs teeter precariously on her arm and he reached past her, snatched up the ham himself, then blocked the doorway when she would have left.

He waited for her to look up at him. Absently, he

noted there were still small splotches of yellow dotting her skin like freckles only brighter than the rest. Then he said, "Tell me what's goin' on and maybe I *can* help."

"There's no time," she muttered and shook her hair back. Immediately, it fell back down to hang on either side of her face again.

"*Make* time. You about gave me a heart attack running in here like the place was on fire."

"The *stage,*" she told him as if that were explanation enough.

"It's here?" he asked.

"It *is*?" She fell back a pace, clearly horrified.

"You just said it was."

"No I didn't," she argued.

"You just said—"

"I said it's coming. Why would I say it was here if it wasn't?"

Oh, it was way too early for this conversation. He pulled in a deep breath, forced a false calm into his voice, and said only, "Explain."

Hugging the loaf of bread to her chest, she looked at him for a long minute before saying quickly, "The morning stage will be here any minute. I have to feed the passengers. And nothing's ready."

"Is that all?" The tight knot that had lodged in his chest the minute she raced downstairs finally dissolved.

Maggie shoved past him, sending him staggering backward. "Is that *all*?" Shaking her head, she hurried to the counter and set the bread and eggs down. "Don't you understand? You said yourself I don't have any customers. If I lose the stage-stop contract, I won't be able to keep the restaurant open."

"I wondered how you managed to keep going," he

said, narrowing his gaze as she grabbed up a bowl and cracked three eggs into it. He frowned when pieces of shell dropped into the mix and then stepped forward, taking the bowl from her. "Figured you must have a host of Saturday-night cowboys every week."

"I do," she said, barely noticing that he was now breaking several more eggs into the bowl. Instead, she grabbed up the loaf of bread and started slicing. "But they're not enough to keep us going. I *need* the stage contract."

He heard the desperate edge in her voice and reacted to it. Reaching out, he cupped her chin in his hand and forced her to pause long enough to meet his gaze. When he was sure he had her attention, he said softly, "Then you'll have it. Don't worry. The passengers will be fed."

She stared at him for a long minute. Seconds ticked past and it felt to Gabe as though the only things in the world were her eyes, looking up at him. Disbelief, hope, and then . . . *trust* glimmered in her eyes and Gabe was staggered by it. No one had ever looked at him the way she did. No one had ever counted on him to do anything except deal the next hand.

And for the first time in too many years, he worried about disappointing someone.

When, a heartbeat later, she moved back and out of his grasp, he rubbed his fingertips together to take the sting out of the loss of her.

"Maybe you haven't noticed this," she said and had to pause to clear the huskiness from her voice, "but I'm not much of a cook."

Gabe chuckled. "I've noticed. But don't worry," he added. "I'm pretty damned good even if I do say so myself."

"You *cook*?" Stunned, she only stared up at him.

He broke two more eggs into the bowl, whipped them into a lemony froth, then grabbed up the ham and shaved chunks of meat into the mixture.

Nodding, he said, "My mother died when I was a kid, and my father was hopeless around a stove, it was either learn, or starve." He winked at her. "I don't like being hungry."

Maggie looked from his eyes to his hands and back again. He wasn't kidding. He really did know how to cook. And she didn't know whether to feel grateful or humbled. Or both. "What can I do?" she finally asked.

Grinning now, he told her, "Put a pot of coffee on, hand me a skillet, then stand back."

She did just what he said. From the corner of the kitchen, Maggie watched as her handyman, whipped up what smelled like a delicious breakfast in less time than it would have taken her to figure out what to attempt to make.

Gabriel Donovan was an unusual man, she told herself. Though he'd irritated her beyond measure when he'd spouted advice about her son, he was now riding to her rescue atop a battered stove. He was still a stranger to her and yet just his touch was enough to start small fires in her blood. He'd slipped into the fabric of her life in a few short days and somehow had made things . . . easier, simply by being there.

And when the familiar sound of the stage's trace chains reached her, for the first time since taking over the restaurant . . . Maggie wasn't worried a bit.

CHAPTER SEVEN

The passengers left happy.

Maggie sighed and flopped down onto the nearest chair. From outside came the early morning Saturday sounds of Regret gearing up for a new day. Usually by this time, she was scrubbing blackened pots and telling herself that one more bad meal wouldn't ruin her.

Amazing what the right kind of help could do.

Reaching behind her head, she untied the string holding her hair into a long, loose tail, then let her mind drift back over the last half hour. Snippets of images filled her brain and she smiled to herself. Gabe had been a charming host. He'd sweet-talked the elderly woman and then done some backslapping with the whiskey drummer. Even Jason, the coach driver, had shared a laugh or two with him. He'd fed them all a wonderful concoction of scrambled eggs and ham and kept them talking with a steady stream of conversation. Then he wooed them with a smile that could melt butter at fifty paces.

And he'd done it all effortlessly.

Quite a difference from the way she'd been doing things for the last couple of years. Sighing, she let her gaze slide across the empty room. In one half hour, Gabe had shown her plainly how ill suited she was to the task of running a restaurant.

She'd hoped that with time her skills would improve.

But instead, she seemed to be getting worse. Not only was she still a terrible cook, she couldn't make herself really *care* about the situation. Oh, she wanted the business to succeed for Jake's sake. She needed to belong here so that he would too. But there was still a part of her that longed to throw her skillet into the yard and walk off into the sunset.

She was a terrible person, she told herself. How could she even consider her own feelings when her son's future was at stake? It didn't matter that she hated trying to cook. It only mattered that she *learn*. But blast it, hadn't she been trying to do just that for two long, failure-laden years?

"Oh God, I'm hopeless," she said to herself, never noticing that Gabe had stepped back into the restaurant after waving the coach off on the next leg of its journey.

"No you're not," he said and she lifted her head to look at him.

That's what he thought. She laughed shortly. "Until today, I'd never seen a smile on Jason's face as he left here. Not once in the last year and a half that I've had the stage-route contract."

"You can learn how to cook, Maggie," he said softly.

"I don't think so," she said, then added quickly, "But even if I could, I can't learn how to do everything else you did."

"Like what?" he asked as he took a seat opposite her.

Looking at his expression, she could see confusion etched plainly into his features. Did he really not know? Wasn't he aware of how easily he charmed people? Maggie was always so busy worrying about saying the wrong thing that she never said the right thing and ended up saying pretty much nothing at all.

Shaking her head in admiration, she said, "It's easy for you, isn't it?"

"What?" He looked puzzled.

"Being charming."

"Charming?" He cocked his head, gave her a half-smile, and asked tentatively, "Is that a compliment?"

"Yes," she said and leaned both elbows on the table. Cupping her chin in her hands, she said, "You actually had that woman simpering at you like a young girl."

All right, now he looked uncomfortable.

"She wasn't simpering."

"Yes she was," Maggie said. "And I don't mean that in a bad way. You made her happy. She enjoyed herself."

He shifted in his chair. "Look," he said, leaning back in his chair and stretching his legs out in front of him. "I was just trying to help."

"And you did," she said. "That's what I'm talking about. How good you were with those stage-coach passengers." She paused, straightened up, and folded her hands in front of her on the table. "And Jason will go back and tell the stage-route manager how well things went here today and he'll be happy too."

"That's good, isn't it?"

"That's wonderful," she said wistfully.

"So why don't you sound happy about that?"

"Because," she admitted, though it cost her some pride, "when you leave here in two months, everything will go back to the way it was. Passengers grumbling, route manager threatening to pull my contract, Jason grimacing as he chokes down one of my meals."

Gabe smiled briefly and shook his head. "You're not that bad."

"Oh, yes I am," she countered. Lying to herself wouldn't change anything. She was the world's worst cook who owned a restaurant that people stayed away from in droves.

"I can teach you to cook," he offered and Maggie smiled at him.

"Thank you," she said. "I'll take you up on that offer." Because it was imperative that she keep her business alive and well, in spite of how much she loathed cooking. But there was more to running a successful restaurant than simply being a good cook and she knew it.

If that was all she needed, she could hire a cook, assuming that she ever had enough business to make the money required to pay someone.

No. She needed help. Not just any help, either. She needed someone who knew how to talk to people. Someone who could bring in customers and then convince them to stay. In short, as she'd learned so completely just a while ago, she needed Gabe.

"I'd like you to think about something," she said softly and clasped her hands more tightly together.

"What?"

"Now don't say anything yet, just think about it."

"Maggie . . ."

Refusal colored his tone and she plunged ahead.

"Wait. Let me at least say this." She shook her head, lifted her chin, and looked him dead in the eye as she started speaking again. "I'd like us to work together."

"We already do," he pointed out.

"No," she corrected him quietly. "Now, you work *for* me. I'd like you to work *with* me."

"What are you saying?" he asked and she noticed that his features had tightened.

"I'm offering you a partnership," she blurted and the minute she said it aloud, she knew it was the right thing to do. Every instinct she possessed was telling her to listen. To take a chance on Gabe.

For some unknown reason, the Fates had sent her the very man she needed to ensure her business's success. With him, the restaurant would become a paying proposition. With his help, she could build a solid foundation for her son to grow on. All she had to do was convince him to make his temporary job here a permanent one.

"Maggie," he said, already shaking his head, "I told you that I'd be leaving in—"

"Two months," she finished for him. "I know. All I'm saying is that I want you to think about that. To reconsider." If she didn't pressure him for a decision right now, maybe in time he'd come to see things her way.

Still shaking his head, he smiled sadly and said, "I'm not a merchant, Maggie. I don't know the first thing about running a business."

She waved her arms to encompass the empty room around them. "Take a good look, Gabe," she said. "Do you think I do?" Then she let her hands drop to the tabletop. "This morning, you did what I've been trying to do unsuccessfully for two years."

"What's that?"

"Send customers away with smiles on their faces," she admitted bleakly.

"You're learning."

"You could teach me more quickly than I could learn on my own."

"No."

Why wouldn't he at least listen to her? Hear her out and then take the blasted time to consider her proposition. "Damn it, don't say that yet."

His eyebrows lifted slightly. "Damn?"

She smiled ruefully. "Aren't you the one who told me to say it when I meant it?"

"You shouldn't take advice from me," he said with a shake of his head. "Believe me. I can't stay, Maggie, I already told you that."

"Why not?" she demanded and fought down a swell of disappointment rising inside her.

"I told you, I have an appointment to keep."

"So come back when your business is finished."

He snorted a choked-off laugh, pulled himself to his feet in one languid movement, then half turned from her. "Wish I could," he said under his breath.

"Then do it."

Spinning back around, he looked into her eyes. "It's not that easy."

"It could be," she said stubbornly, "if you wanted it to be."

"Wanting and getting are two different things," he ground out tightly.

"Just think about it," she said, still determined not to give up. Couldn't he see that this arrangement would be perfect for both of them? When she'd hired him, he'd asked her not to hold his past against him. Well, she figured that he was no longer interested in being a gambler. So why couldn't he see that this would be a fresh start for him?

"Maggie . . ."

She stood up, too, and reached out one hand to lay on his forearm. The instant she did, she felt a jagged spear of heat lance up her arm, rocket around inside her chest, and shimmer around her heart. Instantly, she pulled her hand back, as if by doing so she could pretend that flash of warmth had never happened.

She needed Gabe to help her with the restaurant, she scolded herself. There was no reason for her body to go all limp and rag-dolly on her just because she touched him. And if she did convince him to stay, she'd have to remember to keep a safe distance between them. Because no matter what her insides told her, she wasn't about to let a man into her heart again.

"All right, if you don't want to say yes now," she said in a rush, to prevent him from refusing again so readily, "at least wait to say no."

He inhaled sharply.

Maggie took a quick breath and kept talking. "Until you go, why don't we *try* a partnership?"

"Try it?"

"Yes," she said swiftly, sensing that he was at least willing to consider something temporary. And if that went well, at the end of two months, she would find a way to convince him to make it permanent. "Then we could both see how it would work out. You can teach me to cook and maybe we can make the restaurant so successful you'll change your mind and want to stay."

"I won't change my mind," he said softly, staring down into her eyes. She saw the glimmering shine of regret in those blue depths. Obviously, he was interested in her proposition. Why was he fighting so hard against it?

"People change their minds all the time," she countered. "You might too."

"I won't. I can't."

She ignored that, determined now to reach him. "Fine. But what do you say about the temporary arrangement?"

A long minute or two passed. Maggie could almost see him thinking, weighing his decision, and she couldn't help wondering why he was so hesitant. Was it being a merchant that bothered him? Or being partners with her? And what appointment was so important that it would keep him from ever returning to Regret? To her.

Finally, though, when she'd almost given up hope, he reluctantly said, "All right. For the next two months, we'll be partners. We'll get the restaurant up and running . . ."

She smiled at him and then felt that smile dissolve as he finished.

"And when I'm gone, you'll have the best damned restaurant in Nevada, all to yourself."

"Sugar!"

Dolly glanced over her shoulder, making sure that no one was within earshot. But she needn't have worried. The Harmon house was at the end of town, set well back from the road. Sugar'd seen to that. The walkway leading from the street to the wide front porch was lined with flowers, now looking a bit frostbitten around the edges. Twin pines with slightly twisted trunks stood at the front corners of the house like crippled soldiers on guard duty.

The windowpanes shone in the morning sunlight and from within came the scent of fresh-baked cinnamon bread.

Dolly knocked on the door again, louder this time. She'd been trying to corner Sugar all week with no success. Durn woman appeared to be hiding out. Redmond must have warned her that Dolly was on the warpath.

"Dang it, Sugar," she called out, bending to one side to peer in the window. She thought she caught a glimpse of movement just beyond the lace curtain, but she couldn't be sure. "I know you're in there, Sugar," she yelled, "and I'm not leaving until I have my say."

Ah. The magic words.

The door was jerked open a moment later and Dolly blinked in surprise as Sugar demanded, "What is it?"

The woman looked sour, as usual. Not for the first time, Dolly told herself it was a shame Sugar had never had children. Maybe it was the lack of them that had made her this way. Because Dolly remembered a time, years past now, when Sugar had even been known to smile occasionally.

But after marrying Redmond late in life and then not being blessed with children, she seemed to have shriveled up inside, finding her only comfort in making other folks as miserable as she was.

Still, she hadn't come to sympathize with Sugar, but to warn her off of Maggie. Dolly straightened up, tugged at the hem of her short, slighty too tight jacket, and asked, "Aren't you going to ask me in?"

"No, I am not," Sugar told her and positioned herself in the doorway's opening, as if she expected the other woman to charge right through, knocking her to the floor if she had to.

And Dolly thought about doing just that. But only briefly.

"Fine," she said instead, "I'll say what I came to say, standing right here."

"Well, get on with it," Sugar snapped. "I've bread in the oven."

"And a razor blade in your mouth."

"I *beg* your pardon?" The woman sniffed and lifted her chin even higher than normal. If it started raining right this minute, she'd probably drown, what with her nose stuck so high in the air.

"You heard me," Dolly told her and wagged her index finger. "Maggie told me how you came around to her place, stickin' that long nose of yours where it don't belong."

Sugar's mouth flattened into a thin line and her eyes narrowed. "I don't know what you're talking about."

"Oh, yes you do."

"I think you'd better go," she said and started to close the door.

Dolly slapped the flat of her hand against the pristine white door and held it open through sheer force of will.

"Let go of my door."

"Not until you swear to leave Maggie and her boy alone."

"I have nothing against her boy," Sugar said, and Dolly thought she almost spotted something wistful in her expression before it was stamped out.

"Then, for pity's sake, stop talking about his father."

She sniffed. "All I said was he had the look of Kersey."

"That's more than enough and you know it." Dolly moved closer. "Maggie doesn't want the boy asking questions about his pa and I reckon you can figure out why without having to be told."

"She should have thought of that before she married the man."

"That's neither here nor there."

A breeze stirred and shot past the two women, lifting the brim of Dolly's hat and teasing at the harsh tight knot of Sugar's hair enough to loosen one or two strands.

Instantly, she reached up to push them back into place. "My bread . . ." she said.

"Fine. You go take care of your bread, I've said what I came to say."

"Good."

As the door started closing again, Dolly let it go, but added, "I'm warning you, Sugar. You shut your mouth about Maggie, or it'll be between you and me."

Sugar's fingers on the edge of the door tightened until her knuckles turned white. "Dolly Trent, you've no call to speak to me like that."

"Oh, yes I have," she said. "Maggie has no one to speak up for her and she's so durned concerned about what folks around here think of her, she won't say anything herself."

Sugar snorted. "If she's all that concerned, then she shouldn't have a strange man living in her home."

"He works for her."

A nasty smile touched Sugar's lips briefly and died an ugly death just as quickly. "That's what she says, of course. But I say, where there's smoke, there's fire."

"And *I* say, where there's venom, there's Sugar."

"Now, you listen here . . ."

"No, you listen," Dolly told her and took a step toward her. Heaven help her, never in her life had she wanted to strike another human being as badly as she did at that moment. To keep from doing just that, she curled her fingers into tight fists. "You've become a dried-up, spiteful woman, Sugar Harmon, but there's no reason for you to spread your bile to those who don't deserve it."

She sucked in a breath as though someone had thrown a punch to her midsection. "Go away."

"Oh, I'm goin'," Dolly told her, "but you mind what I said." Then she stepped back and Sugar slammed the door so hard, the curls on Dolly's forehead fluttered in the resulting breeze. A small thread of satisfaction wound through her as she turned and stepped off the porch to walk back to town. At the end of the walkway, she turned for another look at the Harmon house and was in time to see the lace curtain fall back into place after sliding off the tips of Sugar's fingers.

She smiled, then set off for the mercantile, enjoying the soft mountain breeze that rattled the leaves overhead and stirred tiny dust clouds on the road.

A week later, Gabe stood in the kitchen, waving the back door like a giant fan, trying to clear the smoke out of the room. Every day, they'd worked at this and every day, Maggie found something new to burn.

Nothing was safe. Pies, cakes, meats of all kinds, everything that entered her oven left it looking like a lightning-struck tree—black, twisted, and smoking.

"I told you. I'm hopeless," she said from across the room.

He wanted to say, "yes, you are," and quit torturing both of them. But Gabe wasn't a man to whom quitting came easy. "No you're not," he said and shoved his fingers through his hair.

Maggie coughed and flapped her apron at the last of the smoke still hanging in the room like fog. "I don't know what else you'd call it," she said and walked to the table to pick up her latest failure.

Gabe looked at the two unidentifiable lumps and shook his head. Who would have thought apple pies could blacken so nicely?

"At least the stray dogs in town are eating well," she muttered and, carrying the pies to the open back door, set them on the top step as her latest offering.

When she turned away, Gabe noticed a single hound come skulking toward the back porch. It sneaked up on the pies, gave them a sniff, then whined and backed away from them. He frowned and closed the door firmly. She didn't need to know that even stray dogs had started to avoid her cooking. He'd bury the pies later.

"I don't know why I can't do this," she grumbled and gave the stove a dirty look, as if *it* were the real culprit.

"It just takes practice," he said for what had to be the thousandth time that week. And even Gabe noticed he didn't sound quite so sure as he had when they'd started their lessons.

She gave him a look that let him know she'd heard the disbelief in his tone too.

"Your bread's not bad," he offered. Though silently he wondered how anyone could char the outside of the loaf and have the inside be doughy and underdone.

"Face it, Gabe," she said. "I have. I'm not a cook, will never be a cook."

He scrubbed one hand across his face and looked at her. Flour dotted her hair and the front of her blue dress. Her apron bore the marks of everything she'd tried to cook and even the palm of her right hand was still singed from making an unwise grab at a falling hot pan.

All right, maybe it was time to take a break from their lessons and try something else. The woman had absolutely no talent with a skillet and a stove. Well, except for one thing, he told himself, remembering the huge kettle of beef-vegetable soup she'd made Saturday morning. Apparently, she'd gotten into the habit of making her specialty on the one night she could count on customers.

And he had to say, the cowboys had eaten every drop of that soup and washed it down with gallons of coffee, before heading off to the saloon. But as he'd reminded her as she'd stood back proudly, you couldn't run a restaurant that served only soup.

If it killed both of them, he would teach her to cook at least a few edible things. Then, once the restaurant started making money, she could *hire* a real cook. As for now, though, they could work on something just as important.

If they were going to change things around at this restaurant, Gabe thought, they were going to do it right. It wasn't just Maggie's cooking that had to be fixed, it was the place itself.

"Forget about this for a while," he said and started for the door leading to the dining room. "Come with me."

"Not that I'm complaining about leaving the kitchen," she said as she tore her apron off and started after him, "but where are we going?"

"The mercantile," he said shortly.

* * *

Maggie stood beside him as he placed order after order with Dolly. Nerves escalating, she tried to keep track of the money he was spending and lost count purposely when it climbed past fifty dollars.

Still, she had to say something when he ordered some fancy wine all the way from St. Louis.

"You'll get customers so drunk on your wine," she said, "they'll spill food all over the new tablecloths you just bought and ruin them."

"If they want to get drunk," he told her with a too patient smile, "they'll go to the saloon. If they want fine wine with an excellent meal, they'll go to—"

"San Francisco?" Maggie prompted.

"Very funny." He turned back to look at Dolly, who was busily taking notes on her order pad. "We'll need some china coffeepots, too," he said and got an elbow in the ribs from Maggie.

"China? You can't make coffee in china pots. Even *I* know that." Desperate, she tried to snatch the order pad, but Dolly was too fast for her and moved back out of reach.

"The china's not to make it in, but to serve it in," he told her, shaking his head.

"Dolly, don't order those," Maggie said and looked up at Gabe. "The restaurant's not making any money. I can't afford to buy china when tin will work just as well."

"You can't afford not to," he told her. Then, winking at the storekeeper, he said, "Think you could extend us a little credit, Dolly?"

Clearly getting into the spirit of this, the older woman said, "Well now, there's two things I usually stay clear of—credit." she shot him a knowing smile. "And a smooth-talkin' man."

Maggie groaned.

Gabe slapped one hand to his chest in mock horror. "Me? Why, I'm hurt."

"You'll heal, I'm thinkin'," Dolly said with a smile.

He leaned on the countertop and met her gaze. "A little credit would help me on the road to recovery."

"What are you doing?" Maggie demanded, tugging at his sleeve until he looked at her. "I don't want to be in debt."

Damn the man, he patted her hand as if she were a child and said, "You won't be in a couple of weeks."

"Dolly . . ." Maggie warned her old friend with a shake of her head.

But the woman waved an idle hand at her and kept her gaze locked with Gabe's. "Done," she said and offered him her hand.

Instead of shaking it, Gabe bent and kissed her knuckles and Maggie groaned again.

Gabe heard her and understood why she was so worried. She had to take care of Jake. Had to make her business successful. But to do that, she was going to have to take chances. Be daring. And if that meant getting a little credit to tide them over, so be it. It was necessary to fix up that restaurant and make it a place that people would want to come to.

"You've got to make your restaurant stand out from the rest of town," he said, turning to face her. "Since the food's not enough to draw customers, you have to offer them something else. You've got to be different to be noticed."

Dolly cleared her throat, and glanced at Maggie, who scowled back at her.

"What?" he asked.

"Nothin'," Dolly said.

Maggie ignored her friend. "What if I don't want to be different? What if I want to fit in and have my restaurant make people feel like they're at home?"

He laughed shortly. She really didn't understand showmanship at all. Well, that was one thing he knew plenty about. Gabe had learned early on, while watching his father, that people's perception of things was really all that mattered. How many times had his father been down to his last two-bit piece . . . but to look at him no one would ever have guessed it. His clothes were always well tailored, and brushed clean. Hair neat, fingernails trimmed, shoes shined, Eamon Donovan had always looked the very image of a prosperous man. And so people believed it.

Gabe had done the same thing during his career as a gambler. Look successful and, sooner or later, you *became* successful.

Now, he had to teach Maggie that same lesson. "People don't want sameness when they're out getting away from their routine," he said and shook his head patiently. "If it feels like home when they go out . . . why go out?"

"I don't know . . ."

"Trust me, Maggie," he said and gave her a slow smile. "You don't want to be like everyone else."

Dolly cleared her throat again, louder this time.

Frowning, he looked at the older woman. "Are you all right?" he asked.

"Fine, fine," she assured him, but he noticed her giving Maggie another sharp look. Obviously, there was something going on here that he didn't know about.

"If you're sure . . ."

"I'm fine, young man," Dolly told him and waved her pencil in the air. "Now, go on with what you were sayin'."

Maggie smirked at her.

"Anyway," he said, still sure he was missing something, "besides learning to cook, you need to paint the inside of the restaurant. And I think you should leave that part up to me." He shook his head and tried to say what he had to, kindly. "You don't really have the knack of making a place look . . . *special*.

Maggie gasped, clearly insulted.

Dolly choked and went into a coughing fit that shook her whole body. When Gabe tried to slap her on the back though, she moved out of reach, wiped tears from her eyes, and shook her head. "S'cuse me," she said, "must've swallowed the wrong way."

"What is going on here?" Gabe asked, looking from the restrained humor in Dolly's eyes to the disgust in Maggie's. No one spoke. "Will one of you let me in on the joke?"

But neither of the women were looking at him. Instead, they stared at each other for several long moments and oddly enough seemed to almost be having a silent conversation. Finally, though, one of them broke.

"I don't have the 'knack'?" Maggie asked him.

He'd hurt her feelings. Well, hell. He hadn't meant to, but still, he couldn't back down now. If she wanted his help in fixing up her business, then she'd have to take his advice, even when it hurt. "It's nothing to be ashamed of," he said in an effort to placate her some. "Why, in most big restaurants, the owners hire somebody to come in and make the place look nice." He gave her a conciliatory smile. "And I'll do it for you."

She huffed out a breath, tapped her fingertips against the wooden counter, and looked as if she were counting to ten.

"Is that right?"

He nodded. "Don't worry, it'll look fine."

A muscle worked in her jaw.

"Maggie?" the older woman asked, chuckling under her breath. Maggie slid her a glance. "Why don't you just show him?"

"Show me what?" he asked, looking from one woman to the other, trying to figure out what was going on.

"Hire him to decorate the restaurant for me," Maggie muttered. "I have no talent for the job," she went on, as if prodding herself with his verbal jabs.

"Maggie, I didn't mean to insult you."

"Oh, I'm sure," she said, and tore her gaze from Dolly's to fix him with a steady stare. "But before you go picking out what color you want for the restaurant, I think you should see something." Then shooting her friend a sharp glare, she grabbed hold of Gabe's arm, turned him around to face the front door and said, "Come on."

She let go of him as soon as they left the store, but obviously expected him to follow her. He did. Across the street, into the restaurant, through the dining room and then the kitchen right to the foot of the steep staircase that led to her living quarters.

Her home.

There she stopped, glanced at him, and looked as though she had something to say and then thought better of it. "Never mind," she said softly. "It'll be easier just to show you."

She started up the steps and Gabe was just a pace or two behind her. His gaze strayed to the swell of her hips and the wonderful way she had of swaying when she walked. And when she was angry, that sway tripled in strength and at the same time turned his insides into a swirling pool of heated liquid. He told himself a decent man wouldn't stare, but then, he was a sinner, wasn't he? And who could blame him, if on the road to Hell, he paused now and then to admire the scenery?

Then they were on the landing and she opened the door to a world unlike anything he'd ever seen.

CHAPTER EIGHT

Maggie stood back, held her breath, and watched him.

His jaw dropped as he walked slowly into the middle of the main room, turning his head this way and that to take in everything. And there was plenty to see.

Her breath slowly slipped from her lungs as she tried to look at the parlor of her home through someone else's eyes. The wood walls had been painted a soft meadow-green and the sunset-gold color she'd only just gotten from Dolly decorated the windowsills. Along the bottom half of the walls grew a painted flower garden, with every kind of flower she'd ever seen, caught forever in full bloom. The highly polished floor glistened in the afternoon sunlight, reflecting back a muted rainbow of color. In fact, splashes of color filled every corner of the room, from a small, round table in the far corner on which stood a vase filled with paper flowers, to the fire-place screen that boasted a landscape scene of a lake in midsummer.

In front of the hearth, a semicircle of overstuffed furniture sat clustered together, inviting people to come and get comfortable. She'd covered the sofas and chairs herself with gaily striped fabric in shades of green and blue. And small, round pillows in contrasting shades of each color dotted their surfaces.

At the wide windows, blue and white gingham curtains, stiff with starch, rattled and snapped in the breeze slipping beneath the window sash.

"Maggie . . ." he said in a hushed tone and then snapped his mouth shut and shook his head as if he couldn't think what else to say.

She laced her fingers together at her waist and squeezed tightly. Only she, Jake, and Dolly had ever been in these rooms. Until today. And this was why. It was horrible, standing here, waiting to be judged. Waiting to see if he would laugh at her. Or worse yet, look at her as though she were crazy. She knew only too well that most people would never understand what she'd done here. They wanted their worlds to be in dignified shades of white and gray and brown.

But Maggie would suffocate in a world without color.

She'd made up her mind to fit in in Regret. She'd spent her early years being "different." Now she was determined to be just like everyone else. And it was a safe bet that no one else in town had painted the insides of their homes like she had.

But here, in these rooms, she could be herself. Be who she really was.

Her painted flower garden certainly wasn't the same as the garden she'd had to leave behind for her son's sake, but it was better than nothing. And sometimes, she almost convinced herself she could smell the sweetness of the blossoms and hear their stems brushing together in a breeze.

Oh my, maybe she *was* crazy. Her fingers tightened around each other and still she waited for Gabe to speak.

Was he horrified? she wondered and tried to judge his feelings by his expression. Frankly, she thought, he looked as though he'd been hit on the head with a stick.

But she couldn't tell if he was stunned in a good way or a bad way. Her stomach knotted up and the palms of her hands went damp.

Maggie had moved into town for Jake's sake. And she'd determined to keep the restaurant as plain as anyone could possibly wish. But here, she told herself as she let her gaze drift lovingly around her, here, she indulged her passion for color and warmth and . . . individuality. In these few rooms, she could be herself and no one would ever know that the now always proper Widow Benson loved nothing better than to sit barefoot in front of an open fire and dream to the crackle of the flames.

She inhaled again and shifted her gaze back to Gabe, who was watching her with wide eyes and an amused smile on his face.

"I don't believe this," he said finally.

Well, he hadn't laughed. Still, that didn't tell her if he thought it was hideous or beautiful. And suddenly, she wanted him to like her home. Because in liking what she'd done to this small corner of the world, he would be liking *her* as well.

She didn't even want to consider why his liking her now seemed so important.

"You did all this yourself?" he asked.

She nodded, smiling to herself. "Jake helped when he could, but most of it, yes."

He looked at her solemnly for the length of several heartbeats. Then he smiled. "It's beautiful."

He said it simply, but in his eyes she read admiration. Relief swept her and on its heels came a kind of happiness she hadn't felt in far too long. He hadn't laughed. He hadn't looked at her as though she belonged in someone's attic. For the first time in a long time, she felt . . . accepted.

"I feel like an idiot," he said and shoved both hands into his pockets.

"Why?" Here was a reaction she hadn't expected.

He chuckled, looked around again, and then locked his gaze with hers. Maggie felt the power of that stare go right to the tips of her toes.

"Because," he said, "just a few minutes ago, I believe I said something about your not having any idea how to decorate a place."

Now she laughed.

"Why," he asked, "if you can do things like this, do you keep the restaurant so plain and . . . lifeless?"

Maggie relaxed for the first time since letting him into her private domain. Walking across the floor, she sank down onto the sofa cushion and curled her right leg up under her. Looking up at him, she said, "Because it's important to me that Jake and I fit in around here. And to do that, we have to be like everyone else."

"I don't understand," he said and took a seat on the sofa near her.

Maggie picked up a small, green pillow and hugged it to her chest as if it was a magic shield. Looking up at him, she said, "People don't like 'different.' They gossip about 'different.' I don't want Jake to have to hear that sort of talk."

Realization dawned on his features. "Like you did, you mean?"

A rueful smile tugged at one corner of her mouth as she began to pluck at the ribbed edge of the pillow. "Yes, like I did."

Moments passed quietly, almost comfortably, until he asked the question she knew he would.

"What did they gossip about?"

Maggie inhaled sharply and stared at the fireplace screen. As she always did when she was troubled or worried, or just plain fractious, she imagined herself floating in that lake, lying on her back, with the cool water enveloping her. And while that image was detailed in her mind, she said, "They talked about my father. My mother. Me."

"You?" he asked. "When you were a child, you mean?"

She nodded.

"What could people have said about a child?"

"You'd be surprised," she whispered as old memories poked at the edges of her mind, demanding to be recognized.

"Tell me," he said softly.

And just for a moment, she was tempted. But Gabe had already slipped too deeply into her personal life. Inviting him in even further would only cause more problems than it would solve. Wasn't it difficult enough now to fall asleep without the image of his face in her mind?

"It doesn't matter anymore," she said and stood up to walk toward the front windows, still clutching the pillow to her chest. Better to keep a safe distance between them, she told herself, especially when she was so tempted to close that distance and allow herself to be held, if only briefly. "It was a long time ago," she said, refusing to stroll down old paths. "The only thing that matters to me now is Jake."

"He's a nice kid," Gabe said.

She half turned and smiled at him, wondering if he knew that the fastest way to a woman's heart was to praise her children. But of course he did. Even Dolly had called him a smooth talker. As Kersey had been. Her spine stiffened. "Yes, he is."

"I've never really been around kids much," he said as he moved toward her. "But I like him."

"Then you understand why the restaurant's success is so important to me," she said, steeling herself against reacting to his nearness.

"Yeah, I guess so." He leaned one shoulder against the window jamb and looked at her. "But why a restaurant, for God's sake?"

"Good question," she said softly. "And there's an easy answer." She shot him a sidelong glance. "It was my father's idea, really. He bought this restaurant for me. Said it would be good to live in town now that Jake would be going to school. Easier on me, better for him." Maggie wrapped her arms tighter around that pillow and went on. "It was a good idea, moving off our little farm. Help Jake make friends. Help him to be accepted in Regret like I never was."

"But . . . ?" he asked.

She looked up at him and shook her head, "But belonging isn't as easy as I'd thought it would be."

"Sure it is," he said. "All it takes is closing up your mind and giving up everything you are."

Obviously, he disapproved, she thought and wondered why that irked her so. "If that's what I have to do, fine."

"Why don't you just leave Regret?" he asked. "Start somewhere new?"

He didn't understand at all. "What makes you think any other town would be different than Regret? People are people wherever you go. Faces change, but human nature is the same all over." A flicker of anger snapped into life in the pit of her stomach. "Do you really think I didn't consider moving? But where would I go? This is my home, for better or worse."

"Jesus, Maggie, the world is wide open. Regret is your home only if you're too stubborn to think otherwise."

Disappointment warred with the anger still struggling into life inside her and the disappointment in him won. Why had she begun to think of him as a kindred spirit of sorts? She shook her head and stared up at him. "Why did I think you'd understand?"

"Oh, I understand plenty," he said.

"No you don't," she said and turned away from him to look out at the town again. "How could you?"

He grabbed her upper arm and turned her around to face him. His features were tight and a light blazed in his blue eyes. "I know all about trying to live down your parents," he told her and then rushed on when she might have said something. "And I know firsthand the sharp sting of a harpy's tongue. I've come damn close to being tarred and feathered by upright stalwart citizens, which is something I'll wager you've never experienced. And the feel of a rope around your neck—" He broke off suddenly.

"A rope?" His expression told her he hadn't meant to say *that*.

He cleared his throat, let go of her and took a half step backward. "A uh . . . friend of mine almost got himself hanged one time. Said it was downright unpleasant and I've no cause to doubt him."

A friend? Thoughtfully, Maggie's gaze dropped to the

red bandana Gabe always wore tied tightly around the base of his neck. And she wondered.

"The point is," Gabe said, distracting her, "that 'fitting in' isn't always worth the effort."

"It has to be," she argued, thinking of her son and the future she hoped to give him.

"Only if you're willing to become the same kind of person you've been complaining about."

"I don't have to be one of them to be accepted."

He threw his hands high in the air and let them drop to his sides again. "Of course you do," he said shortly. "Why else would you be holed up in a restaurant you're no good at running?"

"Well, thank you very much," she snapped.

"Damn it, Maggie, you know yourself you can't cook worth a damn."

"You're supposed to be teaching me," she reminded him.

"Yeah, but I'll only be here two months, and from what I've seen, it'll take years."

She sucked in an outraged breath and glared at him. All of those tender, somewhat yearning feelings for him disappeared in a red cloud of anger.

"If you can't do the job, say so now," she told him hotly. "We'll end this partnership and I'll go cancel that order with Dolly."

"And if you do that, you'll be out of business before you can burn another pie."

"You son of a—" Holding the pillow tightly in one clenched fist, she slapped him in the head with it and had the satisfaction of seeing surprise flicker across his eyes. She knew how he felt. She'd never hit anyone in her life. Surprising, really, how satisfying it could be.

"I think you should leave."

Slowly, calmly, he reached up and smoothed his hair back from his forehead. "Because you can't win the argument, you're throwing me out?"

"There is no argument."

"Really? Felt like one to me."

Maggie straightened up, lifted her chin, and said, "That shows how little you know me. *Ladies* don't argue."

"Yeah," he said, one eyebrow arching high on his forehead, "they slap people with pillows."

She dropped the pillow to the floor and didn't even glance at it. Instead, she looked deeply into his eyes and deliberately disregarded the flutter of something warm, unfamiliar, and intriguing simmering inside her. This was a mistake. All of it. She never should have offered Gabe a partnership. Never should have hired him in the first place. Clearly, they weren't going to be able to work together. And it would be better for both of them if he left town as quickly as possible. She couldn't even imagine being around him now for another five weeks or so.

Instincts be damned, she thought. "You know something, Mr. Donovan?" she said. "I believe I've reconsidered our partnership."

His sharp blue eyes narrowed thoughtfully as he looked at her. "Somehow, Mrs. Benson, I'm not surprised."

That stung. "I no longer want a partner," she said, trying to be as clear as possible.

"Too bad."

"What?"

"You offered the partnership, I accepted," he said shortly. "That's a done deal."

"But I've changed my mind," she countered.

"I haven't," he argued.

"Damn it, Gabe . . ."

He wagged an index finger at her and smiled. "Tsk, tsk. 'Ladies' don't say 'damn,' remember?"

Furious, she bent down, snatched up the pillow, and swung her arm back. He stepped forward, grabbed her arm, and held it pinned to her side.

"Don't do it," he warned silkily.

"Why not?" she demanded, trying to jerk free of his grasp.

With his free hand, he tipped her chin up until their gazes met and held. Then he smiled wickedly and said, "The only time I indulge in a pillow fight is when I'm in bed."

She gasped and dropped the pillow.

Gabe knew he'd shocked her. And maybe he'd wanted to. Maybe he wanted her to know that he thought about her far more often than was wise.

Staring down into those chocolate eyes of hers, Gabe told himself he was being a fool. Nothing could come of a connection between him and Maggie. She was warmth and life and sweet promise. He was dead and on a short road to Hell. Damn it, he should have left when she asked him to.

But even as he thought it, he knew he wouldn't be leaving Regret a moment before he absolutely had to. If he couldn't have a *future* with Maggie, he at least wanted the present. He wanted to fill his mind with images of her so that when he was standing hip deep in flames, he could . . . what? Bring them to the front of his brain to torture himself further?

Yes, damn it.

If all he could have of her was memories . . . then he wanted them. Wanted as many of them as his mind could hold.

Gabe released her abruptly and stepped away from her, uncertain whether or not he could trust himself that close to her.

"Look," he said tightly, keeping a firm rein on the want invading him, "for the time being, we're stuck with each other. Let's make the most of it, shall we?"

She folded her arms across her breasts and he wanted to thank her for hiding her curves from him. Twin spots of color flagged her cheeks as she asked, "Fine. What first, *partner*?"

The tone of her voice scraped against his nerves. Well, this should be fun, he told himself and let his head fall back on his neck. He frowned to himself and let his gaze drift across the painted surface, then, staring straight up, he asked, "Why is your ceiling sparkling?"

"It's the quartz dust," she told him.

"What?" He looked at her again, silently demanding more of an explanation.

Taking a deep breath, she blew it out again in a rush and said, "I ground up quartz crystals, then mixed it in with the lavender paint." She tipped her head back and couldn't help smiling up at her ceiling. "In the evening, with the oil lamps on, it looks like stardust on a twilight sky."

Even in sunlight, the ceiling had a special, unearthly appearance that made a person think of dreamscapes and fairy tales. Gabe looked at her for a long moment and was still looking at her when he said, "It's beautiful."

She shifted her gaze to him and shifted uncomfortably beneath his steady regard. "Thank you."

They stared at each other for several long moments before Gabe intentionally broke the spell growing between them. What in the hell was happening here? How could they go from being at each other's throats to hot, yearning glances in a few seconds' time? Getting a grip on his own desires, he asked, "Could you do this again? For the restaurant, I mean?"

Obviously surprised at the question, she shrugged and said, "I suppose so, if you think it's a good idea."

Had no one ever told her how talented she was? How beautiful her paintings were? Probably not, he decided, or she wouldn't be spending so much time trying to deny the very gifts he so admired.

"I do," he said with a smile he hoped would erase any lingering hard feelings. "We'll even put up a sign out front with the restaurant's new name."

"It's never had a name before," she said.

"As of right now," he told her, "it does. We'll call it Twilight."

Slowly, a smile curved her mouth and pride shone in her eyes. Pleased that he'd given her at least that much, he smiled in return and felt a warmth he'd never known before slide through him. And before he could really enjoy it, he warned himself silently that there was no reason to get used to such feelings.

"Thank you," she said and, after a moment, added, *"partner."*

Damn. That smile of hers hit him low and hard and he almost staggered from the unexpected blow. When had Maggie's feelings become so important to him? When had her smiles come to mean so much?

And why would he find the woman he might have loved when he was already dead?

* * *

That night, for the first time since arriving in Regret, Gabe went to the saloon.

What he needed, he told himself, was some perspective. He needed to be surrounded by his world again. By the kind of people he'd lived his life with. He needed to remember exactly why he'd come to Regret. Why he'd met Maggie and why he couldn't let this . . . *attachment* to her get any stronger.

He walked through the batwing doors and stepped into a noisy, smoke-filled room that should have welcomed him. Always before, he'd felt right at home in a good saloon. Usually, the jingle of coins, the click of poker chips, and the scent of cheap, flowery perfume was enough to ease his soul like a lullaby soothed a fretting infant.

But not tonight.

Tonight, it was just a crowded, noisy place where he wouldn't have to think. Glancing around him, Gabe let his gaze stray to the poker tables, where cowboys sat losing their money to professional dealers who strove to keep satisfied grins off their faces. Three or four girls wandered through the crowd in dresses short enough and tight enough to feed any man's fantasies.

But strangely enough, the sight of their feather-decorated flesh did nothing for Gabe. Instead, his mind filled with images of freckle-dusted noses and gingham dresses. Scowling, he moved determinedly through the mob of men to the front of the saloon where he leaned his elbows on the bartop and studied the array of bottles lined up in front of a huge mirror reflecting the rest of the room.

"What'll you have?" a voice asked and Gabe slid his gaze toward the bartender, a big man with a completely bald head, a barrel chest, and forearms the size of ham shanks.

Ordinarily, Gabe limited himself to one beer. It didn't pay a gambler to have a foggy head while trying to deal. But tonight was different. He wasn't here to play poker. He was here to try to forget everything Maggie was making him feel. And to do that, he'd need a sight more than one lousy beer.

"Whiskey," he said, "and not the rotgut stuff."

The bartender grinned at him, reached below the counter and grabbed a brown bottle. As he yanked out the cork and poured some of the amber liquid into a shot glass, Gabe told him, "Leave the bottle."

The man's eyebrows lifted slightly.

Reaching into his pocket, Gabe pulled out a handful of coins and tossed them on the bar. "Paid in advance."

The bartender nodded, scooped up the money, and tucked it away. Then he leaned his elbows on the bar, looked at Gabe as he tossed the first drink down his throat and asked, "Thinkin' drinkin', or forgettin' drinkin'?"

Gabe grimaced and poured another. "A little of both."

"You work for Maggie, don't you?"

His gaze narrowed thoughtfully. Jesus. Even bartenders gossiped. "Yeah?"

The bartender laughed and shook his head. "Relax, mister. I like Maggie. Always have."

"Known her long?"

He huffed out a breath. "Most all her life, I guess." He held out one hand. "Name's Deke Conroy."

Gabe shook hands with the man, then threw his second drink back. "Gabe. Gabe Donovan."

He nodded and picked up a bar towel. "Seen you around some. Been meaning to come have a talk with you."

"About what?" Gabe slanted a look at the man and mentally figured that if he had to fight this fella, he was surely going to come out the loser.

The big man shrugged and his shoulders looked like a mountain range shifting in an earthquake. "Her pa ain't around much, so I look out for her. Wanted you to know that."

Gabe wondered if Maggie knew she had a protector looking out for her. "Consider me told," he said and took another drink.

"Fair enough," Deke said and dried another glass before setting it in place beside the others.

"Where *is* her father?" Gabe asked, more to make conversation than anything else. Still, you'd think the man would stick around and help out his daughter. Surely he had to know how Maggie's business was suffering.

But the big man's features closed down and a shutter dropped over his eyes. "Out of town," he said flatly in a tone that invited no more questions.

One more drink and Gabe might have pushed the subject, if he'd had the chance.

Instead, though, Deke looked up, saw something he didn't like, and muttered thickly, "Damn the man, can't he stay home for once?"

"Hmm?" Half turning, Gabe followed Deke's gaze to the front door, where a man stood alone just over the threshold. His ruddy features were drawn into a ferocious scowl.

"Every damn week," Deke complained, more to himself than to Gabe. "He comes in here and busts up the place."

"Tell him to get out," Gabe suggested as the stranger waded into the crowd, shoving man after man out of his way with an eagerness that bespoke a willingness to fight.

"I do," Deke said, "every damn week."

"Why's he keep coming back?"

"For the fights," the barman grumbled just before adding, "Here we go."

Just then, one of the men who'd been shoved, jumped up off the floor and drove his fist into the ruddy-faced man's stomach. He bent over, gasped, then came up swinging.

In seconds, the saloon was in an uproar.

This place was no different than any other watering hole. A fight spread quicker than cholera.

Tables flipped over, bottles smashed, and man after man paired up with the opponent of his choice. The piano player ducked behind his instrument, covering his head with his hands. The dance-hall girls ran behind the bar and kept low.

Deke clambered over the bar and sauntered into the crowd, throwing people out of his way as he passed, headed for the main troublemaker. And Gabe, feeling a dark need to release some of the pent-up emotions crowding too close lately, was right behind him.

CHAPTER NINE

She heard the crash of breaking glass first.

Maggie looked out her upstairs window in time to see a man land on the boardwalk atop a carpet of jagged shards of glass. Another fight, she thought in disgust and almost dropped the curtain back into place. She stopped when she recognized the man crawling to his feet.

Gabe?

Pulling the curtains back farther to give herself a better view, Maggie stared down as her "partner" staggered a little, dusted himself off, then raced back into the saloon. Her jaw dropped. Was he out of his mind?

She pulled the window sash up and instantly a rush of noise filled the room. Men shouting, chairs breaking, glass shattering. At least once a week, there was a fight big enough to warrant the sheriff's wandering out of his office to break it up. And it looked as though tonight was the night.

And Gabe was right in the middle of it.

Up and down the street, windows opened and heads poked out into the darkness, trying to get a good look at the goings-on.

But none of them were as interested as Maggie.

"Mom?" Jake called from the next room. "Is everything all right?"

"Everything's fine, honey," she assured him. "Go back to sleep."

Fine, she thought as she turned back to the window. Gabe was in the middle of a brawl, he'd already been thrown through a window and was probably, right now, getting his head bashed in. Just fine.

But why should she care what he did? she asked herself. She didn't, she thought in her own defense. All she was interested in was making sure her partner wasn't so beaten up that he couldn't do his share of the work.

But not even *she* believed that lie.

Whirling around, she ran for the door and the stairs beyond. If he survived, she just might kill him.

Gabe felt as though tiny knives of glass were working their way through his clothes to scratch at his skin. And it felt damn good, he thought. At least here, he knew what he was doing. Throw a punch, then duck. Hit your opponent before he could hit you.

Simple.

Much easier than trying to do battle with Maggie.

Damn it, here in this smoke-filled, violent saloon, he was at home. This was his place, among the thieves, liars, and whores. Here, he knew what was expected of him and he delivered. In Maggie's world, he was a fish out of water. Lost. And he didn't like it one damn bit.

Someone slugged him on the chin and he saw stars. Reacting instantly, he threw a short, hard punch to the other man's midsection and watched him double over before moving on to his next target. Over and over again, Gabe waded into the fight, relishing every punch thrown and taken. At least for these brief, painful minutes, he felt alive again. And in control of his surroundings. Here, all he had to worry about was physical pain. With Maggie, the danger was to his heart and his already claimed soul.

And then two gunshots rang out and the whole saloon full of men came to a sudden standstill.

Wobbling on his feet, Gabe looked blearily toward the door and saw a man wearing a badge. The sheriff, a man about sixty, gave the crowd a disgusted look, then announced, "Party's over, gents." His gaze wandered over the faces before finding the bartender. "Deke, close the place up. That's it for tonight."

Once the sheriff had disappeared back into the night, the crowd sullenly made their way to the door. A few grumbles of complaint lifted into the air as the piano player and the girls came out of hiding. Gabe didn't move, though. He wasn't ready to stop. He still had too many demons riding his soul. And he hadn't had enough time to drown them or beat them into submission.

"You fight pretty good for a gambler," Deke said from behind him.

Gabe turned slowly, trying to focus with one eye, because the other was already swelling shut. The big man looked a little blurry, but Gabe figured he was just going blind. "How'd you know I was a gambler?" he asked and winced as his apparently split lip sent shivers of pain right down to the soles of his feet.

The bartender laughed. "You been in business as long as I have, you notice things."

Gabe snorted. "Then you should have noticed the secret to keeping your place in one piece is to keep that man out."

"True, true," Deke muttered and looked about him at the wreckage.

His problem, Gabe told himself and slowly started

across the room. He stepped gingerly over fallen men and busted chairs and kept moving until he was on the boardwalk, his boots crunching the glass pieces into dust.

Absently, he noted that the glass sparkled just like Maggie's ceiling.

"You told me not to hold your past against you."

Gabe winced at the familiar voice and looked up to see Maggie, standing at the foot of the steps, staring up at him.

Those whiskeys he'd had were just starting to make themselves felt. And between the liquor and the jabs to the head, he was in no shape for another go-around with Maggie. Especially when just the sight of her sent his body on a wild ride of desire and his mind into turmoil.

But one blurry look at her told him he didn't have much choice. He started down the steps, trying to keep from staggering, which wasn't easy under the circumstances.

She was hoppin' mad and damned if she didn't look even prettier than usual. Didn't seem right somehow, a woman to get prettier when she was mad at a man. Put the fella at a disadvantage. Just when he wanted to be arguing his case, he ended up thinking about kissing her senseless.

And right now, he could almost taste her.

"We just talked about the gossips in this town," she reminded him.

"So we did," he agreed, feeling as though he were doing an excellent job of holding up his end of the conversation, considering.

"And what's the first thing you do?" she demanded.

He opened his mouth to answer, but she jumped in ahead of him.

"You get into a saloon brawl."

He shook his head and wondered idly why his brain felt like it was sliding from side to side. Didn't seem like that was a healthy thing. "Not exactly," he said. "The first thing I did was have a few drinks."

She sniffed and wrinkled her nose. "More than a few by the smell of you."

He took a good sniff himself, frowned, then ran the flat of his hand down his jacket, finding the material soaking wet. "Ah, someone must have spilled on me during the fight."

"Uh-huh."

The doors behind him opened and a man, helped by a shove from the bartender, started for home.

"Evenin', Maggie," Deke said politely.

"Deke," she said and waited until he'd gone back inside to face her partner.

"The whole town will be talking about this tomorrow," she said then, lowering her voice into a hiss of sound that seemed to strike at his aching head like a snake.

Still, he couldn't quite contain a snort of laughter. "Hell, Maggie, *most* of the town was *in* that fight."

She didn't look amused.

Ah, well. Gabe scrubbed one hand over his face, trying to avoid all of the sore spots.

"Can we talk about this tomorrow?"

"We talk about it now."

"Jesus," he muttered again and tried to focus his one good eye.

"Make a choice," she said, folding her arms over her chest and glaring at him.

"A choice?" Hell, couldn't she tell by looking at him that he was in no shape to be choosing anything?

"I'm not going to give the gossips even more to talk about, so decide," she said. "Right now."

"Decide what?" Ah, sweet heaven, he needed a place to lie down.

"You either work for me, or you're a gambler. You can't do both."

"I wasn't gambling," he felt obliged to tell her.

"Doesn't matter," she snapped and took a step closer to him. "It's either the restaurant or the saloon."

The pale shaft of lamplight streaming from the saloon gilded her hair and her skin and made her eyes shine so that Gabe had all he could do not to reach out and grab hold of her. Damned he was and damned he would stay, but this woman touched something in him that the Devil would never claim.

The heart he would have bet money he didn't have.

"Well?" she prodded.

"I choose you," he said, realizing that for the first time in his life, he was choosing light over the dark. Did she know what she'd done to him? Did she have any idea how unusual this was for him? Hell, he was turning his back on the one place that he'd ever felt comfortable. For her. His gaze moved over her features and lingered on her too wide mouth before drifting back up to her eyes.

"Good," she said softly then stepped close and wrapped her arm around his waist. Lifting his left arm, she draped it around her shoulders and looked up at him.

"Now, let's get you home before the rest of Regret sees you."

God, she felt good close up. Every one of her curves imprinted itself on his body and fed the inner flames the liquor hadn't come close to extinguishing. And she was taking him home.

"Home," he repeated, and even in his whiskey-hazed mind that word sounded out loud and clear. He hadn't had a home since he was a boy and now that it was too late to stake a claim, he'd found one.

He'd found her.

At the edge of the steps leading up to the restaurant, Gabe stopped dead and turned toward her.

"What is it?" she asked.

He shook his head, ignoring the tiny stabs of pain and lifted one hand to cup her cheek. His thumb traced gently across her cheekbone, and when she tried to pull her head back, he held her still beneath his touch. He studied her eyes and read confusion along with a trace of the same desire he felt swamping him.

And though he knew he shouldn't, Gabe also knew he couldn't let her go, not without at least a taste of her.

"I've gotta do this before I sober up," he muttered.

"Gabe," she said as he lowered his head toward hers.

"Hush, Maggie," he whispered, looking deeply into her eyes. "Just this once, hush."

And then his lips came down on hers, gently, tenderly, as he explored the mouth that had fueled his dreams. His split lip ached but he ignored the pain in favor of the almost overwhelming pleasure rushing through him.

A second passed, then two, as she held perfectly still, allowing but not participating in, the kiss. And still, he kissed her, because she wasn't refusing him. She hadn't pulled away and asked him to stop. Slowly, he sensed the change in her. Her body shifted closer to his. Her arms slid up to encircle his neck and she tilted her head to one side as if silently asking for more. She kissed him back, then, giving as good as she got, and when he parted her lips with his tongue, hers was there, waiting for him.

Touching, tasting, their mouths mated as the world around them stood still. Yesterdays and tomorrows disappeared and *now* became all that mattered.

Her breath dusted his cheek and Gabe groaned from deep in his chest. He held her tighter, wrapping his arms around her, pulling her flush against him.

And Maggie knew she wasn't close enough. Her breasts flattened against his chest. She felt his heartbeat thundering in time with her own. Sensation flooded her body and every inch of her skin seemed to suddenly spring into life.

Somewhere deep inside her, Maggie had always known this moment would come. From her first sight of Gabe, a part of her had recognized him as the one man who could breach her defenses. And even as she gave herself up to the glory of being held again . . . kissed again . . . after so many years of loneliness, she wondered if she was doing the right thing.

She should stop this now, she told herself. Before it went too far.

But it felt so good, she thought wildly. So good, so different from anything she'd ever known before. This hot, burning need to belong, to be a part of him. To feel Gabe's body cover her own.

Yet that need was the very thing that gave her the

strength to pull back and away from him. She couldn't do this, in spite of how badly she wanted him at this moment. Gabe was temporary in her life. He was the one who kept insisting that he'd be gone in less than two months. He was the one with one foot out the door already.

And if she *did* surrender? What then? She was trying to avoid gossip, not feed it. What if she became pregnant? Then what? What chance would she have of giving her son the kind of life she wanted him to have?

No. Heart pounding, body still trembling, Maggie looked up at him and ignored the hunger tearing at her insides. There was too much to lose by giving in to her own desires. Shaking her head, she said a bit breathlessly, "I'm sorry Gabe, but I can't do this."

He only looked at her.

Steeling herself against a change of heart, she turned for the door. His voice stopped her.

"Maggie—"

Quickly, she spoke up, not daring to look at him again. "Don't ask me to stay," she said softly, then added, *"Please."*

He nodded and watched her go, wondering how he could still be standing when his heart had been torn from his chest.

"Nicely done," another, too familiar voice said from close by.

Damn it.

"Not now," Gabe ground out, slanting a glance at the shadows where the Devil stood, watching him.

The black-clad man sauntered toward him, casting one quick glance at the darkened restaurant. "Get drunk,

get in a fight, then seduce a good woman." He smiled.
"A busy night."

Head pounding, every square inch of his body aching,
Gabe stared at the gunfighter. "Don't you have somebody else to haunt?"

"You know," the other man said as he studied him,
"I don't think I gave you near enough credit."

"What's that supposed to mean?"

"The first day we met, when I said your sins weren't
remarkable."

Gabe ran one hand over his eyes, but it was no use,
the Devil was still there when he looked again. "What're
you talking about?"

The gunfighter stepped out of the shadows and bits
of light fell on his face. "I'm talking about using your
extra time on earth to seduce a good woman. Planning
on taking her then disappearing?"

Gabe reared back as if he'd been slugged in the stomach.

"If you're lucky, maybe you could even get her with
child. Leave her with her reputation in tatters and a bastard child to boot." The gunfighter gave him an admiring
nod. "Impressive."

He hadn't even considered that, Gabe admitted. But
then, all he'd been thinking of was his own need to hold
her, to touch her. He hadn't deliberately set out to seduce
her.

"Didn't you?" the Devil asked, once again plumbing
his mind for stray thoughts.

Gabe snapped him a sharp look. "Stay the hell out of
my head."

"I go where I please."

Wasn't it bad enough he was on his way to Hell? Did

he really have to keep putting up with these unannoun-
ced visits from Satan himself? A body would think the
Devil had better things to do.

"Not at all."

Gabe sucked in a breath through clenched teeth and
started along the boardwalk to the side of the building.
Just as well he keep his distance from Maggie at the
moment. Better to take the long way around and go in
the back door.

"Don't trust yourself?" the Devil asked, keeping pace
with him.

"Go to Hell."

The Devil laughed, a hollow, dark sound. "I will,
when I have what's mine."

Gabe stopped at the back door, his hand on the latch.
Turning, he looked at the other man, cloaked in shadows, and said, "You'll have it. I promised you Henry,
and I'll keep my word. But hear me, Devil. You stay
clear of Maggie. And until my time is up, you stay clear
of me."

The other man's features tightened perceptibly. "I'm
not going anywhere," he said, then pointed out just before he vanished into the shadows, "And you're the one
toying with Maggie. Not me."

When the Devil had gone, Gabe looked up at the
night sky and scowled at whatever God might be watching. "How come I see so much of him and so damned
little of You?" he asked tightly. But as he'd expected,
there was no answer.

The darkness surrounded him and Gabe found himself
alone. Again.

CHAPTER TEN

"Well now, that'un weren't bad, Miss Maggie."

Weren't bad. Well, that was certainly a better reaction than she was used to, Maggie told herself. Before Gabe's cooking lessons, her customers had been known to lurch for the door with their hands clapped over their mouths.

Still, she was in no danger of giving a real cook a run for her money. But then how could she be expected to keep her mind on cooking lessons when all she could think about was kissing the teacher?

Oh, good heavens, how had this happened to her?

"Uh," the cowboy said, distracting her from her thoughts, "if you don't need me anymore, I'll be goin'." He started to get up but Maggie laid one hand on his shoulder and pushed him back into his chair.

"One more, Woods," she said, adding of course, "if you wouldn't mind." She sliced a wedge of yet another pie—this one dried peach—and set it in front of Woods Harper.

"Now ma'am," he said, shaking his head and eyeing that slice of pie as he might a rattlesnake coiled to strike. "I already tried your apple and a piece each of mince and . . . *prune*."

As he said it, Maggie thought she noticed him going

a little green around the gills. And though she felt a bit sorry for him, she still needed an unbiased taste tester. Hands at her hips, Maggie tilted her head and gave the young cowboy a cajoling smile.

"Just one more, Woods?" she asked.

He sighed. "Ma'am, for another one of those smiles, I might could even choke down another piece of that"— he shuddered—"*prune.*"

She grimaced slightly. One of the things she'd discovered was that not all fruits were meant to be in pies. "That's all right. I think we can call prune pie a mistake."

He nodded and rubbed one hand across his whiskery jaw. "Prob'ly wise, ma'am." Then, steeling himself, he picked up his fork and let it hover momentarily over the slice of peach pie as if trying to decide if he could actually eat it or not.

Maggie bit back a sigh and reined in her impatience. She couldn't really blame people if they didn't want to taste her cooking. But how would she improve if she didn't get people to tell her what they thought?

For two weeks now, she'd put every ounce of her will and concentration into learning how to cook. Which hadn't been easy, since it had meant spending so much time with Gabe. But it had been worth it. It was days now since she'd incinerated anything beyond saving.

And in all that time, she thought, neither of them had once referred to that kiss. Just as well, she thought. Better to simply pretend it had never happened. And yet . . .

She closed her eyes briefly and remembered it again. The moonlight, the barest touch of his hand on her face. His mouth on hers, breath mingling, tongues twisting.

Maggie opened her eyes instantly, sucked in a gulp

of air and hoped it would be enough to quell the sudden burst of heat that had lit up her insides. Mistake, she told herself firmly. That kiss had been a huge mistake. And thinking about it was driving her insane. She had to forget about it. Put it out of her mind completely.

And apparently, Gabe felt the same. As much time as they'd spent together in the last two weeks, he'd been distant, polite . . . in other words, completely unlike the man she'd been getting to know. She wasn't entirely sure if she was grateful or angry that he could dismiss what they'd shared so easily.

But then, maybe the kiss hadn't affected him as it had her. Maybe he'd kissed so many women in his life that one more was just that. One more kiss. It didn't necessarily follow that because she'd been knocked off her feet, he had too.

"Hey, now . . ." Woods said around a mouthful of peach pie.

She blinked and looked down at him.

Still chewing, he smiled at her and ducked his head. "This one here's a winner, Miss Maggie," he said and swallowed before tucking up another forkful.

"Really?" A flush of success warmed her through as she stared at him in raw wonder. Finally. And all it had taken was six pies baked to get one good one.

"Yes, ma'am," he said and polished off his slice of pie in record time. Then he stood up, pushing away from the table almost in self-defense.

Maggie couldn't really blame him. She'd spent the last two weeks literally dragging people in off the street to taste her latest efforts. It had gotten so bad now that the citizens of Regret actually crossed the street in order to pass the restaurant safely.

Poor Woods was too polite for that, and in exchange for his "Good morning," she'd kidnapped him and plopped him down at a table.

"You actually liked it?" she asked and glanced at his crumb-laden plate as if for confirmation.

"Yes, ma'am, I surely did," he said, backing toward the door, keeping a smile fixed on his face.

"Thank you, Woods."

He waved one hand at the restaurant and added, "I really like how you're fixin' up the place too."

So Gabe had been right about that too. They hadn't even done much yet. Just a few knickknacks here and there and some brightly colored tablecloths. But Woods had noticed. Maybe others would too.

"I really appreciate your help."

"Proud to oblige, ma'am. But I really do got to be going now." Close to the door, he grabbed hold of the knob and turned it. "The foreman's expecting me back long before this, I'm thinkin'."

"Of course," she said.

"But it was good, Miss Maggie," he repeated "and I'll be back with the boys come Saturday night."

She nodded and refused to take offense at how quickly he slipped through the door and made his escape. "See you—" The door closed behind him and she finished lamely, "Then."

Alone, she glanced around the restaurant and noted the new yellow and white tablecloths and the cushions on the chairs. She still didn't have any customers beyond the stage passengers and her Saturday-night cowboys. But they would come, she told herself.

They had to come.

* * *

Gabe shoved his hands into his pockets and walked down Main Street. He just needed to get out of that kitchen. Away from Maggie. At least for a while.

"Hey, Gabe," someone called and he turned to his right and nodded at the barber.

"Afternoon, Bass," he yelled loud enough so that the mostly deaf man would hear him.

"Saw the smoke signals comin' from Maggie's kitchen this mornin'," the older man shouted on a snort of laughter. "She on the warpath again?"

Gabe smiled. "No more than usual."

"Hell," another voice piped up and Gabe half turned his head to look at a man just stepping out of the barbershop. "I think she must be comin' along," he said, grinning. "The smoke today looked a lot lighter than last week's."

All right, so she was still burning a few things. But not as many as before. "She's doin' fine," Gabe told them both. "You'll have to stop by the restaurant and give it a try."

"Ain't likely," Bass shouted, shaking his head. "I'm too old to die of poisoning. Rather go out with a bullet."

"You keep cuttin' hair like you do," the cowboy said in disgust, "and it'll happen."

Gabe chuckled and kept walking. Up and down the street, voices hailed him and he was stopped once or twice just to chew the fat. People smiled at him. Men he'd fought beside in the saloon a couple of weeks ago compared their fading bruises and rehashed the fight.

He'd left the restaurant to be alone for a few minutes.

And for the first time in his life, "alone" was a hard thing to find.

Since he was a boy of seventeen, he'd never stayed in one town more than a few days. Before coming to Regret, at least. Being a gambler didn't afford a man the chance to make many friends. And those friends he did have were men who shared his vagabond way of life. Or men constantly on the run . . . like Henry, for instance.

Gabe stopped at the end of the street, turned around and let his gaze drift across the now familiar houses and stores. He saw Tessa Hardy sweeping the front of the millinery and knew that when she was finished, she'd head to the mercantile for a chat with Dolly. Bass Stevens was arguing loudly with a customer and Kansas Halliday had slipped so low in his porch chair it looked like he might just slither right off to sprawl in the dust.

He knew these people, Gabe thought, frowning to himself. All his life, he'd never really belonged anywhere. Why was it, now that he was dead, he'd found a home of sorts? With friends. And neighbors. And Maggie.

And which of these friends and neighbors would he be hurting when he took Henry off to Hades with him?

Hell. Dead just kept getting more complicated.

As he stood there, school let out and the air was punctured by high-pitched shouts of triumph and laughter. Turning into the sun, Gabe squinted at the small crowd of kids, looking for one particular face. He wasn't even surprised when Jake was the last kid out, shuffling his feet and taking his own sweet time about heading home. After all, what was the rush? When he got there, Maggie would just set him down for more schoolwork.

The kid walked down those few steps as if each of his legs weighed fifty pounds. Gabe shook his head and smiled sadly. When the boy finally reached the bottom, instead of going on down Main Street, he turned and sidled along the edge of the building until he reached the back and there he stood, a solemn little guy all alone.

Gabe's gaze followed the boy's and he saw that the kids were choosing up teams for a baseball game and he could almost feel Jake's loneliness. Poor kid was looking at that open pasture as if it was paradise. And as Gabe looked between Jake and the other kids, he had an idea. And he smiled.

Maggie had one wall and most of another painted an absolutely lovely shade of blue when she finally stopped long enough to look at the clock.

"Three-forty?"

She turned toward the front door as if expecting Jake to magically appear on the threshold. When he didn't, she set her paintbrush down on the edge of the can and walked to the front door. Looking up one side of the street and down the other, she futilely searched for her son.

"Well, where could he be?" she muttered and started walking toward the school. Wiping her paint-streaked hands on the old apron she wore to cover her dress, she paid no attention to the interested stares she received as she passed. But even if she'd noticed, she wouldn't have cared what they thought about the colorful splashes of paint dotting her face and clothes. At the moment, she wasn't worried about gossips or being a "lady." Right now, the only thing on her mind was her son.

Stepping off the boardwalk into the street, she hurried her steps, telling herself she wasn't really worried. She knew perfectly well that Jake was as safe in this town as he would be in his own bed. But still, she could admit to being curious. He knew he was to come directly home.

As she neared the school, she heard the muted roar of a dozen or more young voices, shouting, cheering. Her hem snapped around her legs as her long strides carried her along the side of the schoolhouse to the back. And there she stopped.

Out on the field, a baseball game was in progress and in the pitching position stood Gabe Donovan.

She should have known.

The wind ruffled his dark hair and tugged at his white shirt. A wide grin creased his face as he went through an elaborate series of moves. Then one of the kids yelled at him to hurry it up and Gabe lobbed the ball to the batter. The child swung and missed to a chorus of hoots and howls.

"Strike one!" the catcher called out and tossed the ball back to Gabe.

He caught it and turned to wave at the boys and girls standing in different positions on the field. That's when Maggie spotted Jake. Her breath caught. He looked so small out there. Much smaller than the other children. She almost started for him. She actually took a step toward him and then she noticed the smile on his face. Proud and scared and excited, he practically vibrated with the thrill of being a part of the game.

So she waited, hands twisting in the folds of her apron. Gabe threw the ball again and this time the solid crack of ball meeting bat sounded out. The baseball lifted straight up into the air. The batter ran for first base, the children shouted, Gabe turned, head back, to follow the ball, and Maggie's gaze focused on Jake.

"It's all yours, Jake!" Gabe called.

It was as if everything slowed down.

The ball looked glaringly white against the gray cloud-swept sky. Jake stood stock-still, hands outstretched, waiting for the ball that was headed straight for him.

Maggie held her breath and gripped her apron so tightly her fingers ached. She strained forward as if she could help her son if she concentrated hard enough.

The ball dropped. Jake cupped his hands. And caught it, making the out.

Maggie's breath left her in a rush. She smiled to herself as one of the other boys ran to Jake and slapped him on the back hard enough to make him stagger. Gabe strode across the field and formally shook his hand. And Jake's proud smile was so bright it almost hurt Maggie's eyes to look at it. He actually *glowed*.

She slumped back against the school wall and barely noticed as the game continued. She kept seeing Jake's pleasure and pride in himself. Over and over again, the images raced through her mind. And she'd been within a breath of taking him home and depriving him of that sense of accomplishment. The feeling of belonging to the team, being a part of something.

Isn't that why she'd moved to town in the first place?

Gabe walked up to her, his steps silent on the still mostly green pasture grass. He tossed one glance over his shoulder, saw that the kids were too busy with their game to pay attention to the adults, then he looked back at her as she stared at her son. Her expression was so wistful it tugged at the edges of his heart.

He wanted to hold her again and this time wasn't even surprised at the strength of that desire. But it was more than wanting to feel her pressed close to him. He wanted to offer comfort and to somehow ease the confusion he read in her eyes. He didn't dare touch her though. Because one touch wouldn't be nearly enough.

"I should be sorry," he said softly and she turned her head to look at him. "It's my fault Jake didn't go straight home."

"I guessed as much," she said, a smile almost curving her mouth.

He walked closer, shoving his hands into his pockets. "I'm not sorry though."

She laughed shortly. "And I'm not surprised."

"Maggie, that kid needs to run around. Get some fresh air. Have friends."

"I know that," she said quietly, still keeping her gaze on her son.

"I don't think you do," he said and took up a spot beside her. He noted her hands, clutching at the folds of her apron. "When I was a kid, we moved around so much, I never had many friends. I know how lonely it is."

She shot him a glance. "So do I," she said, remembering her own childhood and the taunting and teasing she'd endured. "But at the same time, I have to think of his future." Her posture stiffened as she said, "His father was a complete wastrel. Kersey Benson never did an honest day's work in his life. And I want so much more for Jake. I want him—" She shook her head and groped silently for the right words. "I want him to have a good life. To be someone. To have people look at him and know he's trustworthy. Reliable. He's got to learn responsibility now. Got to learn that work comes before play. That rules are there for a reason." Then she was quiet for a moment and muttered, "I can't find the words to tell you what I mean."

"You're worrying for nothing, Maggie," Gabe said. "He's a great kid," he added, looking out over the field to where Jake was taking his turn at bat. As he swung and missed, he said, "Not much of a hitter, but a great kid." He turned his gaze back to Maggie and said firmly, "He'll be a good man."

"Yes, he will," she said, "despite his father."

Gabe sighed and shook his head. "Tell me something."

"What?"

"Are you like your father?"

Maggie frowned slightly and turned to look at him. He could see she was thinking about the question, really considering it. "No," she said at last. "My father is a wonderful man, but he's got a wanderlust in him. I like my home, being in the same place every morning and night."

He nodded. "So, if you're nothing like your father, why should Jake be anything like his?"

She opened her mouth to argue the point, but after a second or two, she closed it again and smiled ruefully. "I see what you're saying."

He gave her a slow smile and said, "Good." Then he took her hand and led her closer to the field. "Now, how about we watch the game? You can finish painting later."

"How'd you—" She stopped. "Oh."

Gabe reached up and touched a slash of blue across her forehead. "It looks good on you."

"I'll bet."

"Never bet with a gambler," he warned her. "You'll always lose."

She followed him, her hand warm in his. A brisk wind shifted across the pasture, but Maggie didn't feel the cold. Warmth and an unfamiliar sense of *ease* filled her. He was right, she thought and couldn't understand why she'd never thought of things in that way before. She'd worried so much about Jake and his future, she'd almost sacrificed his childhood. Hadn't she moved to town to help Jake belong? Hadn't she wanted this very thing for him?

"Run, Jake!" Gabe yelled when the little boy hit the ball and stood there, stunned motionless.

Maggie grinned as Jake suddenly realized what he should be doing and took off for first base, pumping his short legs as furiously as he could.

She looked at her son and realized that for the first time since moving to town, he looked utterly and completely happy. A sharp, bitter pang of regret echoed inside her and tears welled up in her eyes. In her quest for the future, Maggie had forgotten all about just how important being a child was. In worrying about tomorrow, she'd nearly lost today. She'd pushed them both so hard to *belong,* she'd lost the magic she and her little boy used to share.

Flashes of memory darted across her mind. Images of the times they'd had together when they were still on their farm. When she'd thought nothing of spending hours with Jake as they lay on their backs in a field, watching faces in the clouds. When she wouldn't have traded a picnic and a day of fishing with her son for all the money and respect in the world. When it had been just the two of them and nothing was as important as time spent together.

How had she lost so much? she wondered and swallowed around a tight knot in her throat. Blinking back tears, Maggie silently vowed to do things differently from now on. Looking at Jake's shining face as he stood proudly on first base, Maggie felt freer suddenly than she had since moving to town. It wasn't this town's acceptance that she needed to concentrate on. It was being the best mother she could be. If Jake loved her. If Jake became the man she wanted him to be . . . then nothing else mattered.

For the first time in two years, she forgot about what had to be done. She put work out of her mind and concentrated instead on a few simple joys. The wind on her face. Jake happily waving to her. And sitting on the grass beside Gabe.

For now, that was enough.

As always, the children's voices drew her.

Sugar stayed deep into the tree line so no one would see her and she wrapped her arms around her waist and held on tightly to compensate for the gnawing ache she felt within. The pain inside blossomed and grew as it always did when she watched the children play. But she had to be here. She needed to hear their voices, see their faces, even though being so near to them all was like rubbing salt in an old, festering wound.

She should have had children.

Would have, too, if she hadn't been so old when she married Redmond.

But then, it wasn't Redmond she was supposed to have married. It should have been different, she thought, squinting into the wind and focusing her gaze on one boy, smaller than the rest. Handsome child, she thought and let her gaze slide to the boy's mother, sitting on the grass as undignified as you please, with that man.

She looked just like her mother, Sugar thought, gritting her teeth and leaning into the quickening wind. Long hair, big eyes, and a wide mouth designed to tempt men from their rightful places.

The wind turned colder and bit at her flesh with gusty teeth. She shivered but she refused to leave. She wouldn't let that woman chase her away. This was *her* place. Her time to be with the children she should have had if she hadn't been cheated out of what was rightfully hers. No. She wouldn't lose this too. She would stay and watch the children.

Like always.

CHAPTER ELEVEN

Moonlight streamed in through the narrow window above his bed and Gabe stared blankly at the slice of silver piercing the darkness. He couldn't sleep. In fact had stopped trying. Throwing one arm behind his head, he let his mind wander and, naturally, it wandered straight to Maggie.

He couldn't get her out of his mind. Not that he wanted to, but he damned sure should. For both their sakes.

Grumbling to himself, he sat up and swung his legs off the side of the bed. Bracing his elbows on his knees, he cupped his head in his hands and speared his fingers through his hair, squeezing his skull between his palms as though, with enough pressure, he might push her from his mind. His heart.

But it wouldn't be that easy. Maggie wasn't the kind of woman a man forgot. Even when he was trying to. Hell, all he needed now was that damned Devil to show up and open the wound inside him a little wider. He lifted his head and looked to the darkest corner of the room, waiting for the man to show himself. When he didn't, Gabe figured even the Devil didn't have the stomach to be around a man as miserable as he was tonight.

"Damn it," he muttered as he shoved himself to his

feet, snatched up his pants, tugged them on, then walked barefoot to the window. Sighing, he stared out at the street, craning his neck to look at the buildings lining the opposite side. Darkened windows stared back at him like blind eyes. The whole damn town looked as dead and lifeless as he felt.

Yet come morning light, the town would come to life again. And right now, inside those buildings were normal, everyday people, with normal, everyday problems. Not a damn one of them was dead and falling in love.

He snorted a choked-off laugh and caught sight of his own reflection in the glass. His gaze dropped to the scar at the base of his throat, a physical reminder of one fact he couldn't forget. His own hanging. Lifting his gaze again, he stared into his own eyes and saw a man at the end of yet another rope. Pitiful. He'd gone his whole life without running into a woman who had even come close to reaching him. And now, there was Maggie.

Images of her face flooded his mind. He remembered the shine of unshed tears in her eyes only that afternoon as she watched her son playing baseball. He'd expected an argument from her. Hell, he'd expected her to draw and quarter him for keeping Jake away from the extra schoolwork he was supposed to do each day.

"Wouldn't you know she'd surprise me," he muttered and turned away from the window, unwilling to look at either himself or the images of Maggie his mind insisted on drawing.

When a noise sounded from the kitchen, he grasped at the distraction eagerly. Crossing the small room in a few quick strides, he pulled the door open, stepped into the kitchen, and stopped dead.

Maggie whirled around to face him, one hand clutching at the base of her throat. Her incredible hair flew out in a wide arc around her only to settle down again and fall gently across her shoulders and down her back. She wore a white cotton nightgown that covered her completely from neck to toes, yet Gabe's senses leaped into life at the sight of her. A worn pale green crocheted shawl lay atop her nightgown and was knotted between her breasts. Long fingers of fringe hung from the hem of the shawl and swayed as an echo to her quick movement.

She held a lit candle in one hand and by the wavering light of that tiny flame her eyes seemed huge and fathomless. She was a vision, a dream—and the fact that he couldn't have her made all of this a nightmare.

She lifted her free hand to clutch at the knot in the shawl and said breathlessly, "You have to quit scaring me like that."

A fleeting smile curved his lips briefly and he nodded. "Sorry. But you kind of surprised me too. What are you doing down here in the middle of the night?"

What indeed? Maggie asked herself and clutched tighter to the pale green shawl she'd thrown over her nightgown. Fingers twisting in the knotted, crocheted threads, she stared at Gabe and knew the real reason she was standing here was him.

She hadn't been able to sleep. Every time she closed her eyes, she saw Jake again, smiling. Happy. Triumphant. And it hurt more than anything she'd ever known to admit that she'd had nothing to do with his happiness. That she owed her son's smiles to a man who'd known him little more than a few weeks.

And surrendering to that knowledge had brought Gabe's face to the front of her mind and she hadn't been able to rid herself of the image. Although she had to admit she hadn't tried very hard.

"I couldn't sleep," she finally said.

"Me neither," he said and stepped into the room.

It was only then she noticed that he was only half dressed. He wore pants but no shirt and even his feet were bare, making this candlelit scene even more intimate somehow. Her own bare toes curled against the floor and she tried desperately to look away from the sculpted muscles of his chest. But he came closer, into the narrow circle of light, as if inviting her gaze.

Maggie took a deep breath and told herself it was foolish to be so . . . aroused. After all, she was a widow. She'd seen a shirtless man before. But, another, more traitorous corner of her mind pointed out, she'd never seen a chest quite so impressive. There didn't seem to be an ounce of extra flesh on his body. And his skin didn't have the same ghostly white pallor that her late husband's had.

Oh, beans and biscuits—damn. She could be in serious trouble very shortly. Her blood seemed to be simmering in her veins and even breathing wasn't as easy as it had been a couple of minutes ago.

In a desperate attempt to get control of the situation, she turned abruptly and asked, "How about some coffee? Or, tea maybe?" Although just the thought of having to try to swallow at the moment was more than she could bear.

"No," he said. "Thanks."

But she needed to be busy, so she set the candle down onto the table and walked past him toward the pantry. "Well, if neither of us wants anything, maybe I should just get a head start on the morning's chores."

"At midnight?" he asked and her footsteps faltered. At the pantry, she rested one hand on the doorjamb and glanced at him over her shoulder.

"I guess that would be silly, wouldn't it?"

"Yeah." He waved to a chair on the opposite side of the table from him and said, "Why don't you just sit down for a while, Maggie?"

Just sit there? In the dark? With him at arm's reach? Oh, that probably wasn't a good idea. She shook her head and said, "Maybe we should just go to bed."

Even in the half-light, she saw one of his eyebrows lift dangerously high. In the next instant, she realized just what that had sounded like.

"That's not what I meant," she said.

"That's quite an invitation," he said at the same time.

She gaped at him for a long second or two, then he grinned at her and she muttered, "Oh, beans and biscuits."

Shaking her head, she walked to the table and flopped down into the chair he'd indicated. Ridiculous, she thought, to be so nervous around him suddenly.

"So," he asked, when she was sitting across from him, "why couldn't you sleep?"

A question with too many answers. She leaned forward and the fringe from her shawl fell onto the table. Idly picking at the wool threads, she tried to find the right words to answer his question without being completely truthful.

"I was thinking," she finally said, keeping her gaze on the frayed thread as her fingers plucked at it.

"About what?"

You, she wanted to say, but didn't. That answer would only lead to more questions. Questions she couldn't—or wouldn't—answer now. Instead, she gave him a part of the truth. "About what you said today." She shot him a glance. He was leaning back in his chair, away from the candle's glow, keeping his face in shadow.

Just as well, she thought, admitting that she was a bit too vulnerable right now to be looking into those blue eyes of his.

"And?" he prompted.

"And," she repeated with a sigh, "you were right."

"Always glad to hear that," he said. "What was I right about?"

Her fingers twisted a line of thread until it had wrapped itself around her fingertip tightly. "Damn near everything," she muttered.

He chuckled briefly. "You don't sound real happy about that."

"I'm not," she admitted and stood up abruptly. Holding on to the knot of her shawl as if it was a lifeline, she paced back and forth across the darkened kitchen. Her bare feet made no sound, the soft glow of the candle was no more than a tiny circle of light in the shadows.

"What's wrong, Maggie?"

Shaking her head, she said, "Wrong? Me, that's what."

"Explain."

She wished she could. "I don't know," she started and once she'd actually begun speaking, words came tumbling from her mouth, falling over each other in their haste to be heard. "I thought I was doing what was best for Jake. Moving here"—she waved one arm at the kitchen—"trying so . . . *damned* hard to fit in."

"Maggie—"

"No—" She lifted one hand to silence him. She didn't want to stop now. Saying all this out loud was actually helping. Making it all clear in her mind. "But today . . ." She stopped, wrapped her arms around her waist and closed her eyes. "Seeing him playing with the other kids, having so much fun—" She sighed again and opened her eyes. "I really made a mess of everything, didn't I?"

"No."

One word. So sure. So confident. God, she wanted to believe him.

"No?" Maggie looked at him, wishing she could see his face, his expression.

"He's a good kid. He loves you."

"Yes, but—"

"No buts. You were doing your best. It's all anyone can expect."

"Maybe," she said, unwilling just yet to forgive herself for cheating both herself and Jake out of so much. How could she ever have believed that having a town approve of her was more important than time spent with her son?

What would it matter if all of Regret thought she was a paragon of virtue if Jake didn't even *know* her anymore?

"Before we moved to town," she said, more to herself than to him, "things were different." Maggie laughed shortly. "*I* was different."

"You could cook?"

"Not *that* different," she assured him, smiling.

"So, who were you then?"

"Me," she said simply, thoughtfully. "I was just me and I didn't worry about anything but taking care of Jake and myself."

"Sounds about right."

"It does, doesn't it?" She looked at him. "And I *miss* that. Maybe even more than Jake does." Slowly, she walked back to the table and sat down again. Resting her forearms on the table, she leaned in and said, "Do you know how long it's been since I just sat in a field and did absolutely nothing?"

"Too long?" he asked and she could hear the smile in his voice even before he sat forward, bringing his face into the light.

"Far too long," she agreed. Somehow, sitting here in the darkness with him, it seemed easy to talk. Her earlier nervousness was gone now and she felt herself relaxing, enjoying the moment.

"So," he said, giving her that half-smile that always served to curl her toes, "you've decided to *not* become a 'lady'?"

"Not exactly. I've just decided to be me."

"And to hell with what Regret thinks?"

"Well," she said with a shrug, "I haven't exactly impressed them with my efforts to be ladylike. And heaven knows they're still staying away from my restaurant. So maybe I don't have anything else to lose by being myself."

"And maybe," he pointed out, "they'll surprise you and prefer the real you."

"Anything's possible," she mused, looking into his eyes. "But you know something? I don't care anymore. And I owe that to you."

Gabe smiled as he watched her. Damned if the woman didn't have a talent for saying just the thing to twist his heart. If anyone owed a debt here, it was him. She'd shown him life in the sunlight. She'd given him a place to spend his last two months and a chance to see what his life might have been like if he'd made different choices.

The fact that the knowledge would only serve to torture him through an eternity in Hell was his fault, not hers.

She looked beautiful in candlelight, he thought. Studying her features, he etched the lines of her face into his memory so that no matter what else happened in the future, this one moment in time would forever be caught in his mind. He took a deep breath, inhaling the scent of her, drawing it deep inside him, making it a part of him.

Giving in to the urge to touch her, he reached across the table and laid one hand over hers. Surprisingly enough, she turned her hand over and held on to his.

"You smell good," he whispered.

She laughed gently and shook her hair back from her face. "That's turpentine."

His thumb moved across the back of her hand. "On you, it smells good."

"Gabe?"

"Yeah?" he asked and leaned in even closer to her.

"What's happening here?"

"Happening?"

"Between us."

"I think you know."

She licked her lips and his gaze followed the sweep of her tongue. Something inside him turned over and his heartbeat quickened until it sounded like a horse running at a full gallop across the prairie.

"Yes, I suppose I do," she said then and held on to his hand tightly. Her eyes shone with the same desire rising in him. He knew she felt what he did. Knew she wanted him as badly as he wanted her. He also knew, by the grim determination on her features, that it wasn't going to happen. Not tonight. Probably not ever. As if to prove him right, she whispered, "But . . ."

"But," he repeated and reluctantly let go of her hand. He knew damn well that nothing could come of them. Good women, even one who'd just decided to stop dancing to convention's tune, didn't go to bed with a man who wasn't her husband.

And he wasn't about to marry a woman like Maggie just before he left for Hell, for the sole purpose of bedding her.

Even a sinner could have standards.

"It's not that I don't want—"

"I understand, Maggie," he said tightly, but still managed to give her a small smile. "It's better this way, anyhow."

"Gabe—"

"Let's just let it be, huh, Maggie?"

"No," she said and reached for his hand again. Then she pulled him farther into the light and he saw her eyes narrow as she stared at his throat. Whatever she'd been about to say was forgotten as she lifted her gaze to his and asked, "What happened to your neck?"

Shit.

He pulled away from her and stood up, moving back from the table and the light, edging deeper into the shadows. The scar on his neck. He'd forgotten all about it, damn it. Why hadn't he left the damned bandana on when he went to bed? Now that she'd seen it, she would be bound to have questions.

"It's nothing," he said.

"It's a rope burn," she whispered.

"Yeah," he admitted tightly, knowing it was useless to try to hide it again now. "It is."

She swallowed and laid both hands flat on the table. "The kind a man would get if he was hanged?"

"That's right." He shoved his hands into his pockets, turned away and walked to the window. Staring out at the darkness beyond, he deliberately kept himself from so much as looking at her candlelit reflection in the windowpane.

He didn't want to see disgust in her eyes. Or worse, pity. It was for damn sure the desire she'd felt for him would be gone now. Women like Maggie didn't take up with men who'd been dancing at the short end of a rope.

"So the 'friend' you told me about before was—"

"Me."

"You were *hanged*?"

"Yeah."

"Why?"

A short, harsh laugh shot from his lungs before he could stop it. "Why didn't I tell you? Or why was I hanged?"

"Both," she said and stood up from the table. He heard her chair legs scrape on the floor and then the soft sound of her bare feet as she walked toward him. And still he didn't turn, despite the fact that everything inside him wanted to grab her, hold her close, and have her tell him it didn't make any difference to her.

But that wasn't likely to happen.

"I didn't tell you," he said, forcing a light tone he didn't feel into his voice, "because it's not easy to work something like that into a conversation." And because he was a damned coward.

"Why were you hanged, Gabe?"

He took a deep breath and inadvertently inhaled the scent of turpentine that still clung to her. She was standing right behind him. He felt her warmth, sensed her gaze arrowing into him.

"Believe it or not," he said, hoping to high hell she *did* believe him, "I didn't do anything. They made a mistake."

"Who did?"

"The mob of upstanding, righteous citizens who tossed a rope over a tree and tied me to it."

"A mistake? How could anyone hang a person by mistake?" She sounded outraged on his behalf, God love her.

"They got the wrong man," he said and one more time called down a host of curses on Henry Whittaker's head. Damn the old liar anyway. Not only had he escaped the lynch mob, but it was because of him that Gabe was standing here explaining to this woman why he'd been hung.

"How'd you get away? How could you live through something like that?"

I didn't, he nearly said, but figured there was only so much a body could hear in one night. Besides, he didn't like the idea of having to explain to her that she was talking to a dead man.

Instead, he muttered a half-truth. "The rope snapped." It wasn't a lie. He just wasn't telling her the whole truth. That the rope had snapped *after* he was dead.

She touched him and he almost winced at the gentleness. He didn't deserve it, he knew. Yes, he'd been innocent of the charges for which he'd been hanged. But he was by no means an *innocent*. Hell, just ask the Devil who was waiting on him.

Turning him around, she reached up and laid one fingertip on the raw, uneven scarring at the base of his throat. The soft slide of her skin against his rippled down in a torrent of sensation that flooded him. Would she never stop surprising him? He'd expected fury. Disgust. More questions than he could answer. And he damn sure had expected her to throw him out on his deceitful ass.

Instead, he found himself looking into a pair of deep brown eyes glimmering with unshed tears. Her tenderness rattled him, leaving him more shaken than he cared to admit. Tears. For him. As far as he could remember, no one had ever shed a tear for Gabe Donovan.

"Don't cry for me, Maggie." He wasn't worth one of her tears.

She sniffed and shook her head, letting her hand fall back to her side. The absence of her touch was like a knife to the heart of him. How cold it was without her warmth. His hands fisted inside his pockets.

"I'm sorry, Gabe," she said.

"*You're* sorry? For what?"

"For the pain you must have felt," she said softly, tipping her head back to stare up into his eyes.

He felt her gaze right down to his soul.

"For asking you about it and making you remember."

"It's not something I'm likely to forget."

"I know," she said and reached out to lay one hand on his arm. Instantly, the warmth was back again, racing through him, flooding him with a kind of light that no darkness could extinguish.

"I won't ask any more questions," she added quietly,

still looking at him as though he was a much better man than he really was.

Amazing woman.

"Don't you even want to know what they accused me of?" He couldn't believe she was simply going to let this go.

"No," she said, her gaze delving deeply into his. "Because they were wrong. You said it was a mistake."

"I could be lying," he said.

"You're not though."

"Maggie," he said as a rush of emotion swelled inside him, "I might not have deserved that hanging, but I'm no angel either."

She smiled and shook her head. "No, you're more of a fallen angel, I suspect. But you're not the kind of man my husband was either."

"Your husband was a damn fool," Gabe said. "Any man who would willingly leave a woman like you is just too stupid to live."

One corner of her mouth tilted up and he wondered why he'd ever thought that mouth too wide.

"And yet," she said as she backed up a step, "you're leaving me too."

"Not willingly."

"But you're leaving."

"Yeah," he said tightly. "I am."

She turned away then and walked to the table. Picking up the candle, she moved to the doorway that would lead her to the stairs. When she got there, she stopped and looked back over her shoulder at him. Her expression was weary, yet resigned.

He braced himself for whatever she might say, and still felt each of her words as he would have a bullet.

"Then maybe you're not so different from Kersey after all, are you?"

CHAPTER TWELVE

"Just a damn minute," Gabe said and started after her.

"Don't swear at me," she snapped and hurried her steps toward the stairs.

Gabe caught up with her in a few long strides. He grabbed her upper arm and turned her around to face him. Tilting her head back, she looked up at him and a blind man could have seen that all traces of gentleness or tenderness were gone.

Well, fine. Anger was easier for him to take than kindness, anyway.

"Let me go," she said and tried to yank herself free of his grasp.

"Not yet," he told her, tightening his grip on her. "We're not finished talking."

"Oh, yes we are."

"No, ma'am," he argued, looming over her. And even though he was mad, a part of him was pleased to note she didn't back down. If anything, her gaze went even more fiery than before. "You don't get to say something like you just did and then walk away."

"Truth hurt?" she asked.

"It's not true."

"What's different?" She tilted her head to one side and watched him, silently daring him to prove her wrong.

"Your husband left because he wanted to." The words were hard ones and it shamed him to see them strike home. But damn it, it was bad enough he'd been hanged for something he didn't do. He sure as hell wasn't going to get lumped in with the likes of Kersey Benson on top of it. Adding insult to injury was just a bit too much.

She jerked back from him and this time succeeded in freeing herself. As she rubbed her upper arm, he felt a slight twinge of remorse. He hadn't meant to hurt her. He'd just wanted her to stand still for a minute.

"You're leaving too, you just said as much."

"Not because I *want* to," he snapped. "I don't have a choice."

"There's always a choice."

"You're wrong."

"Uh-huh," she said, clearly disbelieving. "So you're saying if things were different, you'd choose to stay in Regret."

"Of course." Hell, who wouldn't choose Regret and Maggie, over eternal flames?

"I don't believe you."

"I can see that."

"Fine. Convince me," she urged. "Tell me why you don't have a choice in this."

He opened his mouth to speak, then slammed it shut again. Frustration roared to life inside him as he realized that for the first time in his life, he wanted to tell a woman the absolute truth and couldn't. How in the hell could he tell her about the Devil and the deal he'd made without sounding like a crazy man? Hell, even *he* wouldn't believe this story. Scrubbing one hand across his face, he glared at her as if this whole thing were her fault and admitted sullenly, "I can't."

"You mean, won't."

"I mean, even if I could tell you, you wouldn't believe me."

"But you're not going to give me the chance, are you?"

"No." He could have used more words. Prettied it up a little. But the end result would have been the same. What would have been the point?

She shook her head and gave him a slow, sorrowful look. "Then there's nothing more to talk about, is there?"

A big, dark hole opened up inside him and Gabe felt its emptiness clean to the bone. Just moments ago, there had been magic in this room. Between the two of them. Now, it was gone and unlikely to come back.

"I guess not," he said finally.

A heartbeat passed, then two. At last, she nodded, let her gaze slide from his and turned for the stairs. Keeping one hand on the banister, she started climbing. When she reached the top, she paused, but didn't turn around. "Good night, Gabe."

Her door closed a moment later. Gritting his teeth, Gabe slammed his fist onto the newel post and was grateful for the throbbing pain in his hand. At least it masked what was happening to his heart.

"What'cha doin'?"

Gabe stopped and looked up at the boy standing on the top step of the back porch. Jake's long-sleeved white shirt was already dirty and one knee of his black pants was torn. His shoes were dusty and scuffed, his hair wildly disarrayed, and his eyes wide and curious. Gabe smiled to himself. Apparently, there hadn't been any extra schoolwork for the boy to do on this Saturday morning. He wasn't surprised to see the kid either. The last few days, it had been like having a four-foot-tall shadow. Everywhere he went, Jake was right there alongside him.

"I'm making a sign for the restaurant," he said and lowered his gaze to the project he'd been working on all morning. Right now, it didn't look like much more than a long, narrow strip of pine. But he had it sanded and ready to be painted.

"Can I help?" Jake asked, flinging his hair back out of his eyes with a quick jerk of his head.

"Where's your mother?" Gabe had hardly seen her since their talk a few nights back. Except for the times when the stage coach stopped and they were forced to work together in the kitchen, she kept him at a safe distance.

There hadn't even been any more cooking lessons and damned if he didn't miss them. But maybe it was better this way. It still stung to know that she was comparing him to her late husband. But if hating him made this easier on her, then so be it.

"In the restaurant dining room," he said. "She's paintin' the ceiling, and I can't help her 'cause I'm too short and there's only the one ladder anyhow and, besides, she said I should go get some fresh air 'cause I ain't got any homework."

Gabe grinned at the stream of information. He was going to miss this kid. Surprising really, since he'd never had much use for children. Still, Jake had a way of sneaking into a person's heart before they had a chance to hold him off. Like his mother. "She said 'ain't'?"

"Nah." The boy shook his head. "She don't say 'ain't' 'cause it ain't proper."

Made sense. He ought to point out that she wouldn't like her son saying it either, but he had a feeling Jake already knew that. "Well, you know your mother's trying to finish painting the dining room so we can have a grand opening."

"Yeah," Jake said and scraped the toe of his shoe against the wood planks.

"You want to help, huh?"

"Yeah," the boy said and came down a step. "I can paint pretty good."

He looked so damned eager.

"Wouldn't you rather be playing with your friends?"

He ducked his head and scraped the toe of his shoe across the wooden plank step. "Nah," he said, "I'd rather help you."

Oddly touched, Gabe nodded. Quite a tribute, he told himself, to be chosen over a game of baseball. His heart twisted a bit as he realized just how much of life he was going to be missing. Hell, since coming to Regret, he'd found that he'd pretty much wasted what life he did have. There was no family to mourn his passing. No friends to tell tall tales about him for years to come.

No, all he had to show for his too short life was a set of old saddlebags, a couple of decks of cards, and a horse. Not much when you added them all up.

Gabe glanced up at the leaden sky and wondered why it was no one ever realized what they had until they lost it. He hadn't been interested in the world around him until he was forced to leave it. Hadn't really lived, until he'd died.

"You all right?" Jake asked hesitantly.

He shook off his depressing thoughts and forced himself to smile at the kid. "I'm fine. And if you're gonna help, you'll need a brush."

The boy grinned and ran down the rest of the steps. Picking up a paintbrush, he dipped it into the can of white paint and carefully scraped off the excess.

"Your mom teach you that?"

"Yeah," he said, smiling. "When I was little, we used to paint together a lot."

When he was little. As opposed to now having reached the nearly crotchety age of six.

"She was always doing something to the farm," Jake was saying and Gabe told himself to pay attention. Enthusiastically, the boy slapped his brush down on the prepared wood and dragged it from side to side. "Near every month, she was changing the color of something."

No wonder she missed the freedom of living out where no one was keeping a watchful eye on her.

"You miss the farm?" Gabe asked, discreetly covering up the boy's misses.

"I used to, lots," Jake admitted. "But now that Mom ain't so worried about me doing schoolwork all the time, town's pretty good too." He dipped his brush again and this time wasn't so careful about it.

Several huge drops of white paint fell into the dirt and the brush splattered when the boy started working again. It wouldn't be the handsomest sign around, Gabe thought. But it would be original. And he was glad to think that even long after he was gone, the boy would remember this day and painting with Gabe every time he looked at this sign.

Unless, of course, Maggie changed it once he'd gone.

"I have a feeling that if your mother hears you saying

'ain't' every other word, she'll change her mind about the schoolwork."

He grinned up at him. "I already told ya, I don't say it around Mom."

"So you did."

"Besides," Jake added thoughtfully, "maybe she wouldn't care so much. She's actin' kinda different here lately."

"Hmm? Oh, you mean about letting you spend more time with your friends?"

The boy shot him a covert look from underneath a hank of hair. "Yeah, but not just that."

"What do you mean?"

Jake shrugged his narrow shoulders and dipped his brush again. As he lavished white paint onto the thirsty wood, he mumbled, "She's kinda sad."

"Sad?" Gabe backed up and sat down on the bottom step. Propping his wrists on his updrawn knees, he asked, "What do you mean, sad?"

Again Jake shrugged and again he mumbled his answer. "She told me that you're going away soon."

Ah, hell. He closed his eyes briefly, then opened them again to find Jake staring directly at him.

"Are you?"

"Yeah," he said, and noticed the word left a bitter taste in his mouth.

"Why? Don't you like us?"

"Sure I like you, Jake."

"How 'bout Mom? Don't you like her?"

Like Maggie? With her long, wild hair, deep brown eyes, and too wide mouth? His insides hummed into life at the thought of her.

"Yeah," he said in the understatement of the century, "I like her too."

"Then why don't you want to stay with us?" His eyes went all teary before he blinked furiously to stem the rising tide.

Gabe took a long breath and sighed, knowing that this conversation was about to get a lot more difficult. "I just have to go."

"But grown-ups don't have to do anything they don't want to."

Gabe chuckled wryly in spite of the situation. It must look that way to kids, he thought and only wished it were true.

"You could stay," Jake said, shooting him another sidelong look. "If you wanted, you could maybe even be, well, my pa, sort of."

Damn it.

Jake must have seen the disgust on his face and assumed it was meant for him, because the boy started talking even faster than usual.

"I'd be real good, Gabe. I swear I would. And you'd never have to tell me to do my chores or nothing. I'd always do 'em." He dropped the paintbrush onto the half-finished sign and threw himself into his argument. "And you and my mom could get married and then I'd have a pa like everybody else instead of just being that no-account Kersey's boy."

"Where'd you hear that?" Gabe interrupted the flow of words and latched onto that last phrase.

Jake didn't answer, just ducked his head again and started smearing paint with the tip of his finger.

It didn't matter really. Gabe had a pretty good idea where the boy had heard such talk. Sugar Harmon, no doubt. The damn woman needed to be muzzled like a wild dog.

"Don't you pay attention to what folks say, Jake. Some people have nothing better to do than talk about other people."

"But he was a no-account, wasn't he?"

Well, he had two choices here. He could lie to the boy to try to ease his feelings. Or he could tell him the truth and help him to accept that he wasn't responsible for what his father had done. Or didn't do.

"Come here, Jake," Gabe said and patted the step beside him.

Slowly, the boy walked toward him and sat down. He made a big show of studying the paint-stained tips of his fingers, but Gabe knew he would be listening not only with his ears, but with his heart.

And what he would say in the next few minutes was more important than anything he'd ever said before. So he'd better damn well get it right.

"I never knew your father," he said softly and reached out to smooth the kid's hair back from his face. When Jake scooted closer to him on the step, Gabe's heart cracked a little around the edges. Nodding to himself, he draped one arm across the boy's shoulders and continued. "But from what your mother's told me, I figure your pa was just . . . confused."

" 'Bout what?" Jake tipped his head back to look up at him.

"About a lot of things," Gabe mused. "But mostly, I guess, about what was important."

"Huh?"

Chuckling, he shook his head slightly and told him,

"Sometimes grown-ups don't really know what they want, Jake."

"How can you not know what you want?" Clearly, he was astounded at the thought. Jake, like every other little boy, knew just what he wanted. To be grown-up.

"Too many choices in life, I guess," Gabe said and remembered all of the bad choices he'd made during his lifetime. But then again, every one of those poor choices had led him to this precise moment. To this town. To Maggie and Jake. So how could he regret even one of them? "Sometimes," he went on, "folks choose the wrong thing and don't even know it until it's too late to get the right thing."

"That don't make much sense," the boy said softly.

"No, it doesn't," Gabe agreed.

Jake tossed his hair back out of his eyes again and said solemnly, "My pa didn't leave my mom until I got born, you know. So I figure he must have been some disappointed in me."

"No," Gabe assured him and silently hoped he got to meet up with Kersey Benson in Hell one day. Because he dearly wanted to pound on that man's face for a while. "Him leaving had nothing to do with you."

"How do you know?"

Gabe smiled at him. "Because I know *you*. And any man would be proud to have you for a son, Jake."

The boy's bottom lip trembled and Gabe prayed silently that he wouldn't cry. His prayer was answered when the child sniffed, rubbed one fist across his nose, and nodded. "I could be *your* son, if you wanted," he said a moment later.

Now Gabe was afraid *he* would be the one to cry. Heart aching, he forced himself to look into the eyes that were so much like Maggie's and deliver more pain.

"I'd like nothin' better, Jake," he said and realized that he meant every word. The boy gave him a teary smile that slowly faded as Gabe kept talking. "But I can't stay here with you and your mother."

"But why not?" Anger and hurt colored the boy's voice and Gabe felt like a bastard. Maybe Maggie had been right. Maybe he wasn't so very different from Kersey after all. Hell, at least the boy's father had just left. He hadn't stuck around to twist the knife in the kid personally.

"Remember I told you about choices?"

"And making bad ones?"

"Yeah." He pulled in a deep breath and blew it out again. "Well, I made some bad ones, too, and now it's too late to change 'em."

"Make new ones."

"I wish I could," Gabe told him, feeling that heartfelt wish to the bottom of his soul. But if wishes were horses, beggars would ride. Wishing had never made a thing so and it wouldn't change now.

Jake studied him for a long minute and Gabe never looked away. It cost him some, because watching the boy's pain and knowing he was the cause wasn't an easy thing to face. But he wanted to make sure that Jake understood he didn't *want* to leave him. He didn't want the boy to feel abandoned again.

"When are you leavin'?"

"A few weeks," Gabe said softly.

"Are ya ever coming back?"

Tickets to Hell were never round trip. Gabe shook his head. "No."

The boy nodded thoughtfully then asked quietly, "Do

ya think it would be all right if I sorta pretended that you was my pa. Just for a while? I mean, until you have to go away and everything?"

Jesus.

The pain in his chest blossomed and swelled until Gabe was sure his heart would simply explode and still it grew. The trust and love in the boy's eyes staggered him. No one had ever looked at him quite like that before. It was a gift. And a responsibility. And Gabe hoped he was up to it, even temporarily, because this was too important to mess up.

Tightening his grip on the boy's shoulders, he gave him a hard squeeze and said gruffly, "I think that'd be fine."

Jake's smile was damn near bright enough to read by. "I won't tell Mom though," he said. "She wouldn't understand."

"All right," Gabe told him conspiratorially, and stood up, drawing the boy with him. "It'll be our secret."

"Thanks . . . Pa."

Standing in the kitchen, Maggie caught her bottom lip with her teeth and bit down hard. She hadn't meant to eavesdrop at first. But when her son had started questioning Gabe about his father, she'd had to hear. Now, she wished to heaven she hadn't.

Listening to Gabe's gentle reassurances had tugged at her heart until the effort to hold back her tears had nearly choked her. Knowing that Jake had been suffering silently, wondering if he was the reason his father had left, only gave her cause to heap more curses on Kersey Benson's head.

What had she done in her life to account for this? She'd had one man who could've stayed, but chose not to. And now she'd found one who said he had to leave, but would have stayed if he'd been able.

Maggie pulled the edge of the curtain back with her fingertips so she could look out at the two men in her life. Gabe had such an easy way with Jake, she thought and her son responded to him as he had to no other man except his grandfather.

She looked at Gabe then and felt her heart turn over in her chest. Why wasn't she put off by him? An admitted gambler, he'd even been hanged by outraged townsfolk. But then, Kersey Benson hadn't been any damn good and she hadn't seen it. Was she making the same mistake with Gabe? Was she only seeing what her heart wanted her to see?

No, she decided a moment later. There was a kindness in Gabe that Kersey had never had. No matter what he'd done in the past, she knew instinctively that he was a good man at heart . . . where it counted.

And just for a moment, she let herself play Jake's game of pretend and made believe that Gabe loved her and that the three of them were a family.

CHAPTER THIRTEEN

"Quite a boy." A short man in a dusty black suit and a white clerical collar stood near the corner of the building, watching Jake sprint off to find his friends.

Gabe spared him a quick glance, then turned his gaze back to the boy, just scampering out of sight. Two hours they'd worked together, side by side, preparing the restaurant sign. And for two hours, Gabe had listened to the kid's steady stream of chatter without once wishing he'd be quiet. If nothing else, that fact said plenty about his affection for the boy.

"Yes, he is."

The preacher strolled toward him and Gabe looked him up and down, taking his measure. He had pale blue eyes that shone with a sort of wise innocence and a kind face that looked as though it smiled often. Apparently he was no fire-and-brimstone preacher. Gabe had had plenty of run-ins with those kind of churchmen and he'd learned to recognize them when he saw them. Saved him riding a rail out of town more than once. Since the preachers were usually trying to shut down the very places Gabe spent most of his time in, he and men of the cloth rarely saw eye to eye.

Which was pretty much why he'd been so successful at avoiding Regret's preacher. Until today.

"I'm Reverend Thorndyke," the man said and held out his right hand.

Gabe wiped his right hand down the front of his shirt, then accepted the handshake. "Reverend. What can I do for you?"

"Strange you should ask," the man said with a smile. "I usually like to come and meet the new people in town straight off, but well . . . I've been busy. We've a new baby in the house and my wife and I aren't getting much sleep these days."

"Congratulations."

"Thank you." The preacher looked down at the stark white sign and said, "What are you doing here?"

Gabe reached up and rubbed the back of his neck. The hours spent sanding and painting were beginning to make themselves felt in his muscles. "Making a sign for the restaurant."

The other man looked at him and grinned. "You think a sign's going to help folks find their way to the place?"

"Couldn't hurt."

"No, but Maggie's food can."

Hmm. Even the preacher, a man who made his living giving succor to the people, was used to ignoring Maggie's place of business.

"There've been a few changes," Gabe told him. All right, not many. But at least when Maggie cooked now, she rarely incinerated things. Most of her food was only scorched these days. Surely that was an improvement.

"I've heard," he said and shrugged. "Small town. People talk."

"Yeah?" Gabe cocked his head and looked at the man, waiting. There was more coming, he was sure of it. The good reverend hadn't come to just talk about the menu. "And you've been listening."

Nodding, the preacher said, "Yes, that's why I'm here."

"Gossip?" A spurt of anger jumped into the pit of his stomach. "Doesn't the Bible disapprove of gossip, *Reverend*?"

The man colored a bit and stretched his neck as if his collar were suddenly too tight. "Yes it does," he said. And so do I."

"But?"

"But," he said, admitting there was a "but." "I prefer to think of this more as a general . . . concern for Maggie's welfare, rather than simply gossip."

Gabe laughed shortly.

The reverend cleared his throat and frowned slightly. "One or two of the women in town have expressed certain, well, *concerns* about Maggie to me and—"

"One or two, huh?" Gabe asked. "I'm betting it's just the one. And you and I both know her name. Sugar Harmon."

"Sugar is a . . . difficult woman," the preacher allowed.

"Difficult?" he repeated incredulously. "That's like saying the Grand Canyon's a little deep."

Reverend Thorndyke nodded glumly. "I will admit to having my patience sorely tried a time or two by her."

Reaching up, Gabe shoved one hand through his hair and too late remembered the still-wet white paint clinging to his fingers. Well, perfect. Now his head would look like the wrong end of a skunk.

"You know, Reverend," he snapped, "I'd think you'd have better things to do than jump when Sugar shouts."

"And I'd think, if you're as fond of that boy and his mother as you appear to be," the preacher said, not a trace of temper in his voice, "you'd want to do what you could to help this situation."

Caught. Damned if the preacher wasn't a fine fisherman. He'd laid out the bait, tugged at the hook, let his prey swallow it good and deep, then reeled him in. He gave the other man an admiring smile, then asked, "And what did you have in mind, Reverend?"

The shorter man smiled broadly. "I think if the townsfolk were to see you at Sunday services with Maggie and Jake, they just might stop listening to Sugar."

"You want me to go to *church*?"

Reverend Thorndyke laughed. "The tone of your voice tells me it's been a while since you've attended."

"Let's just say inviting me into your church is like praying for the walls to come tumbling down."

"I'll risk it," the preacher said.

Risk it? He looked well pleased with himself, Gabe thought. Nothing a preacher liked better than to drag a sinner back into the fold. Only problem here was, it was a little late for the man to be worrying about the state of Gabe's soul.

The Devil had a prior claim.

But this didn't have to be all bad. As an idea glimmered in the back of his mind, Gabe spoke up. "All right, I'll come to services."

The man smiled victoriously.

"On one condition."

The smile faded just a bit.

"What's that?"

"You and your wife come have supper at the restaurant."

"Oh," the man said, already shaking his head and taking a mental step or two backward. "I don't know if that's a good idea."

"Preacher," Gabe said, reeling in his own fish, "if the folks in this town see you and your wife come here to eat, they might try it themselves."

"But my wife is nursing our son; I don't think it would be wise to—"

"We won't poison her, I promise."

He didn't look convinced.

"Reverend," Gabe said, "you're getting me into *church,* for God's sake, and all I'm asking in return is for you to have a nice meal here at the restaurant. I'd say you're still getting the biggest piece of the pie, here."

He was thinking about it, Gabe could see that much. If the little preacher only knew, he thought. Why, there were churchmen all over the west who would count it a real coup to get him through their doors and into a pew.

"When?" he asked on a sigh.

Gabe smiled. "I'll let you know."

"All right, then," he said, lifting his round chin and trying to look courageous, "it's a deal."

"Good."

"But," the little man added slyly, "I think eating at Maggie's is worth at least two Sundays. In a row."

Hell, if he was going to go to church, what difference did it make if he went once or twice? Gabe nodded and grinned at him. "You sure don't look it, but you're a hard man, reverend."

He grinned right back. "My appearance is a bit deceiving, isn't it?"

Their bargain struck, Gabe pointed at the restaurant and offered, "Care for some coffee?"

The preacher's eyebrows lifted and he slid a slow, wary glance at the restaurant. "Coffee?"

"Not afraid," Gabe teased. "Are you?"

Reverend Thorndyke inhaled sharply and briefly lifted his gaze heavenward. " 'The Lord is my shepherd—"

"You shall not want," Gabe finished for him, then asked again, "Coffee?"

The other man nodded though he didn't look happy about it. "Daniel was forced into the lion's den . . . seems the least I can do is drink of cup of Maggie's coffee."

As they walked up the steps, Gabe muttered, "I made the coffee."

"Oh, thank God."

Maggie heard the men talking in the kitchen, though she couldn't quite make out what they were saying. Heck, she wasn't even sure who it was in there with Gabe. And she didn't care, she told herself firmly. Of course, she'd been telling herself that for the last few days and she still didn't believe it.

Grasping the handle of the paintbrush tightly, she climbed the ladder again and carefully applied another coat of lavender paint. She smiled to herself as she worked and glanced back at the portions of the ceiling she'd already finished. She still wasn't sure if this was a good idea or not, but she couldn't help admiring how the quartz crystals shimmered and shone in the afternoon light.

In her mind's eye, she could already see how the restaurant would look when it was finished. And whether or not the town approved, she knew it would be beautiful. The pale blue walls reached up to the lavender sky and thousands of tiny quartz stars glittered on the expansive field. She would have a painted trellis with a fall of flowering vines climbing it on one wall. And on another, she would paint garlands of roses—all colors—in generous swags. And maybe, she thought now, she would add a few soft, dreamy-looking clouds to the twilight sky.

She could see it all so clearly. Lamplight streaming down on the heads of her customers, illuminating her paintings. She could hear their whispered compliments, see their smiling faces.

Oh yes, she told herself as she smoothed the paint onto the rough wood, it would be a beautiful place when she'd finished. And she owed it all to Gabe.

Damn it.

If he hadn't complimented her, encouraged her, she would never have risked being so outrageously different.

And though she still didn't know if she would be a success or not, at least she'd rediscovered herself. For that, she would always be grateful to him.

Even if she had wanted to strangle him just a few days ago.

"Oh, my heavens," a familiar voice whispered throatily and Maggie turned on the ladder to watch the town preacher walk into the room. Gabe was right behind him, a pleased smile on his face.

Reverend Thorndyke's head swiveled back and forth as he took the time to admire the differences she'd already made in the restaurant. Judging by the delighted smile on his face, he approved of the changes.

Maggie tightened her grip on the paintbrush and tried not to remember how she was dressed. But then, she'd only expected to be painting today, not entertaining her minister. She wore a paint-spattered man's white shirt she'd bought for this purpose at the mercantile, and an old pair of her father's trousers, belted around the too big waist by a length of rope. Her hair hung in one long braid down her back and she was barefoot . . . the better to go up and down the ladder. Mentally cringing at how she must look, she slowly climbed down from the ladder and said, "Reverend Thorndyke, what a surprise."

She looked past him to Gabe, who only shrugged and smiled.

The short man turned his wide-eyed gaze on her, briefly noted her wild appearance, then grabbed her right hand and shook it. She didn't have time to warn him about the lavender paint clinging to her—and now *his* skin.

"My dear, this is wonderful," he said, tilting his head back to admire the ceiling. "How it sparkles."

Maggie grimaced as she saw him prop his now paint-covered hand on one hip. She thought about telling him, but really, it was too late to do anything about it. "It's quartz dust," she said. "At night, it will look like star-dust."

"Stardust," he repeated in a voice filled with awe. "How very poetic." He lowered his gaze until he was looking at her again and said, "I'm sure it will be lovely. I had no idea you were so talented."

A flush of color swept into her cheeks; she knew because she felt the heat of pleased embarrassment swamping her. "Thank you," she said sincerely, "that means a lot."

His pale blue eyes looked directly into hers. "This is quite a gift you've been given, Maggie."

"A gift?"

"Oh, yes." He looked around again and, still smiling, turned back to her. "To be able to create such wonderful things is the best kind of gift." Then pausing, he seemed to think about something as he tapped one paint-coated finger against his chin. Dots of lavender remained behind. "I wonder if you would consider a business proposition."

She'd been trying to think of a way to tell him about the paint, but that statement caught her off guard. "A business proposition?"

"Yes," he said, his voice growing more determined as he spoke. "I'd like to hire you, my dear."

"To do what?" She tossed a glance at Gabe, who looked as confused as she felt. He simply shrugged, shook his head, and stared at the minister, waiting along with her.

"Why to paint the church, of course."

"The church?"

"Yes," the little man practically crowed in his excitement. "Inside first, and then perhaps come spring, the outside?"

"But," she said, still more confused than she'd care to admit, "the church was painted just last spring."

"White," he said and waved one hand, dismissing what he obviously thought of as a boring color. "If I'd known that we had a real artist, actually living right here in Regret . . ." His voice faded off as he shook his head.

"An artist?" she echoed, liking the sound of that.

"A talent so fine as yours can't be labeled any other way," the reverend said gently.

"I don't know what to say." Maggie was torn between excitement and disbelief. Turning her head, she looked around her at the blossoming restaurant and felt a rush of pride. Pride in herself and what she could accomplish. It was a heady feeling.

Still. An artist?

She'd never considered herself an artist, for heaven's sake. She simply liked color and beauty. Artists were men who lived in cities like Paris. And New York.

"Say you'll do it," the reverend urged.

"I don't know . . ." What if he wanted her to paint something and she made a mess of it? What if she ruined the town church? What would her neighbors think of her then? Oh, she put a stop to that thought almost instantly. Hadn't she just recently decided to not be swayed by what others thought of her?

"You could use your own imagination of course," he said. "I would never presume to give you instructions."

That would be lovely, she thought, and immediately, a string of ideas unwound through her mind. But as she looked at the preacher, Maggie knew that though he denied it, he had an idea or two of his own that he was holding back. "But you would like something in particular?"

"Actually," he admitted with a grin, "I would, yes." He lifted his right hand toward the ceiling, spotted the paint clinging to his palm and fingers and frowned. "Hmm."

"Oh, I'm sorry, Reverend," Maggie said and whipped out a paint-spattered cloth from her pocket.

"Thank you, I have a handkerchief," he murmured and reached into his inside coat pocket. As he absently wiped his hand, he said, "If you don't mind, I would like to see the sky painted on the wall behind the pulpit. And perhaps a few clouds as well?"

Maggie smiled and nodded. If she were any happier,

she would burst. "Exactly what I would have done."

"Wonderful." Then his smile faded and he warned her, "Now mind, we can't pay much, but—"

"Oh, Reverend," she interrupted him quickly, "I would never charge my church money for something I would gladly do for free."

He reached out to pat her, couldn't find a spot not dotted with paint and thought better of it, letting his hand drop to his side. "That speaks well of your heart, Maggie, but not of your business sense. We will pay for your services."

This was all happening so fast, she thought, clinging to the knowledge that her pastor had not only accepted the real her, but approved of her. And if the rest of the town liked what she did to their church, maybe she would finally feel as though she belonged. On her own terms.

"When did you want me to start?" she asked, already itching to get to work on the blank canvas that was the church walls.

"As soon as you've finished your work here," he said.

Maggie inhaled sharply and nodded. "All right, then, Reverend. And thank you. Thank you for . . . everything."

He smiled and started for the front door. Before he left though, he turned and said, "I'll see you both on Sunday?"

"We'll be there," Gabe agreed and Maggie turned to look at him in surprise. Before she could ask what was going on though, he added, "And we'll see you at our grand opening?"

"You will," the preacher said, though he didn't sound happy about it.

Then he left and Maggie looked up at Gabe as a dark suspicion formed in her mind, substantially dimming the happy glow inside her. "Did you have something to do with him hiring me to paint the church?"

"Me?" He clapped one hand to his chest and shook his head. "Nope, that was strictly his idea. A good one, though, if you want my opinion, which you probably don't."

She sighed and shook her head. "What was all that about you going to church? You haven't gone once since you came to town."

"I know," he said with a shrug. "But by agreeing to go to church, I forced him to agree to bring his wife to supper at the restaurant once it's ready."

"You blackmailed him into being a customer?" she asked, appalled on the poor minister's behalf.

"Now Maggie, don't get mad," Gabe said with a half-grin, "we've just started talking again."

"I can't believe it," she muttered, shaking her head. "You blackmailed a minister."

" 'Blackmail' is a harsh word."

"But appropriate?"

"Let's call it . . . an inducement."

She stared at him. "No matter what you call it, you forced him to come to the restaurant. I don't want to have to march people in here at gunpoint."

He chuckled at the image she drew, then apologized. "Sorry. You weren't trying to be funny."

"There's nothing funny about this."

Stepping close, he laid both hands on her shoulders. "You won't have to force anyone to come here, Maggie."

She hardly heard him. God, it felt good to have him

touch her again. Even knowing that he was leaving. Even knowing that there was no future for them. Heck, even knowing that he'd been hanged for something it was likely she'd never learn about wasn't enough to stamp out the skittering sensations humming through her bloodstream.

He felt it too. She saw it in his eyes. And when he dropped his hands from her shoulders, she wanted to ask him to put them back. Wanted to, but didn't.

For now, it was enough to be talking to him again. She'd missed him the last few days. Which only served to point out how lonely it would be around here when he left for good. Blast him, anyway, for making her care and then leaving her.

And to make matters worse, he'd gone and done something nice like blackmailing her minister on her behalf. How could she stay mad at a man like that?

"Just wait. Once people have seen this place, seen what you've done to it"—he smiled at her—"they'll be climbing over each other to get in."

She liked his optimism, but felt she should remind him of one fairly important fact. "This is a restaurant, Gabe. Not a museum. People will want to eat too, not just look at the paintings."

"Your cooking is—"

"Still terrible?"

"Improving," he corrected. "And after a couple of weeks, you'll be making enough money so that you can hire someone to cook for you. It'll work out, Maggie. Trust me."

Trust him.

Trust him when he refused to tell her why he was leaving. Trust him when he'd been here little more than a few weeks and already he'd torn her heart apart. Trust him, she thought and realized with a start that she did.

Despite everything, despite the pain of knowing he would be leaving soon, she trusted him. Maybe it was the way he treated Jake. Maybe it was the way he'd coaxed her into rediscovering her true self.

But whatever the reason, he'd found a place in her life that she couldn't deny.

She stared up into his eyes and found herself reflected there. The real her. The Maggie she'd always hidden from everyone. He saw her. *Really* saw her. And still, he believed in her.

"You know something, Mr. Donovan?"

He grinned at her, obviously relieved that she wasn't going to start up the war between them again. "What's that, Mrs. Benson?"

"I think I do trust you." She reached up and with one paint-stained hand cupped his cheek, relishing the warm, whiskery feel of his skin against hers. "Everything will work out, just like you said."

He covered her hand with one of his, gave it a squeeze, and pulled it down. Still holding on to her, he said with a smile, "Never bet against a gambler."

CHAPTER FOURTEEN

"Is this some desperate, last-minute bid for mercy?" the Devil asked from the corner of the room.

Gabe groaned inwardly but didn't even look at him. Instead, he concentrated on tying the black string tie around Jake's neck. Hell, he'd been expecting a visit from Old Scratch long before this.

"Sorry to disappoint you." The gunfighter read Gabe's mind again as he took a seat on the boy's bed.

Gabe noticed the mattress didn't shift, dip, or show any signs at all of someone sitting on it.

"Surprised?" the demon asked.

"Go away," Gabe muttered.

"I can't go away," Jake complained. "You're tyin' my tie, remember?"

"So I am," he said with a smile and shot a vicious look at his enemy across the room. "And you're not making this easy. Hold still."

For approximately ten seconds, he did.

Then, jumping from foot to foot, he said tightly, "I gotta *go,* Gabe."

The Devil laughed.

Gabe quickly finished the job, straightened the kid's collar, then pointed him toward the door. "All right, run."

"Thanks, Gabe!" he yelled and raced across the room.

His Sunday shoes clattering against the wooden floor made him sound more like a herd of children than just one small boy.

But the smile on Gabe's face disappeared as he turned to face the Devil watching him. "I already told you. Go away."

The demon settled back against the pillows and threw both arms behind his head. Crossing his feet at the ankles, he sighed and said, "Going to *church*, Gabriel? Getting a little desperate as the days count down?"

Desperate yes, but not out of fear of his own fate. If he was headed for Hell, then it was because he'd earned his way there. No, what Gabe worried about was Maggie. And Jake. They'd be alone again, when he was gone. All he was trying to do now was help Maggie be accepted by this town. Help make her life a little easier.

"So you're doing this out of the goodness of your heart."

Gabe shot the Devil another furious glance. "If you can read my mind so well, why show up and talk to me at all?"

The gunfighter shrugged. "Why not?"

"Y'know," Gabe said, "in less than two months, I'm going to have to spend eternity with the likes of you." And no matter how many times he said that, it didn't get easier. "But until then," he went on, "I can choose my own company."

"That's where you're wrong."

"How do you figure anything I do is your business?"

"Because your soul is mine. *I* gave you this extra time."

"You didn't *give* me anything. I bought this time." By promising another man's soul to the Devil. Gabe scowled at the thought and tried to imagine Henry facing down this devil. The older man's cheerful disposition would be sadly out of place in Hell. But since when had he started worrying about Henry?

"Regrets?" the Devil asked.

His head snapped up and he glared at the gunfighter, still sprawled across Jake's bed. Early morning sunshine slanted in through the windows, making the green and white room shine like a summer meadow. Jake's treasures lay scattered across every flat surface. His dirty clothes were tossed in a pile and a battalion of toy soldiers were frozen in battle in the far corner.

A normal kid's room, he thought, but for the Devil lounging smack in the middle of it. He never should have agreed to live here, he told himself. He'd had no right to drag a demon into Maggie's home. But soon enough now, his time would be up and both he and the Devil would be gone forever.

"I've been thinking," the gunfighter said and sat up on the bed. He fixed Gabe with a steady stare and asked, "How would you like even more time?"

"What?"

"Let's say a year. Maybe even two."

Everything in Gabe yearned for it. More time. Hundreds of days and nights. Sunrises and sunsets. Countless hours spent with Maggie and Jake. Even thinking about the possibility made him nearly light-headed. But at the same time, Gabe knew deep in the heart of him that when the Devil made an offer, there was a price to pay.

"Sounds good, doesn't it?" the gunfighter said in a whisper that urged Gabe to grab the offer. "A year or two—a man could pack a lot of living into a couple of years."

He steeled himself against temptation and forced himself to ask, "What's it cost?"

"Well, now," the Devil said slowly, thoughtfully, "you got two months for Henry."

"Yeah?" he said, past the shame of knowing he'd sold out another human being. Jesus. Stop feeling guilty about Henry. He'd danced all his life. Now it was time to pay the fiddler.

"So to be fair, I'll give you two years for Maggie's soul."

Blackness closed around him until the only light he could see was gleaming in the mocking pale blue eyes watching him. Rage. Dark, burning, overwhelming rage poured into his body like water into a jug. Fast, furious, the feelings swamped him until his body shook with the force of it.

"You stay the hell away from her," he warned, and even his voice trembled at the fury tearing through him.

"Think about it, Gabriel," that cajoling whisper came again. "Two long years—go where you want. Do what you want." He stood up, braced his legs wide apart, and crossed his arms over his chest. "What do you say?"

Gabe moved closer to his enemy and looked him dead in the eye so there would be no mistake. "Not for two. Not for twenty." Hands fisted at his sides, his entire body shaking with helpless fury, he ground out tightly, "She's not a part of this."

"Isn't she?" A half-smile curved the other man's lips and Gabe wanted nothing more than to smash that smile with his fists.

"This is between you and me, mister," he told the Devil. "And I swear to you—if you harm her, or her boy, what I'll do to you'll make Hell look like a Sunday picnic."

"Gabe?" Maggie called from the landing.

He swiveled his head in that direction, then looked back at the Devil only to find he'd gone as silently as he'd come. Anger still rushing through him, Gabe snatched up his hat and headed for the door. Turning back one last time, he said it again, quietly this time, just in case the gunfighter was still lingering in the shadows. "Leave her alone. You hear me?"

Then he left the room and walked to where Maggie waited at the head of the stairs. After the sunlit brightness of Jake's room, he had to squint to see in the more dimly lit hall. But Maggie was worth the effort. Dressed in a pale yellow dress with lace at the high collar and at the cuffs, she looked like a splash of spring in the middle of autumn.

His heart lifted, then staggered at the idea of her being threatened by a demon who never should have been allowed to get this close to her.

"Did you say something?" she asked.

"No," he said and cupped her elbow in his palm.

She gathered up the hem of her dress and started down the stairs. "I swear I heard you talking to someone."

"There's no one else here," he said and tossed one last glance over his shoulder at the door to Jake's room. "Who would I be talking to?"

Was it his imagination? Or did the shadows in the hall tremble and sway?

* * *

"You're pushing him too hard," one voice said.

The gunfighter turned toward his friend. "Don't you think I know that? I have no choice. Before you know it, the two months will be up."

"Whose idea was this two-month thing, anyway?"

"Mine," he said glumly. "It seemed like a good idea at the time."

"Uh-huh. And when the two months are up, then what?"

"Then, I don't know. That depends on Gabe."

"And if he fails?"

Oh, he didn't want to think about that. His superiors were already unhappy with this unorthodox scheme.

"Gabriel won't fail," he said with determination and reassured himself by remembering the look on Gabe's face when Maggie's soul was threatened.

"I hope you're right."

"So do I," the gunfighter said softly and focused his long-seeing gaze on the man in question.

After church, Maggie stepped out into the sunlight and lifted one hand to shade her eyes. Jake scampered past her, dodging in and out of the crowd as he ran looking for his friends. The rise and fall of the conversations around her went unnoticed as she half turned to look behind her for Gabe.

As he stepped out of the church, Maggie was sure she saw relief flicker across his features.

"It wasn't that bad," she said. "I thought the reverend gave a very good talk this morning."

"The wages of sin?" Gabe asked with a shudder.

Their preacher wasn't a fire-eater by any means, Maggie thought, but he did have a way with words. So much so in this case that she caught Gabe shifting uncomfortably in the pew every few minutes. As a professional gambler, he must have felt that the sermon was directed especially at him.

He looked at her and gave her a sheepish grin. "Besides, it wasn't the service I minded so much as keeping a constant eye on the ceiling."

She chuckled and shook her head. "What?"

"Been so long since I've been in a church, I figured the roof would come falling down around me."

"And yet," she pointed out with a quick look at the shingled roof, "you both survived."

"So far," he agreed and took her elbow to guide her down the steps, "but let's get away from the building. No sense tempting fate."

Still smiling, Maggie allowed him to escort her through the crowd, and as she passed, she caught more than a few curious gazes directed at her. But that was to be expected, she supposed. A widow attending church services with her handyman would be bound to stir up talk. And for the first time in a long while, she didn't care. Some people would think the worst no matter what. If given the truth, they'd believe a lie because the lie was more interesting.

The people who knew her wouldn't believe gossip and why should she care what people she *didn't* know thought of her? And she wasn't going to let anything spoil the feeling of having Gabe by her side . . . however temporarily.

She inhaled deeply and smiled to herself, enjoying this new sense of liberation. Then Patsy O'Keefe stepped in front of her and Maggie's inward smile slipped a bit.

"Is it true?" the woman asked, reaching up to tilt her black bonnet farther back on her head.

"Is what true?" Maggie looked at her in confusion.

"I heard," Patsy was saying, "that the preacher hired you to do some painting in church."

"Oh." Maggie shot Gabe a look, then said, "Yes, it's true."

"What kind of paintin'?" Patsy asked, more puzzled than outraged. "And why would he ask you?"

"It's difficult to explain," Maggie said, but was interrupted by Gabe.

"Reverend Thorndyke took one look at Maggie's paintings and hired her on the spot to spruce up your church," he said and Maggie felt warmed by the ring of pride in his voice.

"Well, for goodness' sake," Patsy said. "I had no idea."

Ripples of murmured conversation rolled across the small crowd of people gathered at the foot of the steps. Maggie smiled and hoped she didn't look as nervous as she suddenly felt. Liberation was all well and good, she thought, but what if no one else besides the reverend liked her paintings? Then what?

Oh, she wasn't at all sure she was comfortable with the idea of people seeing her work and then judging it. She remembered all too well how it had felt, waiting for Gabe's opinion. And now everyone in town would feel as though they had the right to judge her work.

But then she reminded herself that Gabe *had* liked her work and remembered, too, how good it had felt to hear his praise.

"I think it's disgraceful," one woman piped up and Maggie didn't even have to turn to identify the speaker.

Only one woman she knew was capable of ruining a perfectly good day with an ill-chosen remark.

Sugar elbowed her way through the crowd until she was standing directly in front of Maggie. Looking her square in the eye, she went on, just loud enough for everyone to hear.

"I for one don't want my church decorated with a bunch of folderol paintings and pictures of heaven knows what."

Before she could stop herself, as usual, Maggie shot back, "I didn't realize it was *your* church."

The crowd around her oohed in approval and moved closer en masse, obviously loath to miss a word.

Sugar gasped, outraged. "You know very well what I mean, missy."

It felt good, standing up to this woman. And now that she'd started, Maggie wasn't going to stop. "I don't think even you know what you mean half the time."

Someone nearby chuckled and sent a rush of dark red color into Sugar's pasty cheeks.

Maggie stared into her enemy's eyes and, not for the first time, wondered what she had ever done to make the woman hate her with such a vengeance. Sugar's rail-thin body nearly vibrated with fury and the warm, friendly faces surrounding Maggie only seemed to feed the pool of venom inside her.

"It's a disgrace, is what it is," Sugar was saying. "You and your fancy man." A gasp from the crowd made the woman smile victoriously. "Coming to church together as bold as brass."

Well, there it was. Right out in the open, a jab about her and Gabe. Meant to deliver a stunning blow, it had missed its mark. Maggie straightened up, lifted her chin, and gave the other woman a pitying smile.

"Is that the best you can do, Sugar? If you'd like to take a minute or two to come up with something better, I'm sure we'd all be happy to wait."

"Sure would," someone called out from the back of the crowd.

Another voice shouted, "You tell 'er, Maggie!"

"You see," Maggie went on, crossing her arms over her chest, "Gabe works for me. That's all. And what you and other petty-minded little people want to think has nothing to do with me." She almost laughed aloud, it felt so good to be saying what she meant rather than what she thought others would want to hear.

"Well, I never!" the woman said on another gasp.

"Never what, Sugar?" Maggie asked sweetly. "Smile? Laugh? Be specific."

Another snort of laughter sprang up from the crowd but Maggie hardly heard it now. She wasn't doing this for her audience's sake, but for her own. And it felt wonderful.

"You're just like her, aren't you?" Sugar asked, her voice low and vicious.

Maggie knew who she meant and lifted her chin another notch. "I hope so."

"Well, there it is," Sugar said loudly, swinging her gaze over the knot of people. "You heard her. Just like her mother and you all know what her mother was—"

"Don't say it," Maggie warned her as her protective instincts came rushing to the surface. The woman could say what she pleased about her. But she'd better keep her vicious tongue off Maggie's family.

"A witch," Sugar finished, victory shining in her eyes.

Maggie squeezed her hands into such tight fists, her

fingernails dug at her palms. This confrontation was her fault, she reminded herself. If she'd simply ignored Sugar's taunts as she used to, none of this would be happening. But she hadn't. She'd made her stand and it was too late to back out now, even if she'd wanted to. Keeping silent all these years hadn't done a spot of good. Maybe what they both needed was a good clearing of the bad air between them. Heaven knew, *she* felt better for getting some of this off her chest. If Sugar wanted war, then she could have it.

"My mother wasn't a witch and you know it." Maggie planted both hands on her hips and said loud enough for everyone to hear, "All she ever tried to do was help people."

"With her brews and potions," Sugar sneered.

"With herbs and remedies."

"True, true," someone remembered out loud. "You recall the time the croup laid everybody low? Maggie's ma kept this town going, doctoring us all in turn."

"A good woman," another voice said.

"She was a heathen and a witch," Sugar said, clearly furious that no one else was agreeing with her. "And I say, like mother, like daughter."

"Thank you," Maggie said, a tight smile on her face. "I can't think of a nicer compliment than being compared to my mother."

A couple of women nearby chuckled and Sugar's features turned to stone. "You're a fool, then," she said, "because this whole town knows what your mother was. What *you* are."

She moved in closer until she and Sugar were standing just a breath apart. From behind her somewhere, Maggie heard Dolly muttering encouragement. But she didn't need it. For the first time in two years, Maggie wasn't backing down from Sugar or from anyone else. From now on, if the gossips in this town wanted to talk about her, they'd have to do it knowing that Maggie would be challenging them openly.

And if they didn't like her paintings, well, that was their right. Just as it was her right to go ahead and paint anyway, whether they liked it or not.

As that last thought flitted through her mind, she felt Gabe's hand come down on her shoulder and she drew strength from his warmth. His support.

She looked into the other woman's eyes and noted a flicker of surprise in the older woman's eyes. Obviously, she'd still expected Maggie to back down. To run away. Well, no more.

"And we all know what you are, Sugar," she said, her voice a low hum of anger. "A mean-spirited, sour, used-up crone of a woman who wouldn't know genuine kindness if it fell out of the sky and hit her on the head."

A man laughed outright. A few women gasped in pretended horror, but to Maggie's satisfaction, the majority of the crowd seemed to be on her side. Gabe gave her shoulder a companionable squeeze.

Sugar huffed and sniffed and reared her head back like a rattler about to strike. What she might have said was lost forever, though, when Redmond pushed his way through the crowd to his wife's side. "That's enough," he murmured, close to Sugar's ear.

"It's not nearly enough," she retorted and pulled free of his grasp on her arm.

"Let her be, Redmond," Dolly shouted, "this has been a long time coming."

Grumbled mutterings from the crowd supported her

opinion, but Redmond wasn't listening to any of them. His entire concentration was focused on his wife. "You're coming with me," he said flatly. "Now."

Furious, she tried to pull free of him again, but Redmond hung on like a bulldog. Damn the man, couldn't he see that she finally had Maggie where she wanted her? She was finally going to have her say and half the town would be witnesses to Maggie's comeuppance. This girl, who looked so much like her mother, was a thorn in Sugar's side. A constant reminder of what could have been. What should have been.

But Redmond wouldn't understand that. How could he? He wasn't a woman. A woman who'd been tossed aside for the first twitching skirt that had come along.

His fingers dug into her upper arm and Sugar shot him a look that should have curled his hair. But he didn't budge, his expression didn't waver. Sugar felt a moment's pause as she stared up into the face of the man she'd married nearly ten years before. She'd never seen him like this before and she wasn't entirely sure she approved. His eyes glittered with banked anger and frustration and she asked herself what in heaven *he* had to be upset about.

Her gaze shifted to the faces of the crowd surrounding her. It didn't improve her mood any to note that most of the people—her friends and neighbors, if you please—were siding with Maggie.

Bitter tears stung the backs of her eyes, but Sugar refused to cry in public. Straightening up, she tugged at her shirtwaist, gave Maggie a brief, barely-there nod, then turned on her heel for home. Redmond kept pace, his hand still keeping a tight hold on her arm.

Her neighbors, her preacher, even her husband, had

taken Maggie's side against her. And the old pain of being second best twisted in her heart again.

It wasn't right.

Maggie stepped down from the borrowed buggy and looked at the ramshackle little cabin as if it were a glorious palace. Her features were lit with an inner glow that dazzled his eyes as he watched her. And Gabe couldn't help wondering how he would survive an eternity apart from her.

She tossed him a quick glance and a brilliant smile that took his breath away, before striding up to the picket fence and the gate hanging crookedly from its hinges.

After her confrontation with Sugar, Maggie had insisted on making this trip to her former home. It was as though talking about her mother, defending her, had lit a fuse inside her that demanded to be recognized. So, leaving Jake with one of his friends, the two of them had set off on the two-hour drive to Maggie's past.

Gabe looked around the place then, trying to see it through Maggie's eyes. But what she saw through a veil of love, he saw in bitter reality.

The picket fence dipped and swayed like a line of old drunks. Each stake had once been a different color and now that paint was peeling and chipping from sun and weather, giving it the look of an aging clown. The cabin itself was small and had once been a bright yellow, with a cherry-red door. But again, the paint had faded away, leaving behind a sad echo of its gaudiness. One windowpane was broken and the others were grimy. The roof sagged in the middle and the pine tree at the edge of the house leaned its branches over the sag, as if protecting it.

The yard was overgrown, weeds and vines clinging to the fence and trailing across the ground as if in search of new life. The whole place looked like what it was. Abandoned. Empty. Lifeless.

But Maggie, headed for the front porch with a spring in her step, obviously saw it differently. When she opened the door and went inside, Gabe climbed down from the buggy and followed quickly after her. God knew what she might find in there. Skunks, snakes, or an assortment of other creatures looking for a warm place to take up roost.

Two birds flew out the front door as he approached and he ducked his head to get out of their way. He took the steps two at a time and called "Maggie?" as he entered the darkened house.

"In here," she yelled back and Gabe started for her, glancing around him as he went. The rooms were small and empty now, but for a stick or two of forgotten furniture. Vibrant color splashed across the walls and even the wooden floor had been painted in swirls of reds and blues. And even though he'd been expecting something of the sort, Gabe was overwhelmed and wished he might have seen the place as it once was. Before it had been left behind to molder.

In the tiny apple-green kitchen, he found Maggie rummaging through shelves, grabbing up jars and crocks and small paper packets.

"Did you find what you came for?" he asked and walked up behind her.

She threw him a glance over her shoulder and his chest tightened at the pure joy in her eyes.

"Yes," she said and turned around, laying her booty on the table. "It's all here. Seed packets, instructions, herbs, oils, everything."

He glanced down. It looked like a jumble to him, but clearly it meant the world to Maggie.

"I left them behind, you know," she said as she thumbed through the seed packets like a gambler fingering a worn deck of cards. "When Jake and I moved to town, I thought I had to leave everything I was here." She paused and let her gaze sweep the tired, dusty kitchen. "In this place."

A bittersweet smile curved her mouth briefly.

"And now?"

She looked up at him and he was lost in the shine of her eyes. "Now," she said, "I want to bring my mother's herbs and things back to town. I'll plant a garden behind the restaurant and—" She broke off and looked at the papers in her hands. "It won't be the same," she murmured, "but I don't want what my mother knew to disappear."

"It won't," he told her gently, "as long as you remember."

She nodded to herself, then looked up at him. "She wasn't a witch, you know."

"I figured that much out for myself."

Maggie smiled. "But she did know about herbs and healing. She learned from the Cheyenne."

"Well, now," Gabe said and crossed his arms over his chest. "That's interesting."

"When she was little, her family died in an accident and a roving band of Cheyenne found her. Raised her."

Maggie looked at him almost defiantly then, as if she expected him to be put off by her story.

He wasn't.

"She was lucky."

"Yes, she was," she said, clearly relieved at his response. "And so was I, to have had her."

"As lucky as Jake is," he said, reaching out to smooth a stray lock of hair back from her face, "to have you."

A flash of heat leaped into life between them and Gabe sucked in a breath at the hard punch of desire. Then he took one long step backward, purposely putting her far out of arm's reach. They were too close here. Too alone. And one more touch, one more spark, might be all that was needed to start up a fire they wouldn't have a chance of extinguishing.

Especially when a part of him didn't want the fire put out at all. Lately, his self-control had been sorely tested and he wasn't sure just how much more temptation he could take.

Shifting his gaze from hers, he said gruffly, "Look, you lay out what you want to take with you and I'll pull the buggy around back. Make it easier to load everything." He started for the door then, but her voice stopped him before he could escape.

"What are you so afraid of, Gabe?"

He did a slow turn, met her gaze with his, and through tightly clenched teeth, told her the simple truth. "You, lady. You scare hell out of me."

Maggie pulled in a deep breath to steady the nerves humming into life inside her. "You scare me too," she said and moved close enough to reach up and lay one hand on his cheek. He turned his face into her palm briefly, and she couldn't be sure, but she thought he kissed her hand. When he looked at her again, she added, "I like how you make me feel."

Gabe smiled at her briefly. "So do I, Maggie. Too much."

CHAPTER FIFTEEN

Late into the night, Maggie painted.

The incident with Sugar, the trip out to the farm, and Gabe's startling confession had all somehow come together to feed her creativity. Or, at the very least, to make sleep impossible so that it was either lie in bed staring at the ceiling, or get up and paint.

Stretching her right arm out, she laid in a darker shade of gray as the shadow line on her nearly finished mural of a trellis. As she worked, her mind spun from one thought to the next and eventually settled on Gabe.

Her brain drew up image after image of him, smiling, arguing, looking at her with a fire in his eyes . . . Her stomach pitched unexpectedly and Maggie pulled in a deep breath, hoping to steady it.

But it was useless.

Almost from the first, he'd unsettled her in a way that no one else ever had. He'd made her think, made her angry, and made her want him with a fierceness she never would have believed possible. That alone astounded her. She was no shy virgin. She'd been married, had been bedded, then discarded. She'd experienced sex and after her wedding night had decided that, for a woman, sex was strictly a means to having children. Oh, kissing was certainly pleasant, but as for the rest, despite how much men seemed to enjoy it, she'd rather sleep.

So to suddenly find herself actually *wanting* Gabe in her bed was surprising, to say the least.

She paused for a moment, let her arm hang at her side as she rolled her shoulder, trying to ease out the kinks in the muscles. And as the ache eased, she turned her mind back to the scene with Sugar, outside the church, and recalled the sensation of knowing Gabe was there, right behind her. He hadn't pushed himself to the front, ready to fight her battles. He hadn't treated her as though she were incapable of defending herself. What he'd done was more important than that.

His hand on her shoulder had shown her that he was there if she needed him. He'd let her know she wasn't alone.

And after years of loneliness, that was the greatest gift of all.

"Aren't you tired yet?"

"Jesus!" Maggie jumped, startled, and whirled around to look at Gabe, silhouetted in the doorway leading to the kitchen. The lamps she'd lit hours ago were beginning to sputter and their flame-cast shadows danced on the walls.

Shaking her head, she told him, "If you don't quit scaring me like that, my hair's going to be snow-white."

He leaned against the doorjamb, and even from across the room, she felt the power of his gaze drift over her.

"You'd still look too damned good."

"Thank you?" she asked. If that was a compliment, he didn't sound happy about it.

He lifted one hand and pointed at the wall behind her. "You don't have to work all night, you know."

"Did I wake you?"

"No." He straightened up and came farther into the

room. Shoving his hands into his pockets, he said, "Couldn't sleep. Too quiet."

"Ah." She nodded and smiled. "You're still not used to Sunday nights in Regret. Even the saloon closes early on Sundays."

He nodded, still walking, and she watched him move in and out of the puddles of lamplight dotting the floor. He was barefoot again and shirtless and Maggie had to wonder why, if she scared him as much as he claimed, he was here. Now. Alone with her in the darkness.

A spiral of warmth started low in the pit of her stomach and then spread even lower. Heat blossomed inside her and made her legs quake so hard, she locked her knees in an effort to stay upright. She didn't understand the sensations rippling through her, but damned if they weren't pleasant. As he came closer, she was acutely aware of her own worn nightgown and the fact that she wore nothing beneath it.

And she wondered what it would feel like to have Gabe's hands on her body. A rush of expectation tempered by experience filled her. After all, she'd had a man's hands on her body before . . . much to her own disappointment.

He stopped a few feet from her and she didn't know if she was glad about that or not.

Looking up at the vine-covered trellis that was nearly finished, he said quietly, "Looks good."

"Thank you," she said and wondered if he heard the raw huskiness in her voice.

A moment passed, then two. And still, neither of them spoke. When the silence became nearly unbearable though, Gabe said, "I've been thinking."

"About what?" Her mouth was so dry, she could

barely form the words. Flickering light played on his bare chest and Maggie couldn't seem to tear her gaze away from the hard, muscled strength of him.

"Maggie," he said on a groan, "I can't talk to you if you keep looking at me like that."

She pulled in a shaky breath and forced her gaze up, to meet his. What she found in his eyes made breathing at all nearly impossible. "Am I scaring you again?"

"Damn right, you are," he said tightly.

"Only fair," she quipped, with a lightheartedness she didn't feel. "You do the same thing to me."

He flinched and she saw the muscle in his jaw twitch. "I won't hurt you, Maggie."

"Yes you will," she said breathlessly. Swallowing hard, she went on before he could argue. "You're going to leave, and that will hurt me." Even saying the words sent small spasms of pain radiating throughout her body.

"I know," he muttered and sighed heavily. In the half-light, his features looked tight. "If I could change things, I want you to know, I would."

"But you can't."

"No," he whispered and she heard the pain and regret in his voice. "I can't."

She nodded, accepting that for the moment. "All right, what were you thinking about?"

He rubbed one hand across the back of his neck and she tried not to watch his chest muscles shift with the motion.

"I've been thinking, maybe it would be better for both of us if"—he paused and looked into her eyes—"I moved out. Took a room at the hotel."

Maggie shook her head. "Why?"

"You know why," he said tightly. Waving one hand

at her, he went on. "We keep running into each other dressed like this, something's going to happen. Something that shouldn't."

She smoothed one hand down the front of her nightgown and, as she did, felt the rapid beating of her own heart. "You want to leave?"

"No, I don't want to, but—"

"Then don't," she said quickly.

The night was so quiet, it was as though they were the only two people left in the world. Old sheets were tacked up over the front windows, shutting out the view of Main Street and enveloping them in a quiet, candlelit, shadow-filled room. It was as if there were no town right outside, no sleeping son upstairs. Just the darkness and she and Gabe. Together.

On that word, her mind filled with delicious images. Gabe kissing her, holding her tightly, laying her down across a bed and then lowering himself to lie alongside her. Gabe joining his body to hers and her holding him while pleasure took him to a place she couldn't share.

"God, woman," he muttered, "get that look off your face."

"What look?" she asked, her voice low and dreamy.

"The look that asks me to do everything I've thought of doing to you for weeks."

"Oh my." Her heartbeat tripled and she struggled to draw air into heaving lungs. "You've thought about it too?"

He snorted a choked laugh. "Only every minute I'm around you and then when I'm not." Shoving one hand through his hair, he grumbled, "Why the hell do you think I said you scared me? Why else would I be looking to find a room somewhere else?"

"Would your moving be enough to quiet what's between us?"

He snorted. "Hell, no. But it might make it a little easier to live with."

"What if I don't want you to go?"

He threw his hands wide and let them fall to his sides again. "It wouldn't be any good. I can't offer you what you want. What you need."

"And what's that?" she asked.

His gaze found hers. "Forever, Maggie. You're the kind who needs forever."

She dropped her paintbrush to the nearby tabletop and moved toward him. "And what if I said I wasn't interested in forever?"

He gave her a sad, tired smile that tugged at her heart. "Then you'd be lying."

Yes, she thought. She would. She'd always wanted forever. But she'd stopped believing she would find it. Jake's father had convinced her to never seek love again. But then Gabe had arrived, and in just a few weeks, he had become more important to her, more a part of her life, than her late husband ever had.

And she didn't want to lose it, though she knew she would, the moment he left.

But that time was weeks away and they still had now. So for right now, tonight, she wasn't interested in tomorrow, or the day after that. All she cared about was this moment. This small piece of forever that she could claim and remember in the years to come.

She took another step closer to him and noted that he braced himself as if for battle. But this was one battle Maggie was going to win. For just a little while, she wanted to pretend that the world outside this room didn't exist. She wanted to feel alive. She wanted to feel his hands on her. And tomorrow could take care of itself.

"For tonight," she whispered as she took the last step that brought her right up against him, "there is no tomorrow. No forever. There's only us."

"Maggie, you don't know what you're saying," he said tightly.

"Yes I do," she told him and reached up to put her arms around his neck. Her hands slid up his bare shoulders, loving the feel of his warm skin beneath her palms. Spearing her fingers through his thick hair, she watched a glazed look cross his eyes and knew that he wouldn't fight her much longer. "I'm not a virginal spinster being lured off into the shadows by some unredeemable rake."

He choked out a short laugh.

"This is my idea. What I want. You're not forcing me into anything." She leaned in close to him, brushing her breasts against his chest. Her breath caught at the sensation of worn fabric scraping across her nipples and she heard him groan as his arms came around her like twin bands of iron.

He buried his face in the crook of her neck and murmured, "Maggie, Maggie, this isn't why I came in here tonight."

"I know. You wanted to leave me."

"No."

"Are you sorry you came in here?"

Lifting his head, he stared down into her eyes and said, "No, God help us both, I'm not. I only hope you won't be tomorrow."

She shook her head gently and reminded him, "There is no tomorrow, remember?"

Moving one hand up to cup her face, he nodded and

whispered, "No tomorrow. Only tonight. And you." Then he lowered his head and claimed her mouth with his.

Maggie sighed and gave herself up to the wave of sensation pouring through her. He parted her lips with his tongue and laid siege to her soul. Again and again, he teased her, his tongue tasting, exploring, twining with hers. Her hands clutched at him, fingers digging into his shoulders, then moving up and down his broad, bare back, loving the feel of him, wanting more. She fell against him then and he held on to her as he slowly sank down onto the floor.

Then they were kneeling and he rained kisses all over her face. His lips dusted across her eyelids, her cheeks, along her jaw and back up to her waiting mouth. His hands fisted in her nightgown at the small of her back. He held her tighter to him, as though he was trying to pull her inside him, make them one.

Her mind spun out of control as too many sensations presented themselves at once. She held on to his shoulders as if her grip on him meant her life and let him take her where he would.

This was all so new to her. This desire. This wrenching, pulsing need soaring inside her. She'd never known this kind of pleasure. To her late husband, a kiss had been only a prelude to the business of bedding her, and though she'd enjoyed the kissing more than what had followed, she'd never felt what she did now. This rush of heat and light, as if her entire body was aglow with the flames of a thousand candles.

He tore his mouth from hers then and she sucked in air like a drowning woman. Gently, he laid her down on the shining wood floor and leaned over her, propping himself up on one elbow. Mind spinning, body humming, she tipped her head back and stared blindly at the glittering ceiling overhead as his lips trailed along her neck, leaving a warm, damp trail of kisses behind him.

When he reached the high collar of her nightgown, he lifted one hand to the buttons and quickly undid them, pulling the fabric aside to allow him access to the tender skin at the base of her throat.

More sensation. More warmth.

While his mouth teased her, she felt him lift the hem of her nightgown, pulling it up, over her calves, past her knees and high on her thighs. The cool air of the room dusted her bare skin and gooseflesh sent another shiver up her spine.

"Cold?" he whispered, lifting his head to look down at her.

Oh, she didn't think she'd ever be cold again. Her skin was on fire. Her blood was boiling and everything inside her felt as red-hot as the glowing end of a piece of firewood.

"No, I'm not," she said and reached up to cup his cheek. It was good of him to make this coupling nice for her as well, but she wanted to get the uncomfortable part of this business out of the way so that she could lie in his arms and enjoy being cuddled up beside him. Smoothing her thumb along his jawline, she smiled softly. "It was nice of you to spend so much time on me," she whispered, "but you don't have to worry. I'm ready."

"Nice of me?" He smiled. "I don't know what you're talking about. Ready for what?"

"Ready for you to take your pleasure," she said and reached down to bunch her nightgown at her hips.

"What are you doing?" he asked quietly, and she noted that he wasn't smiling anymore.

"Helping," she said softly, then drew her knees up and planted her feet firmly on the floor.

He glanced down at the open invitation she was affording him, then shifted his gaze back to hers. Clearly confused, he shook his head. "Are you in a hurry? Have a train to catch?"

"No," she said and, beginning to feel just a bit confused herself, lowered her legs and tugged the hem of her nightgown down far enough to cover herself modestly. "But," She shifted slightly, looked up at him and whispered, "I don't understand, we've kissed and now it's time for you to . . ." She let the words fade off.

"To?"

Frowning slightly, she took a deep breath, blew it out, and said bluntly, "To bed me."

"Ah . . ." He nodded, understanding. He bent over her, planted a quick kiss on her mouth, then lifted his head again to look down at her. "You know something, Maggie?"

"What?"

"You were wrong. You *are* a virgin. In every way that matters."

"Don't be ridiculous. I'm a widow. I have a child."

"Yet you've only known the touch of a man too stupid to appreciate what he had when he had it."

"I don't understand," she murmured, staring up at him.

"I know," he told her, "but you will." Then he reached out and laid one hand atop her fabric-covered breast.

"Oh my."

Maggie sucked in another gulp of air through clenched teeth. Tingles sparkled into life deep within her and she shifted again on the floor. His thumb and fore-finger rubbed her hardened nipple, tugging at it, pulling the cotton fabric across its tip. "Gabe . . . ?"

No one had ever done *this* before.

"Trust me, Maggie, we're not near ready yet."

"We?" she whispered and caught her bottom lip with her teeth as he tugged at her nipple again.

"We."

Then he took his hand from her breast, and before she could moan the loss of his touch, he reached down, slipped his hand beneath her nightgown, and ran his palm up the length of her body until he was touching her bare breast without the barrier of cloth separating them.

"Oh my," she said again and her eyes widened. His fingertips traced a slow circle around her nipple and then he cupped her fullness in the palm of his hand, fingers kneading the soft flesh gently.

Strange, incredible feelings skittered through her. She'd never known anything like it. Wouldn't have guessed that something this amazing existed. She reached for him and held on to his arms as he continued to explore her body beneath her nightgown. First one breast, then the other. First one sensitive nipple, then the other. Over and over, his hands and fingers touched, stroked, caressed.

Maggie's body trembled with the force of sensation rocketing around inside her. Her grasp on his arms weak-ened as her strength was drawn from her and still she wanted more.

Then in one, seemingly effortless motion, he pulled

her nightgown up and over her head, baring her body to his gaze. In the candlelight, she watched him as he looked his fill of her and she realized that this was the first time a man had seen her body.

Kersey had never seemed interested. His quick, hard fumblings had been performed in the dark and were usually over and done with before Maggie had time to complain.

This was new. This was . . . exciting.

Until Gabe smiled at her before lowering his head to her breast. And suddenly, it was so much more than exciting. It was thrilling.

Stunned, Maggie watched him as he took her nipple into his mouth and rolled his tongue over the sensitive tip. She arched her back and moaned gently, surprising herself with the helpless sound.

He lifted his head long enough to look at her and murmur, "Easy, Maggie. Just enjoy. Feel." And then he dipped his head again and went back to his ministrations.

Maggie clutched at his shoulders, holding on for dear life to keep from sliding off a suddenly wildly tilting world. Again and again, she arched into him, helpless to hold off the swirling sensations crowding her body and mind. And then he suckled her and Maggie knew she would die from pure pleasure.

Drawing, tugging, pulling at her body, it was as though he was trying to take her inside him. When that thought presented itself, Maggie groaned again, giving in to the needs erupting within. She reached for him and held his head to her breast, loving the feel of his mouth on her. His tongue. His hot breath dusting her skin. If she could have, she would have kept him there forever, intimately linked with her, *loving* her.

Her body hummed with a frantic need.

He redoubled his efforts when she touched him and his fierce loving brought a new rush of sensation that seemed to be pooling at her center. She lifted her hips and as though he heard her silent plea, Gabe slid one of his hands down, across her abdomen, past the soft triangle of hair to the juncture of her thighs.

Maggie gasped, lifting her hips into his touch. He smiled against her breast and continued to suckle her as his fingers delved into her warmth. In and out of her heat he went, sending her higher and higher with every stroke.

She didn't know what to do. Her hands moved over his head and shoulders, as if searching for purchase. Her hips rocked of their own accord as she instinctively reacted to his intimate caresses. Her body tightened. Her breath caught and held in her lungs, making her lightheaded.

She stared blindly up at the twilight ceiling over head. Her heartbeat jumped erratically. Mouth dry, throat closed, she yearned for something she didn't recognize. It was waiting for her. Just out of reach, it hovered so closely she could almost see it. Feel it. Never had she known anything like this. Never. The wonder. The fire of it.

His thumb rubbed an especially sensitive piece of flesh and Maggie's body jerked as she gasped his name aloud. "Gabe," she whispered brokenly. "Help me. Oh, God." Her hips rocked. Her body reached. "Please. Help me."

He lifted his head from her breast, looked down into her face and smiled gently. "Let go, Maggie."

"I can't," she told him, almost paralyzed with the fear

of the unknown. What if she gave in to this overwhelming sensation and her mind shattered. What then?

"Trust me, Maggie," he said softly and bent to give her a quick, hard kiss. "Trust me, and let go."

"Gabe . . . ?" It seemed she had no choice. Her body overruled her mind. She dug her short fingernails into his shoulders, lifted her hips again, and as his fingers dipped inside her one more time, felt an explosion detonate deep within her. Bright light filled her. A pulsing shimmer of sensation coursed through her body over and over again like waves pounding onto the shore. She trembled with the force of it, moaned his name again, and held on tightly as the tremors continued to wrack her body.

And as the last of it faded, Gabe moved, peeled off his trousers, and knelt between her thighs. She looked up at him and, through dazed eyes, watched him join his body to hers.

Gabe pushed himself home and paused long enough to enjoy the rightness of being within her. Still pulsing with the last of her release, her body closed around his, and the tight, close feel of her was almost enough to spark his own climax.

But he wanted more. He knew he'd given her something tonight that she'd never known. He'd shown her what a man and a woman could find together. But along with Maggie's discovery, Gabe had discovered something himself. Making love was so much more than simple pleasure. When it was the right woman, the right time, "joy" wasn't a big enough word to describe what happened between them.

"Gabe," she said and limply reached for him.

He leaned over her, loving the feel of her arms coming around him. Her heartbeat thundered in her chest and he felt her shiver as he moved within her.

"Now you," she whispered, catching his face in her hands. Pulling him down for a kiss, she said, "I want you to feel what I just felt."

He turned his head to plant a kiss on her palm before saying, "I felt everything you did, Maggie. And more."

It was the truth. He'd never experienced anything like it before. He was a man who had always believed in sharing the pleasure of lovemaking. But not once before tonight had he ever taken such joy out of simply watching a woman experience a soul-shattering release.

His life before this night, this woman, had been an empty thing. And it was finding this treasure trove of feeling that underlined that simple truth. Here in this place, with this woman, Gabe had discovered what wonders life could offer.

And there was a part of him still rational enough to know he'd found it too late.

But tomorrow would be soon enough to mourn what he could never have for his own. Tonight was a time to be thankful that he'd found her at all.

Staring down into her liquid brown eyes, Gabe felt a rush of warmth rise up and take over. He wanted to give her so much. He wanted to be with her. Be a part of her life.

She gave him a languid smile and trailed her fingertips across his back. Gabe shuddered and surrendered to his most immediate need. He needed to find the end of his own desire. He needed to empty himself into her warmth and feel the slow slide into oblivion.

Desire simmered inside him, urging him on. He rocked his hips against her then, pushing himself even deeper inside her. Her body cradled his in a gentle, tight grasp. Maggie moaned, tipped her head back and sighed as he moved again, increasing the rhythm of the dance.

His blood roaring in his ears, Gabe gave himself up to the joy to be found with Maggie.

She locked her legs around his hips, holding him to her. Her hands gripped at his shoulders, and as the end came near, Gabe bent his head and took her mouth in a soul-searing kiss that bound them together even as the world around them splintered in a sea of light and magic.

CHAPTER SIXTEEN

Gabe collapsed atop her and used the last of his strength to brace some of his weight on his hands, at either side of her head. But Maggie had other ideas and, wrapping her arms around his middle, pulled him fully atop her.

"I'm too heavy for you, Maggie," he said and brushed a kiss along her neck.

"It's a good weight," she told him quietly. "And I'm not ready to let you up just yet."

Truth be told, he wasn't any more ready to disengage himself from her. He liked things just as they were, thanks. "Whatever you say, ma'am," he said and rested his head in the crook of her neck.

"Besides," she added, "if you move right now, I think I might shatter."

He knew just what she meant.

"Gabe . . ." she said, what could have been minutes— or hours—later, he wasn't sure which. And didn't care, either.

"Mm-hmm?"

"What *was* that?"

"What was what?" he asked, though he knew damn well what she was talking about. No matter what happened to him in the coming eternity, he would never forget the rush of stunned pleasure that had crossed her face.

"What I felt," she said. "It was . . . almost like dying and then coming back to life again."

There he'd argue. It was nothing like dying. He knew.

"That," he murmured, "was something you should have felt long before tonight, Maggie."

"You mean," she asked, still a little breathlessly, "that's supposed to happen every time?"

He smiled to himself and, groaning quietly, pushed himself up onto one elbow so he could look down into her face. "Ah, Maggie," he said and reached to brush her paint-spattered hair back from her face. "Making love should be a pleasure to both people."

"Pleasure," she repeated and shook her head gently. "Seems a small word for such a huge . . ." Her voice faded off, as she gave up trying to find a word to describe what they had shared.

"Yeah, I know."

"And I used to wonder why Kersey enjoyed himself so much." She shook her head and shot him a look. "So, it's like that for a man every time?"

She almost sounded outraged on behalf of her gender. And a part of him didn't blame her. A half-smile curved one corner of his mouth. "It's good," he admitted, then confessed, "but for me, tonight was different. Better."

"How?"

He grinned at her. "Fishing for compliments?"

"Maybe," she said and lifted one hand to stroke her fingertips along his chest.

He sucked in a breath, shifted position, and Maggie gasped, her body still sensitive. Going perfectly still, Gabe looked down at her and said softly, "Hard to move, just yet."

"Then don't."

"All right." He'd just as soon stay right where he was, anyway. Actually, he'd prefer staying this way until forever ended.

"Tell me," she said softly as she ran her palms up and down his back. "Have you always felt that . . . *amazing*?"

"No," Gabe told her honestly. "Like I said, tonight was special. It was better this time, because of you."

"Good." She smiled. "That's what I wanted to hear."

"It's true."

"I believe you. It *was* special." She shifted slightly and practically purred. "Well, Gabriel Donovan, you can do that to me anytime."

Anytime.

Her words hit him unexpectedly hard. His features tightened and he did a slow roll to one side, carefully separating his body from hers. She moved into the curl of his arm and cuddled close to his side.

Anytime? There was no time for them. His last remaining weeks on earth were winding down faster than he would have thought possible. All too soon, he'd be separated from her forever. And suddenly, forever sounded a damn sight longer than it had a couple of months ago.

"Gabe?" she asked. "What's wrong?"

What wasn't wrong? he asked himself silently. Jesus, what had he been thinking? He lifted one hand, pushed his hair back from his face, and stared up at the glittering, quartz-starred ceiling. But he wasn't seeing Maggie's creation. He was seeing the face of the Devil he knew was expecting him in less than a month.

Damn it, how could he have forgotten, even for a moment, that he didn't have the right to lie with Maggie?

How could he have given in to his own desires at her expense? God, what if she was pregnant? Then what? She'd be forced to carry the child of yet another man who'd abandoned her. A hard, short laugh shot from his throat. And he'd called her late husband all kinds of a bastard for hurting her?

Hell, compared to him, Kersey Benson was a damned saint.

At least *he'd* married her before bedding her.

Shame rippled through him with the realization that maybe the Devil wasn't all wrong about him after all. Hell, this was pretty damned low. He'd taken a good woman he cared about without thought for what the future would bring her.

And as long as he was silently admitting to being a bastard, he had to admit that most of his life had been led the same way. Selfish pursuits had guided him, always. What *he* wanted. *When* he wanted. He'd never gone out of his way to help a living soul. No worse than most of the men he'd known, he was certainly no better either.

Gabe had slid through life, never touching anything real. He'd existed only in smoky bars and whorehouses. His friends were those on the wrong side of the law. His enemies . . . or *marks* . . . the very people he should have admired. At least they worked and sweated and prayed and tried to do the right thing.

Not like him. When he died, there'd be no one to mourn him. And the world would go on nicely with one less cardsharp. There'd be no sign that Gabe Donovan had passed this way. He'd never made a mark on the world to show that he'd lived.

Never once loving and taking a stand.

All at once a flicker of a wild-haired, completely insane idea jumped life from some dark corner of his brain. And as soon as it did, Gabe knew it was the only thing to do. The one thing he could do for Maggie to protect her after he was gone. And maybe, just maybe, it might be enough to wipe away some of the shame of how he'd frittered his life away.

"Gabe!" She went up on one elbow, stared down at him and gave his chest a slap with the palm of her hand.

"Huh?" Pulled abruptly from the whirling thoughts spinning through his mind, he blinked and looked up at her.

"What's going on? What's the matter?"

"Never mind, Maggie," he said quickly and grabbed her upper arm, "there's something more important we have to talk about. I want you to marry me. Soon. This week. Hell, tomorrow."

She stared at him blankly for a long moment and he watched several different emotions cross her features. Excitement, joy, confusion, and finally, regret.

"Don't say no," he warned her before she could speak the doubts obviously plaguing her.

"Of course I'm going to say no," she said.

"Damn it, Maggie . . ."

"I'm not going to marry you," she told him. "I hardly know you."

"You just got to know me pretty damned well," he reminded her. Damn it, she couldn't turn him down. Not when he'd finally found a way to make amends. Not only for what he'd done to her, but for what he'd done most of his life.

"That was different," she said and whipped her hair behind her shoulder.

"How is that different?" he demanded and pushed himself up into a sitting position. "You slept with me. So marry me."

"No."

Dumbfounded, he stared at her. He'd never considered for a minute that she might turn down his proposal. What sane man would have? Hell, any woman in her right mind would say yes to a marriage proposal from the man who'd just made love to her.

"What do you mean, no?"

"Why are you so suddenly set on marriage?"

"Jesus!" He threw his arms wide and glared at her. "How can you ask me that after what just happened?"

Not to be outdone, Maggie sat up, too, and matched him glare for glare. "Excuse me," she said, "but aren't you the man who not so long ago told me to stop worrying about what other people think? To be who I am? To do what *I* thought best?"

Now she listens to him? "I was talking about your painting and not trying to be a cook when you're so obviously not."

"There's no reason to be insulting."

"I was *not* talking about your carrying a child that didn't have a father."

She blanched slightly and he knew he'd struck a nerve.

"That's right," he said, his voice low and hard, demanding to be heard. "Think about it, Maggie. A baby. And you unmarried."

"I'm probably not pregnant," she said, though her tone lacked conviction.

"Yeah. And I wonder just how many women have

said that over the centuries." He cocked his head. "Don't you?"

"Some of them were right."

"Most of 'em were wrong," he reminded her. "You feeling lucky?"

She inched backward on the floor and stretched out one hand until she found her nightgown. Then she grabbed it up and yanked it on over her head. Shoving her arms through the sleeves, she said, "Fine. You want to get married. Does this mean you love me?"

He rubbed one hand across the back of his neck. "I *care* for you."

"Well, you certainly know how to sweet-talk a girl."

"Damn it Maggie," he complained, still rubbing his neck.

She pointed at him. "I've noticed that you do that a lot when you're trying not to lose your temper."

He let his hand drop to his side, looked at her and snapped, "Well, it's not working."

"Uh-huh," Maggie said. Shoving her long sleeves up to her elbows, she stood up, planted her hands on her hips, then looked down at him. "So. You want to marry me and you don't love me."

"Yes," he said, then paused. "I mean, no. At least—"

"I know," she interrupted. "You *care* for me."

She made it sound like nothing. Well, it was a damn sight more than he'd ever felt for any other woman in his life. "Yes. I do."

"Uh-huh." She folded her arms across her chest. "And if we get married, does this mean you'll be staying in Regret?"

Shit.

A moment ticked by. Then two. Images of the Devil waiting on him flooded his mind. He thought seriously about lying, but then figured if he lied to get her to marry him, that would pretty much take all the good out of what he was trying to do.

"No," he said tightly. "I can't stay."

Buttoning up the collar of her nightgown, Maggie shot him a furious glare. "So you're still leaving me, you don't love me, but I should marry you anyway. Why would I do that?"

"Because," he grumbled, grabbing up his pants and standing up to tug them on, "even when I'm gone, if you're married, it won't matter if you're pregnant."

"I'll still be alone," she told him and stepped close enough to poke him in the chest with her index finger.

Judging by the glint in her eye, he should have been grateful she wasn't holding a knife. Damn it, he didn't want to hurt her. He was trying his best to find a way to take care of her from the grave. Why couldn't she see that?

"Nothing more to say?" she asked.

"One more thing," he said.

"Go ahead."

"Marry me and you'll still be alone, granted. But your baby wouldn't be a bastard."

She actually flinched at the hard word.

"You think that would matter to me?" She clapped one hand to her breast.

"No," he said and finished buttoning his pants. "But it would sure as hell matter to my kid."

My kid. Jesus. Two little words. Who knew how hard they'd hit him? Instantly, his mind filled with images of the child he and Maggie could have had . . . might have . . . together. Her wide mouth, his blue eyes. Her laughter, his card sense. Her gift for loving. His gift for . . . what? Messing up?

Poor kid.

"Damn it, Maggie," he said abruptly. "Can't you see I'm trying to do the right thing, here?"

"All I see is, you're awful bloody anxious to leave."

"No I'm not," he muttered thickly and speared his fingers through his hair.

"Then stay. If you'll stay, I'll marry you," she said.

"It's not that easy," he told her bleakly, his gaze meeting hers. Silently, he tried to convey just how much he'd like to stay with her. He wanted her to believe that if he had a choice in this, he'd choose her.

"Of course it is," she snapped. "You said you had an appointment to keep. Cancel it."

He laughed. A short, harsh sound that scraped against his throat and nearly choked him. "Oh yeah," he muttered. Then shaking his head, he said, "No one cancels an appointment with this fella, Maggie. No one."

"Who *is* this man?" she demanded. "Who is so damned important you're willing to walk away from me?"

"I'm not willing. I have no choice."

"Tell me," she said simply. "Tell me or we're through talking right now."

"You won't believe me."

"Tell me anyway."

"Fine." Nodding, he started pacing. Walking just a few steps, he turned right around and came back. Stepping up close to her, he picked up her right hand and held it to his throat. To the scarred flesh that was a constant reminder of what he'd gotten himself into. "Feel that?"

"Yes," she said and curled her fingers into her palm. "You were hanged. And you escaped. What's that have to do with this? With us?"

Gabe released her hand, grabbed hold of her shoulders and held on tightly to keep her from turning away in either disgust or disbelief.

"Yes, I was hanged," he said flatly, his gaze boring into hers. "But I didn't escape. I *died*."

"What?" Shaking her head, she stared at him as if he was crazy and she hadn't even heard the best part yet.

"That's right," he told her, "I died. Hanging from a damned tree, my life choking out of me. And that appointment I have to keep?" He let her go as he finished. "The Devil's expecting me, Maggie. In less than a month now, I'm going to be hip deep in flames with a front-row seat in Hell."

CHAPTER SEVENTEEN

Maggie yanked free of his grip on her shoulders and took a hasty step back. Looking up at him, she could see he actually believed what he was saying. Either that, or he was a much better actor than she would have given him credit for being.

Well, she didn't believe it. Not for a damned minute.

Shaking her head, she said, "I've heard some tall tales in my time. God knows, my father has told some real beauties, over the years."

"Maggie—"

She held up one hand to silence him. It was her turn to talk now. "But this." A choked-off laugh shot from her throat. "This is the winner by a long shot."

"I'm not lying."

"Oh, of course not," she said and her sarcastic tone let him know she wasn't really agreeing with him.

Good God. Staring at him, looking into his eyes, she had to wonder why she kept falling in love with the wrong man. First Kersey Benson, a lying, no-good, who'd left her as soon as he'd discovered she didn't have enough money to make living with her worthwhile. And now Gabe.

An ache around her heart throbbed low and heavy and she silently admitted that Gabe's deceit hurt far more than anything Kersey had done to her. Because what she felt for this man was deeper and bigger than anything she'd ever known before.

But Lord. The *devil*?

She was supposed to believe that she'd been living with and talking to and *making love* with a dead man? How stupid did he think she was anyway? She took a long, deep breath and held it, hoping to steady herself. But as it slipped slowly from her, she knew nothing was going to help at this point.

"Maggie," he said quietly, "I told you you wouldn't believe me."

"And you were right," she quipped and started to walk past him. "Congratulations."

He grabbed her as she passed and Maggie whirled out of his grasp, fixing him with a stare hot enough to burn eggs. "Don't touch me."

"How can I make you believe me?" he asked.

"You can't," she assured him. "But you should know this, you didn't have to concoct this wild story just to leave me. I've been left before with far less imagination."

"I told you I don't want to leave," he said tightly. "I have to."

"Uh-huh," she said. "Because you're dead."

"Exactly."

"Well, then, lie down for pity's sake. You must be exhausted."

"Maggie . . ."

"Just stop it," she said, lifting both hands palms out toward him. "Stop all of this nonsense."

Hard to believe that only moments ago, she'd been happier than ever before in her life. Her body still thrummed with the aftereffects of the pleasure she'd found in his arms. She could still taste him on her mouth. She could still feel the glorious rightness of his body joining with hers.

And now this.

Why had he even bothered to propose? she wondered. To make himself feel better? That had to be it. Because it certainly hadn't been a proposal designed to win a woman's heart. *I don't love you, will you marry me, and oh, by the way, I still have to leave because I'm dead.*

She wrapped her arms around her waist and held on tight. That ache around her heart began to build and grow, uncoiling ribbons of pain that seemed to reach out to every corner of her body.

She loved him, damn it. And damn him for making her feel and then ruining it.

"Maggie," he said and reached out a tentative hand toward her. When she eyed it like a snake, he let it drop to his side. "You have to listen to me. You have to believe me."

"Why should I?" she asked quietly.

He lifted both hands and raked them across the top of his head before shrugging. "There's no reason at all why you should. I'm just asking you to, that's all."

"Oh well," she said. "That's different. Of course I'd be *happy* to do you a favor just now."

"Maggie . . . damn it, don't you think I know how this sounds?"

"If you knew, you wouldn't keep talking," she told him.

He snorted a laugh. "Think about it, Maggie. If I was going to lie to you, wouldn't I have made up a better one than this?"

"Maybe," she conceded. "And maybe you're just not

that clever." But he was, she knew. He was a smooth talker and probably had a legion of lies for just such a situation as this to choose from. So why would he tell her such an outrageous fable?

All right, she was curious enough to keep listening.

Curious. That was all.

He must have read her acquiescence in her eyes because he started talking again. As he spoke, the words came faster and faster until it was all Maggie could do to keep up. And strangely enough, as the story unwound, it even began to make an odd sort of sense. Which told her she was either desperate to believe him or just as crazy as he was.

Her own thoughts raced to keep up and when he finally finished talking she asked the first question she could think of. "Why come here to wait for your friend the thief?"

Gabe shrugged. "He comes here from time to time."

"What's his name?" she asked, as if that would prove anything.

"Damn it, Maggie, that doesn't matter," he snapped. "That's not why I told you all of this."

"Why did you, then?" Maggie asked and walked toward him. With every step, pain seemed to throb inside her. Aching sorrow rose up and she fought to battle it down. To keep her mind clear and pain at bay. When she was no more than a step or two from him, she stopped and looked him squarely in the eye.

In the guttering candlelight, his features looked different, somehow. Less real, more elusive. Or maybe it was simply her imagination, colored now by his ridiculous story.

"I wanted you to know. To understand why I have to leave."

"Well, I don't," she said simply with a shake of her head. "What I understand is that you're going to leave and you want me to marry you so you can go with a clear conscience."

"Maggie—"

"But I'm not going to," she said, cutting him off before he could get going again. It was her turn to talk now. "You see, I don't believe a word of what you just said."

His chin dropped to his chest briefly, then he lifted his head again and looked at her. He didn't say a word, simply waited for her to finish.

"You say you're dead? Well, for a dead man, you've a pretty strong heartbeat." She moved in closer and slapped one hand against his naked chest. Just the touch of his skin beneath her hand sent off sparks of heat and wonder shooting through her bloodstream, but she desperately fought to ignore the sensation. "I can feel it. It's pounding every bit as hard as mine. Dead men don't feel. Dead men don't walk and talk and make love and *lie*."

Her hand dropped to her side as she looked up at him. "And you're doing all of that."

"I can't explain any better than I have," he said, and his voice was a low groan of frustration.

Sorrow welled inside her and she battled to keep her voice steady. "You don't have to," she said. "I think you've already said more than enough."

In his eyes, she read the same pain she was feeling, but since he was the cause of all of it, she couldn't feel sorry for him. He studied her sadly for a long minute before asking quietly, "Do you want me to leave now?"

"Leave town?" she asked and wondered how she could possibly feel even *more* pain.

"No," he said. "I can't leave Regret yet."

"Oh." She nodded and shook her head at the same time. "That's right. Your appointment with the Devil."

"Yeah," he said tightly. "But I'll move to the hotel if you want me to go."

She looked at him then, asking herself silently if his leaving would make this better? Or worse? Her gaze lingered on his features. So familiar now. Such a part of her life. Blue eyes that seemed to hold every secret she'd ever yearned to know. Strong cheekbones and the smile that had at first dazzled and then warmed her.

No. There would be no help in his leaving because, despite everything, she would miss him utterly. She would miss the sound of his voice, the flash of that smile, even the stray lock of his hair that tended to flop down across his forehead. She would miss his touch, his easy way with Jake, and the pleasure of sitting across a table from him at the end of the day.

"Maggie?" he whispered and his voice brought her out of her thoughts and back into the candlelit room that had been the scene of such joy and, now, such misery.

"No," she said softly. "I don't want you to leave."

He took a breath then and she nearly felt his relief.

She quashed it a moment later.

"Your leaving now would only make things worse." Her fingers twisted together at her waist. "What I want is for you to have never come."

"Oh, Maggie, don't."

"I want to not have this pain in my heart," she went on, her words tumbling out, one after the other, carried on a tide of disappointment and frustration. "If you'd never been here . . . if I'd never discovered what it was to really *love* someone, then I wouldn't miss it when it was gone."

He took a step closer to her and she backed up, keeping that safe distance between them.

There was nothing left to say and yet so much seemed to have been left unsaid. But she was so tired. Heart aching, head pounding, she turned then, headed for the doorway that would take her to the stairs and the shelter of her room. She made it to the threshold before his voice stopped her.

"Think what you will, Maggie," he said softly. "I can't stop you. But think about what I said too. Not about the Devil or anything else. But about marrying me before I leave. Not for my sake or yours. But for the sake of the child we may have created."

His words hit her like a blow and one hand dropped protectively to her flat abdomen. Glancing over her shoulder at him, she said solemnly, "I sincerely hope I'm not pregnant. But if I am, I'll protect *my* child any way I can."

Then she was gone and Gabe was alone in the guttering candlelight.

One week passed and then two and still Gabe and Maggie circled each other warily. He'd tried to talk to her, but each time, she'd blithely insisted that nothing was wrong. That she was fine. That nothing had changed.

But her eyes looked bleak and she held herself so stiffly, he was afraid she might shatter.

Grumbling under his breath, Gabe lifted his end of

the new restaurant sign and, taking a nail from the corner of his mouth, set it in position and hammered it home.

Keep busy, he told himself repeatedly. Stay too busy to think. To dream. To entertain idle wishes and make plans for a future that would never come.

Still, he watched her and let the pain inside gnaw at him. It was nothing less than he deserved. It was fitting that a man destined for Hell should already be feeling the torments that awaited him in the eternity to come.

For the time he had left, he would concentrate on helping her prepare for the day when he'd be gone. He'd have the restaurant up and running and hopefully make it easier for her and Jake to thrive without him.

Then voices drifted to him from the crowd gathered below and Gabe listened to them instead of his own depressing thoughts.

"Don't see how a fancy sign's going to make a spit's worth of difference here," one man said. "Maggie still can't cook."

One corner of his mouth lifted. No, she couldn't. But she was getting better.

"Twilight what?" another man asked.

"You'll see," Gabe answered, glad they were curious. To find out what had been going on inside the restaurant the last few weeks, they'd all have to come to the grand opening. "You show up on Saturday night and have your questions answered."

"Oh, I don't know about that," Bass Stevens shouted. "Seems mighty risky lettin' Maggie cook for me."

Gabe turned his head and looked down at the small group of men watching him and Deke Conroy hang the new sign. Singling Bass out with a fixed stare, he reminded the man, "Maggie brings Jake to you for haircuts, doesn't she?"

Bass rubbed his jaw with one beefy hand. "A haircut can't kill you." He snorted. "But Maggie's cookin' surely could."

Woods Harper, the young cowboy, spoke up. "I don't know. I ate her pies and they weren't bad. 'Cept stay away from the prune . . ."

Deke dropped his end of the sign and Gabe lurched to hang on to it.

"Prune?" the man repeated.

"Here now," Kansas yelled from below. Pointing one finger at the burly bartender, he accused, "You coulda killed me by droppin' that sign."

"Yeah, if you were ever out of your chair."

They were getting way off the subject here, Gabe thought and, speaking up, told them all, "It wouldn't kill any of you to show up."

"You guarantee that, Gabe?" Deke asked.

Gabe glared at him. "I thought you were her friend."

"I am, but—"

"No buts," Gabe told him, then spared another glare for the rest of them. "She's one of you. She's a part of this town. Maggie shops at your stores. It's time to repay the favor."

Maggie looked at her reflection and saw a woman wearing her best green calico dress and a forced smile.

She should be happy. The restaurant's grand opening was in less than an hour and she'd worked hard for weeks preparing for it. They'd all worked hard. She and Jake and Gabe. It hadn't been easy, working alongside him, seeing him every day, dreaming of him every night, feeling her body burn for his touch. Often in the last couple of weeks, she'd come close to taking him up on his offer to move out. Especially late at night when she couldn't sleep and when wanting him seemed as much a part of her as breathing. Yet she hadn't. Because knowing he was close by was better than feeling the loss of him earlier than she had to.

Time was rushing past her. Only another week or so and Gabe would be gone. Oh, she still didn't believe a word of his story. But he was leaving. Did it really matter where he was going?

"C'mon, Mom," Jake called and she turned from her reflection to look at her son, standing in the doorway opposite her. "Gabe says we should get ready for the people now."

Gabe says.

How many times had Jake started off his sentences with those two words? Did Gabe know how much her son loved him? Depended on him? How much he would miss the man who'd become such an important piece of his life?

Jake hopped from foot to foot in his excitement. Clean and shiny from the top of his neatly combed head to the toes of his polished shoes, her little boy was once again the happy, carefree child he used to be. And damned if she didn't owe Gabe for that too.

"Go ahead down," she said. "I'll be right along."

"Okay, but hurry up," Jake said, and in the next instant he was gone, the only sign of him, his footsteps clattering on the wooden stairway.

Briefly, Maggie stood in the silence of her room and tried to imagine the time when Jake would be grown and gone, leaving her for his own family. She'd be alone then. With no one to talk to, to share secrets with, to hold during the long, dark nights.

Wrapping her arms around her waist, she let her head fall back on her neck and closed her eyes. Emptiness welled inside her, growing and blossoming until it threatened to choke off her breath.

She gulped back a knot of tears crowding her throat and told herself to get used to the silence. Because when Gabe left, he would be taking her last chance at love with him.

Then, steeling herself, she straightened up and headed downstairs to face the man who'd taught her to dream again only to turn those dreams into nightmares.

Gabe peered through the front window at the darkened street outside, craning his neck this way and that, looking for the people who should be lining up to help Maggie rechristen her business.

But Main Street looked deserted. If not for the lights blazing away in windows, he would have thought Regret was a ghost town. Apparently, he and Maggie were throwing a party and no one was coming.

"Where is everybody?" Jake asked from behind him and Gabe turned around to look at the kid.

"No one's here yet," he said and thought about the Preacher. At least *he* should have shown up. Gabe had kept his part of their bargain, taking a pew in church every Sunday.

The little boy across the room from him ducked his head and scuffed his shoe along the floor. "Nobody's comin', huh?"

"They'll come," Gabe said, silently vowing to get people into the restaurant if he had to go to each of their houses and drag them out by the hair.

Maggie stepped up behind her son and Gabe's breath caught in his chest. She looked beautiful, her long hair curled and pulled back from her face only to fall in a thick wave down her back and across her shoulders. Her simple green calico dress hugged her body enough so that his palms itched to hold her. And even from across the room, he could see the shine of imminent tears glimmering in her brown eyes.

The last two weeks had been the longest of his life. To be so close to her and unable to touch her. To hear her speak to him as politely as she would a stranger. To lie in his bed at night, remembering the peace he'd found in her arms. To know that his time with her was nearly at an end. And that he would spend eternity missing her as he would a part of himself. Because that's what she'd become. A part of him. The best part of him.

She laid one hand on Jake's shoulder and guided him into the room. When they were just a few feet from Gabe, she stopped and looked around at the beautifully appointed and completely empty restaurant.

"It seems there are lots of things neither of us can change," she said and he heard the hurt in her voice.

Back teeth grinding together, Gabe stiffened and met her gaze when she looked at him. He wouldn't let these people ignore her. By damn, he'd bring her in customers. "They'll come. It's early yet."

She shook her head and he tried not to notice the lamplight shining on her hair, gilding it. "No they won't."

"Why not, Mama?" Jake asked, tipping his head back to look up at her.

"Because, honey, some things can't be changed." She never took her eyes off Gabe. "No matter how much you try, or how much you wish it were different."

"That don't make sense," Jake muttered.

"Doesn't," she corrected.

"Doesn't," the boy muttered, then a moment later snapped, "But it don't. Gabe says it's never too late to change things. Gabe says if you want something bad enough, you can get it. Gabe says you gotta keep tryin' even when it looks like you ain't never gonna get it."

Maggie flinched at the boy's words and Gabe felt that flinch as he would have a slap. Everything he'd told the boy came back to haunt him now. He'd only tried to instill in the child a sense of hope. A sense that no matter what happened in his life, he shouldn't quit trying to succeed.

But hearing those words quoted back at him only made him feel like a heel. How she must want to shout at him, to tell Jake that Gabe was a liar and that trying only brought pain. Still, being the amazing woman she was, she didn't do it. Instead, she patted Jake's shoulder, pasted a smile on her face and said, "He's right, Jake. It's just that sometimes changing things takes time. It doesn't happen overnight."

"Don't see why not," the boy muttered.

And neither did Gabe. Damn it, he didn't have time. He couldn't sit around waiting for Regret to come to its senses and accept Maggie and her business. They had to do it now. Mind racing, searching for a way to bring in customers, he finally hit on an idea and smiled to himself.

"You two wait here," he said and turned for the front door. "I'll be back."

"Where you goin'?" Jake called.

"To make some overnight changes," he told him. Gabe threw the front door open and almost ran smack into the preacher and his wife. "Reverend," he said, smiling.

" 'Evening, Gabe," the little minister said and slid a glance toward Maggie before whispering, "A bargain's a bargain. We're here, as promised."

And his wife didn't look very happy about it. Her face was three shades of pale and she clung to her husband's arm with a grip that told everyone she'd rather be anywhere else than where she was.

Well, two customers were a start, Gabe thought and shook the minister's hand. "I'm pleased to see you, reverend," he said. "I was beginning to wonder if you remembered our little deal."

"Oh," he said and ran one finger around the inside of his collar. "It would have been hard to forget."

Gabe chuckled at the man's obvious nervousness. "Relax, Preacher," he said, "we haven't poisoned anybody in nearly a month."

"You've been closed," the other man pointed out.

"A man of the cloth? With so little faith?"

"Let's just say I believe in heaven, but I'm in no hurry to visit."

"Go on in, reverend," Gabe said. "Maggie will take care of you. I'll be back directly."

"Into the lion's den," the minister muttered, then swallowed bravely, nodded, and took a step inside, dragging his reluctant wife behind him. But as Gabe closed the door, he heard the woman's gasp of delighted surprise.

"Why," she said on a breath, "it's beautiful."

Smiling to himself, Gabe sprinted toward the saloon. With any luck, Maggie would soon be hearing more of those compliments.

Two customers weren't enough to build a restaurant on, Maggie told herself, but listening to the reverend's wife chattering on and on about the dining room's beauty was certainly a balm to a wounded heart.

"Why, now I see why the reverend asked you to paint the church," the tiny woman was saying, her head still turning this way and that, taking time to admire even the smallest details of the paintings decorating the walls. "At first, I thought . . ." She stopped herself and smiled at Maggie. "Well, it doesn't matter what I thought. The point is, I just love this. Oh, my dear!" She poked her husband's upper arm. "Look, there are even butterflies hovering above the rose vine on the trellis."

"I see," her husband said, reaching up to rub his arm. "You've done wonders here, Maggie."

Jake flashed her a proud grin and Maggie felt a flash of happiness for the first time in two weeks.

"You know," the other woman was saying thoughtfully, "if it wouldn't be too much trouble, perhaps when you've finished painting the church, I might hire you to spruce up our home?"

Maggie simply stared at her. "I beg your pardon?"

The minister smiled as his wife kept talking. "I would love a flower garden on our bedroom walls," she said dreamily. "I can't imagine waking up to something this beautiful every morning. Oh! And perhaps something simple and lovely in the parlor. Perhaps a twine of ivy around the windows and doors?"

Maggie opened her mouth then closed it again. She didn't know what to say. She'd never expected this.

"What do you think, dear?" the woman asked her husband.

"I leave the house to you, my dear," he said with a smile and a wink for Maggie. "Just remember, I asked first so the church has priority on Maggie's talents."

"Oh, naturally, but I would love to make plans with you, Maggie, when you're not too busy . . . ?"

"Of course, but I—" Whatever she might have said was lost in the sudden burst of piano music that seemed to leap into existence out of nowhere. "What in heaven . . . ?"

Maggie hurried across the room, her customers and son right behind her. Flinging open the front door, she stepped out onto the boardwalk to find the piano player from the saloon seated at his instrument in the middle of Main Street. An oil lamp on top of the piano spilled light across the old man's features and the keys his talented fingers flew across.

As she watched, a stream of men flowed from the saloon, carrying tables, chairs, and oil lamps, which they scattered across the street in random fashion.

"What are they doing?" she asked no one in particular.

Just then the sound of a well-played fiddle joined the piano and music soared up into the night sky.

"Well, my goodness," the preacher's wife said as her toe started tapping against the boardwalk.

"This looks like a party," the reverend muttered.

"It certainly does," Maggie agreed, noting that one by

one, her friends and neighbors were leaving their houses and wandering out onto the street. Called by the music and the lights, the citizens of Regret were being wooed to Maggie's grand opening whether they liked it or not.

And only one man could have come up with such an outrageous plan. Her gaze raked the familiar faces crowding the street. Finally, she spotted him, rearranging a row of chairs into a semicircle facing the piano player and the fiddler.

He laughed at something someone said and Maggie's heart lurched in her chest. How could she let him go, knowing that nothing in her life would ever be the same once he'd left her?

As if he sensed her gaze on him, he straightened up and looked at her. Slowly, deliberately, he shrugged and smiled. Maggie's toes curled. Despite the crowd of people and the distance separating them—despite their harsh words and the emptiness of the last two weeks—she stared into his eyes and felt an invisible cord bind them together. And she vowed to do everything she could to keep it from being broken.

CHAPTER EIGHTEEN

"Just look at her," Sugar muttered, eyes narrowing as she stared through the crowd at the woman of the hour. "Smiling and carrying on as though she was the belle of the ball."

Beside his wife, Redmond shifted and huffed out an exasperated breath.

The music and lights had drawn Sugar here, and for one brief moment, she'd been entranced with the oil lamps glittering in the street and the couples dancing and laughing. But as soon as she'd discovered that the impromptu party was all for Maggie's sake, the magic had gone out of the scene.

"It's not right," she whispered viciously and threw a quick glance at her husband's stoic features. "It's just not right that she should have so much when her mother ruined my life."

Redmond inhaled sharply and Sugar thanked him silently for being so outraged on her behalf. A chill wind shot down the length of the street, tugging at the hem of Sugar's dress and whipping free a few graying blond strands of her hair. She lifted one hand to futilely smooth them back into place.

"You see it, don't you, Redmond," she said, her voice so low, the piano and fiddle nearly drowned it out. "You understand."

"I do," he murmured, shaking his head.

"I can't let this go on," she continued. "I have to tell her what I think of her. I've tried to be a lady, Redmond, but sometimes, you simply must speak up. Or something inside you will burst."

"I know just what you mean," he assured her.

Nodding, she said, "Then wait for me at home. I'll be there as soon as I get a few things off my chest."

She took a step toward Maggie, but Redmond's hand came down hard on her shoulder. Glaring up at him, she said, "Let me go."

"No."

She tried to yank free, but his grip was surprisingly strong. This was so unlike Redmond. He rarely spoke up and never tried to force his will on her. Now was not the time for him to start. Frustrated, she snapped, "You just said you understand. I have to face her. I have to tell her what I think of her and her fancy man."

"You've already said enough to Maggie," Redmond said quietly, locking his gaze with the woman he'd loved so long. How could she be so blind to everything but her own hatred?

"Redmond," she said, "you're hurting me."

He winced and eased the pressure on her shoulder, but he didn't let her go. Not this time. He'd waited long enough. Some might say too long. Tonight he'd say what needed saying if he had to tie her in a chair to make her listen. "You're coming home with me."

"I am not."

A few people nearby turned to openly watch the confrontation going on. He paid them no mind.

"There are a few things I want to say to you, Sugar,

before *I* burst," he said, not caring who was listening. "And I'm not doing it here."

"Well, I'm not leaving," she snapped and folded her arms across her chest.

"Oh, yes you are," he murmured and bent down quickly. He tucked his shoulder into her middle and stood up, lifting her too thin body with no effort at all.

Gasping wildly in outrage, Sugar pounded on his back with her fists and whipped a furious glance at the men daring to laugh at her. "Put me down this instant, Redmond Harmon."

"Not this time, Sugar," he said and started off down the street for home. Absently, he noted that the music had stopped. Snatches of laughter rippled around them and he didn't care one whit.

"Blast you, Redmond, put me down!"

At least she was paying attention to him. Most days, they walked through their lives, each of them separately, polite strangers occupying the same house. And it was his fault, he knew. He should have told her long ago how he felt. Should have made her feel the same.

He walked faster and he heard her grunt as her breath shot from her lungs every time he took a step. As they neared home, the music behind them started up again. The townspeople went on about their business and that was just as it should be. This was between Sugar and him. No one else.

He set her on her feet as soon as he walked in the door and blocked her way when she would have pushed past him in an effort to escape.

"What has gotten into you?" she demanded, her usually pale face flushed with a deep pink color.

"Years of waiting," he said tightly and took her hand

to drag her into the main parlor. Once there, he pushed her into a chair, then turned around and poured himself a healthy drink of whiskey. Downing it in one gulp, he slammed the glass onto the tabletop and looked at his wife.

"You're being a fool," she said, but didn't make an attempt to get up.

"No, I've been a fool up until tonight."

"What's that supposed to mean?"

"It means, Sugar, that I've waited for you to wake up and see me." He crossed the room, grabbed her up from the chair, and pulled her close. "*See* me. The man who married you. The man who loves you."

She twisted in his grasp and the color on her cheeks brightened. "Of course I see you, you ninny."

"No you don't. When you look at me, you see the man I'm not. You see Maggie's father. The man who left you for another woman."

She gasped as if he'd struck her.

"You've spent years mourning a man who wasn't worthy of you."

"I wasn't mourning him," she snapped.

"Then what? Pining?"

"No, he . . . *hurt* me. Humiliated me."

"I know that, Sugar," Redmond said and pulled her even closer, wrapping his arms around her until they were so close that when she drew a breath, air filled his lungs. "But instead of seeing what we could have together, what we could build, you focus everything you have on the past."

"Redmond—"

"No more, Sugar," he interrupted her. "I knew you didn't love me when we married."

"I—"

"No lies tonight, Sugar. There've been enough lies and half-truths between us." He paused, took a breath, and admitted, "You didn't love me, and it didn't matter to me."

"It didn't?"

She stared up at him and Redmond saw the world in her eyes, as he always had. But in the years they'd been married, he hadn't pushed himself on her. He'd wanted her to come to care for him. Maybe even to love him. But maybe he shouldn't have been so damned patient. Maybe he should have taken her to bed every time she got spiteful or resentful. Maybe then they'd be happy today. Maybe they'd have a family.

"No, it didn't," he said, "because I loved you so damn much."

"You never said—"

"I didn't want to push you."

"But—"

"But that's over. I'm through apologizing for being the wrong man."

"I never asked you to—"

"I love you, Sugar," he interrupted her again. "And we can still have those babies you always craved."

"I'm too old," she said softly, her voice filled with defeat.

"No you're not," he said and let one hand slide to the curve of her bottom.

"Redmond!"

He looked her dead in the eye. "Neither of us is too old. But if we wait much longer, we will be."

She squirmed in his grasp. "We haven't waited. We've tried."

He sighed and shook his head. "Making babies requires us having sex more than once every couple of months."

"Redmond . . ." Her eyes widened, her mouth fell open.

"Sex, Sugar," he went on, loving the embarrassed flush on her cheeks. "Hot, sweaty, wonderful sex. I've tried to be patient, hoping you'd come to care for me. But I need you, Sugar. I need to be inside you, filling you. I need to hear you crying out—"

"I did no such thing!"

"Oh, yes you did," he said, with a soft smile of remembrance. "One night a couple of years ago, you forgot about being a lady long enough to enjoy yourself." He sighed. "I still think about that night."

She bit her lip then ducked her head. "I do too."

"Thank God." Redmond smiled and tipped her chin up. "Enough of the past, Sugar. It's finally time to build a future."

"I don't know . . ."

"I do," he told her, bending his head lower. "I'm sure enough for both of us this time too."

Then he kissed her, hard and long and deep, with all of the passion and love he'd been holding back over the years. Seconds passed and then she melted against him, her body going limp in his arms. Finally, he broke the kiss long enough to shift his mouth to the line of her throat and when his lips closed over her pulse point, he felt the rapid rate of her heart and smiled inwardly.

"Oh, Redmond . . ." she murmured.

* * *

Maggie watched the faces of the people she'd known most of her life and smiled to herself as she had all evening. The fried chicken was too dark brown to be called golden. The biscuits were a bit underdone and the mashed potatoes and gravy both had enough lumps in them to pave Main Street, but her restaurant was a success in spite of it all.

Even Sugar hadn't been able to spoil this night, she thought and wondered just what had happened that had pushed Redmond Harmon into taking a firm hand with his wife.

Smiling to herself, Maggie walked to the shadowy end of the boardwalk and leaned tiredly back against a porch post. Her head was ringing with the compliments she'd received all night. Everyone loved what she had done to the place and the minister's wife wasn't the only woman who'd asked Maggie to help them decorate their own homes.

Gabe had been right, she thought, when he'd advised her to be different. To not be afraid to be herself.

Her gaze swept the crowd until she found him. He stood across the street at the edge of the party he'd created. A part of things, yet separate, distanced. As always, her breath caught in her chest as a swirl of emotion rippled through her. She wondered if forty, fifty years from now he would still have the same effect on her? But that was foolish. They didn't have years. They had only weeks now. A handful of days before he would be as much a part of her past as childhood scrapes and bruises.

A sudden sheen of tears filled her eyes and she blinked them ferociously back. She wouldn't cry. Not now. Not while he was still here. There were long, empty years to come when she could fill the cold nights with buckets of tears. As she had the last two weeks.

That thought ricocheted around inside her mind for a full minute before she realized exactly what she'd been doing. There was so little time left to them and she'd already wasted the last two weeks. By nursing her anger and her disappointment in him, she'd cheated herself out of time she might have spent with Gabe. Instead of lying alone in her bed missing him, she could have been with him. He'd never made any promises. He'd told her that first day that he wouldn't be staying. And now she was punishing them both because he wouldn't—or couldn't—change those rules. It wasn't fair. To either of them. Time was passing too quickly and every minute gone was another stolen from what they might have had. Another memory that might have been.

Everything inside her screamed to go to him and Maggie finally stopped fighting that urge.

Stepping down from the boardwalk, she moved through the crowd, her gaze fixed on Gabe. Around her, people talked and laughed, but she heard only the voice in her head telling her to claim the happiness she could, *while* she could.

And then he was there, in front of her, just a touch away.

"Hello, Maggie."

"Gabe." She smiled and waved one hand to indicate the crowd. "You did it. You said you'd bring the customers to us and you did."

"No," he said with a sad smile. "I may have brought them out onto the street, but they stayed because of you." He looked at the people nearby then shifted his gaze back to her. "You're one of them. A part of this town. You always were, though you didn't know it."

"Maybe," she said. "And maybe you had more to do with this than you're willing to admit. Maybe you're just as much a part of this place as I am."

He sighed and shoved his hands into his pockets. "I'm not a part of anything, Maggie. It's just me. Always has been."

Lamplit shadows fluttered across his face, illuminating and then hiding the sadness in his eyes. But Maggie saw it. Felt it. And reacted.

Reaching out, she laid one hand on his arm. His eyes closed briefly at her touch and she knew he felt the magic between them as strongly as she did.

"You're a part of me," she told him softly. "And a part of Jake. You always will be, whether you're here or not."

He actually winced. "Maggie, don't make this harder."

"Nothing could make it harder, Gabe," she said and swallowed back a knot of pain lodged in her throat. "If you leave—"

"*When* I leave . . ."

She nodded and lifted her chin. "Fine. When you leave, you'll be missed. Desperately."

"Maggie," he said, then sighed and stopped.

"But I'll survive and so will Jake."

"I know that."

She smiled at him and knew it was a sad smile, still, it was the best she could manage under the circumstances. One corner of his mouth lifted in a vague shadow of the cocky grin that had first captured her heart.

Absently, Maggie noted that the piano had gone si-

lent. After a moment, the fiddler ended the quiet by drifting into a haunting melody. The soft, sorrowful strains
of "Barbara Allen" lifted into the night and its tale of
love and loss seeped into Maggie's bones until she
thought she might weep for the pain.

But hadn't she already decided that there would be
no more tears until after Gabe had left her? Firmly re-
solving to snatch what happiness she could, Maggie
stepped up closer to him and held out her arms. "Dance
with me?"

His features twisted briefly into a mask of pain before
he reined in his emotions and took her into the circle of
his arms. He looked down into her eyes and Maggie
ordered her mind to etch this moment on her memory.

Years from now, she wanted to be able to look back
at this night and feel the strength of his arm around her
waist, the firm yet gentle way he held her hand, the shine
in his eyes as he stared into hers. She wanted nothing
lost.

And then he began to move, but instead of guiding
her into the circle of dancers, he instead shifted them
farther into the shadows. There, they danced alone, as if
the fiddle played only for them. The hum of conversation
and laughter faded away. The lamplight strained to reach
them and failed and still they danced. Gently swaying,
whirling in slow, lazy circles. His touch at her back. Her
hand in his.

Maggie closed her eyes, tipped her head back and
trusted in Gabe to keep them safe in their shadowy
world. She could have gone on forever in silence, but
when he spoke, she opened her eyes and looked up at
him.

"Nothing's changed, Maggie."

"Everything's changed," she said, shaking her head.

"How?"

"I won't try to make you stay."

"And you'll marry me?"

"No," she said gently and watched that word hit its mark on his heart. In an effort to ease the pain creeping up on both of them, she laid her head on his chest and whispered, "I won't marry you, but I will love you."

He stiffened slightly and she heard his heartbeat stagger.

"Maggie," he said on a groan, "I can't let you."

"You can't stop me." She lifted her head again and looked up into his eyes.

"I won't risk leaving you with another child to raise alone."

"But—"

"No." He shook his head slowly and gave her a smile that spoke more of hurt than happiness. "I'm already halfway to Hell. I won't buy myself a bigger share of the flames at your expense."

"Don't deny us the little time we have left," she said.

"Then marry me."

Marry him and have him in her bed again. Know the rush of pleasure, the tingle of anticipation. The glory of his mouth and hands on her body. Tempting. So tempting. Yet even as she considered it, she knew she wouldn't do it.

"I can't marry a man I know is going to leave me," she said softly. "I won't be the deserted wife again."

He smiled grimly and executed a slow turn, keeping her tight against him. "That's it, then."

She laid her head on his chest again, and listened to

the solid, comforting beat of his heart beneath her ear. "You're a stubborn man."

"That's been said before."

"I'm stubborn too," she pointed out.

"I've noticed."

She tipped her head back far enough to be able to plant a quick, soft kiss to the base of his throat. He shivered. "Think you can resist me?" she asked.

He swallowed heavily. "I'm gonna try."

"I'm going to be trying too," she said, feeling it only fair to warn him.

He sighed. "I know." His arm tightened even further around her waist and he stepped into a series of turns, their bodies moving together as if made to fit one against the other. And as the fiddle music soared to a heart-wrenching end, she thought she heard him murmur, "Ah, Maggie . . . what a time we would have had together . . ."

When the last of the revelers had stumbled home to their beds, Gabe took a slow look around at the town he'd grown so fond of. Hard to believe that in just a couple of weeks, he'd be leaving it and the world behind. He pulled in a deep breath and cast a furtive glance up at Maggie's darkened windows. He yearned to go inside, climb those stairs, and slip into her bed and her body. To find the warmth that only she could offer him. To bask in the love she wanted to give.

But he couldn't. Because the dead have no place with the living.

Shifting his gaze from the one place he wanted to be, Gabe shoved both hands into his pockets and set off down Main Street, headed for the dark beyond. For the first time since dying at the end of a rope, he was going to seek out the Devil who'd claimed him—and try to strike a new bargain.

Maggie slipped out of the shadows and quietly followed him. Hugging her worn green shawl tightly around her, she stepped softly, not wanting to make any sound that might alert him to her presence.

Mooncast shadows seemed to reach for her, stretching out long, black fingers as if trying to keep her from him. But she wouldn't be stopped. She wanted to know what he was up to. Who he was meeting. If it was the friend he claimed to be waiting for, she'd intervene, try to make him stay here. With her.

And if he hadn't lied? If there was a devil waiting in the darkness? Her fingers tightened in the wool threads and a shiver of apprehension rippled along her spine at the thought before she stiffened her spine and lifted her chin defiantly. If there *was* a devil out there somewhere, then he'd better be set for the fight of his life. Because Maggie was ready to charge Hell itself if she had to.

Jake crouched low as his mother hurried down the street, following after Gabe. He'd watched them dancing and even seen them kiss once when they thought nobody was looking. It had felt . . . strange, watching Gabe kiss his mom. But it was a good kind of feeling too.

His friend Mickey told him that his ma and pa kissed all the time and how it was kind of disgusting. But Jake thought it would be a fine thing to have Gabe stay with them forever and kiss his ma and take him fishing sometimes. He'd figured on following Gabe himself and telling him to marry his mom, but then she'd shown up and now everything was a mess.

He looked around to make sure there was no one to see, then he sneaked out of the alley and started after his mother, who was following the man Jake had to talk to. But he sure wished it wasn't so dark.

Gabe didn't stop until he was well outside of town. When he was sure he was alone, he turned in a slow circle, his gaze sweeping the distant, shadowed treeline, and called out, "All right, Devil, you and me need to talk."

Seconds passed and dripped into minutes. The only sound was the hollow sigh of the wind in the grass. And still he waited. Sure, now when he wanted the demon to show up, he couldn't be found. Overhead, threads of clouds chased each other across the face of the moon. From somewhere in the distance, an owl hooted and the bushes close by rustled with the passage of a night creature.

Loneliness was almost a taste in the air.

"What do you want?"

Gabe jumped and spun around. The gunfighter stood staring at him, a sardonic smile on his face. "I *want* to not die of a heart attack in this damned meadow," Gabe snapped as his heartbeat slowly returned to normal.

"You've got your wish already. Remember that noose?"

"Yeah," he said and wished to hell the Devil could go the length of one conversation without bringing up that rope.

"I think I can manage," he said, plucking the stray thought from Gabe's mind.

A spurt of irritation swept through him but he tamped it down again. Couldn't afford to get testy with the Devil just now. "I want to talk to you."

"So I gathered," he said and crossed his arms over his chest. "About what?"

Gabe rubbed the back of his neck and glanced at the Devil. "About making a new deal."

Twin black eyebrows lifted. "I like the deal we have. You bring your 'friend' to this meadow, on the night of the full moon."

A cold wind raced across the meadow, wrapped itself around Gabe briefly, then ran on, down the lane and into the town where it would rattle shutters and shake windowpanes.

The full moon. It was too soon. The two months he'd been given had gone by too fast.

"I want more time," he blurted.

"Not surprising," the Devil commented.

He'd known it wouldn't do any good and still he'd had to try.

"It's the woman, isn't it?"

Gabe's gaze snapped to the Devil.

"It is," the gunfighter said and smiled broadly as he walked a slow circle around Gabe. "You're in *love*."

"I told you before, leave her out of this."

"I have no interest in her," the Devil said. "She has no part in our bargain."

"That's where you're both wrong." Maggie spoke up and had both Gabe and the Devil turning to stare openmouthed at her as she marched up to join them.

"Go home, Maggie," Gabe told her and stepped between her and the demon.

"I will not," she said and darted around him to face the gunfighter down. She'd watched that man appear out of nowhere and still she could hardly believe it. Now, as she looked into the gunfighter's pale blue eyes, she tried to find a spark of kindness there, but all she saw was irritation.

"You can't have him," she said, forcing a calm she didn't feel into her voice.

"Ah, but I can."

"Maggie, damn it." Gabe grabbed her arm and tugged her back from the other man.

But she yanked free and went right on talking. "You like deals, I'll offer you a new one."

The gunfighter looked suddenly wary. He straightened up and gave a quick glance around the empty meadow as if expecting to see someone else appear out of the darkness. "No more deals."

"Maggie, I swear, if you don't shut up and go back home I'll—"

"You'll what?" she snapped, turning on him with a vengeance. "*Leave* me? You're already planning to, remember?"

"Don't you be a damn fool, woman," he shot back. "You have a son to take care of. He needs you. You can't do this. I won't let you do it."

"He needs you too, don't you see that yet?" She stared up at him, desperate to make him understand. Gabe grabbed her and, even in this tense moment, she relished the warm strength of his hands on her. She would fight to keep him here. Where he belonged. With her.

Even if it meant facing down Satan himself.

She pulled free of him and whirled around to once again confront the man in black.

But he was gone.

She turned frantically, searching the shadows for him, but there was simply no sign of him anywhere. "Blast and damn, he's gone."

"Thank God!" Gabe shouted, torn between hugging her and throttling her. He'd never been terrified and touched at the same time before. Figured it would be Maggie to manage showering those opposing emotions on him all at once. And as much as it meant to him that she'd been willing to knock down the gates of Hell in his name, he was furious that she'd endanger herself . . . her soul . . . like that.

"Where did he go?" she demanded.

"Back to Hell I suppose," he snapped.

Maggie threw him a wild look. "Well, get him back!"

"I can't and wouldn't even if I could," he told her, reaching out to grab hold of her shoulders. "Damn it, Maggie, what were you thinking?"

"I wasn't thinking," she muttered, shaking her head. "When I saw him . . . *appear* out of nothing, I just—"

"Rushed right in?" His grip on her tightened.

"I didn't believe you," she said, staring up at him. "When you told me about this before . . . I didn't believe you. How could I?"

"But you do now."

She threw another searching glance around the meadow before looking at him again. "Yes. But God, I wish you'd been lying."

He let her go, then shoved his hands into his pockets. "So do I."

"A devil. Right here in Regret." She shook her head as if still trying to convince herself of what she'd seen. Then she slapped his arm. "And *you* wouldn't let me talk to him!"

"Are you out of your mind?" he asked, dumbfounded. "You have no business talking to the likes of him."

"And you do?" she countered.

"Damn it, Maggie, what did you think you were doing?" Gabe glared at her as his hands fisted in his pockets.

"Fighting for what I want," she said. "*You* taught me that."

He looked down into her face and saw the wild glint in her eye and, for one brief moment, he wondered if she might not have beaten the Devil at his own game. But that moment was gone in a flash and he knew without a doubt that his soul wasn't worth risking hers over.

"This fight is finished, Maggie. It's done. Bargain sealed. Soul practically delivered." It cost him to say the words aloud, but she needed to hear them. To believe them. So she wouldn't do something stupid when he wasn't around to protect her.

"I won't let you go," she said, her voice low and fervent.

"You can't hold me, darlin'," he whispered and, yanking his hands out of his pockets, pulled her close, wrapping his arms around her. He inhaled the scent of her and told himself to remember it forever. She burrowed in closer and he took some comfort in the fact that she wanted him so much. It had taken him a lifetime, but he'd finally found a home. Love.

And he'd give anything to be able to claim it.

She threaded her arms about his waist and laid her head on his chest. "I don't want to lose you."

He closed his eyes and rested his chin on top of her head. Sighing, he glanced up at the star-strewn sky and silently prayed for her safety. For her happiness. And he hoped that the prayers of a condemned sinner would be heard.

Then he cradled Maggie against him and, for one long moment, in a moonlit field, they were together for a small piece of forever.

Jake hunched his shoulders against the cold and wiped the back of his hand across his face, scrubbing at the tears rolling down his cheeks. He stared at his mother and Gabe, then looked at the spot where the other man had disappeared. That old Devil wasn't gonna take Gabe anywhere, he told himself, scowling furiously. Then he shot a long, angry glare at the heavens before running back to town.

CHAPTER NINETEEN

"Michael, you have to tell your gambler the truth."

"It's not time," the gunfighter argued.

"It's past time," his friend said, shaking his head. "It's bad enough when an angel masquerades as a devil, for pity's sake. But when he stoops to frightening innocent women and children . . ."

"Children?" the gunfighter asked.

"The boy. Jake. He saw you too. He's been praying for Gabe."

"Oh no . . ." This couldn't be good. His superiors wouldn't look kindly on an angel, no matter how well-meaning, if he was upsetting a child. To God, there was nothing so important as a child.

"Oh yes," his friend countered. "He actually said a prayer asking God to, and I quote here, 'Beat up the Devil.' And I have to say, our superiors are not happy that a child is expecting the Almighty to get into a fist-fight with Satan."

Michael frowned thoughtfully and rubbed his head. The boy must have been following his mother. Good heavens, just how many people had been trotting through the darkness tonight, anyway? And why couldn't these mortals stay out of Heavenly business? How had this gotten so out of hand? the would-be gunfighter wondered. It had seemed like such a good idea at the time.

And relatively harmless to all but Gabe Donovan.

Then he remembered the look on Maggie Benson's face and gave silent thanks that he was already long dead and so beyond her reach. He had a feeling that female could be downright dangerous.

"You've been ordered to straighten this out."

Michael looked up guiltily. "I plan to."

"When?"

"Soon."

The other angel sighed. "Michael, your plan didn't work. Admit it."

"It is working though," he insisted, remembering how Maggie had flown to Gabe's defense. Surely his superiors could see that if a good, decent woman was willing to fight for his soul, then Gabe was worth saving.

"It's your wings you're risking on this."

"I know," he said and glanced at his still-wingless shoulders. Two centuries of eternity had passed and still he hadn't earned the wings that would mark him as a full-fledged angel. But if he could save Gabriel, steer him down a path different from the one the gambler had been on, Michael would finally be able to hold his head up around here.

It was worth it, he told himself, not for the first time. Soon enough, things would come to a head and Gabe would make his choice for good or bad.

"I hope you know what you're doing," the angel whispered.

"Me too," Michael said softly, and cast an anxious glance at the world below, locking his gaze on Regret.

* * *

The next week was a hard one.

Gabe and Maggie didn't speak about what had happened in the meadow. Anytime Maggie tried to broach the subject, Gabe walked away. He wouldn't let her get any more deeply involved than she already was. And he was careful to keep a safe distance from her, despite her protests. Maggie was distracted, worried, and even Jake seemed quieter, more pensive. But while the three of them were quietly miserable, the rest of the world kept on turning.

The stage-coach company, impressed with the restaurant and the comments from passengers, increased the number of stops from twice a week to four times. With the extra money, Maggie hired a cook, Annie Taylor, a widow from an outlying farm, who would be starting work next week. Soon, her business would be blossoming beyond anything she had ever hoped for.

She stood at the back of the now empty building, and realized she had everything she'd ever wanted. The tables at the restaurant would always be full and the stage route manager had even suggested she expand to accommodate overnight guests. She was almost through with her painting at the church, and when she was finished, she had half a dozen more projects to take on. Sugar Harmon hadn't spewed venom in days and Maggie finally felt accepted by Regret.

Yet none of it meant a thing because she was losing Gabe.

Pulling in a deep breath, she turned and stepped out onto the boardwalk. The weather matched her mood. They'd left the days of Indian summer behind them and stepped into the middle of fall. Iron-gray clouds covered the sky, spitting an occasional raindrop at the earth below. Wind howled along the street, and everywhere she looked, people were huddled into coats. Maggie shivered, crossed her arms over her chest, and tried to ignore the cold. She had other things to think about.

Staring out at the busy street, she let her mind wander back to the night in the meadow when she'd come face-to-face with a *devil,* of all things. A twinge of fear tugged at her heart. How could they fight Hell itself and hope to win?

Frowning, she shifted her gaze to follow the flow of Saturday shoppers. When she spotted the reverend Thorndyke, though, an idea leapt into mind and she almost laughed at the simplicity of it. Why hadn't she thought of this before? Jumping off the boardwalk, she hitched the hem of her skirt up and, dodging in and out of the crowds milling in the street, raced to catch up with her minister.

"You're really goin' away, aren't ya, Gabe?"

He looked up from Maggie's ledgers into Jake's eyes and wished to hell he could lie. But staring into a gaze so much like Maggie's, he just couldn't. Not anymore.

"Yeah," he said. "I am."

The boy leaned against the doorjamb of Gabe's room and stared at him long and hard for a minute or two. Then he rubbed one hand under his nose, kicked the doorjamb, and said, "But if you go, who'm I s'posed to call pa?"

A groan bubbled up in his chest and he strained to keep it inside. Damn it. Who would have guessed there was even *more* pain headed his way? In his gambling days, Gabe would have bet cold hard cash that he couldn't feel worse than he had a moment ago. Just went to show how much poker sense he'd lost in the last several weeks.

"Jake . . ." He didn't know what to say. If the truth be known, he didn't want the kid calling anyone but him pa. It tore him up inside just thinking about some other man taking his place here, with Jake. With Maggie. Dropping the pencil, he pushed his chair back from the makeshift desk in his room and faced the boy. Nothing he'd ever done in his life was as hard as looking into Jake's wounded, accusing eyes. "I want you to know that if I *could* stay, I would."

"It's 'cause of that devil, ain't it?"

Gabe choked, coughed, and stared at the boy, stunned.

"I saw him with you and mom the other night in the meadow."

Well, perfect. Like mother like son, he thought.

"You shouldn't have been there, Jake." He ran one hand through his hair and dug his fingers into his scalp. Apparently, it was impossible to have a secret around the Benson family. He'd thought himself alone in that meadow, never dreaming that Maggie had followed him. And now he finds out Jake had followed her.

A reluctant smile curved one side of his mouth. They must have made a hell of a sight, their own small parade in the middle of the night. God, but he was going to miss these two.

"I didn't mean to see nothin'," the boy said and came into the room. Perching on the edge of Gabe's narrow bed, he hunched his shoulders, put his clenched hands between his knees, and stared at the floor. "I only was lookin' for you 'cause I wanted to ask you somethin'."

Staring at the kid's bowed head, Gabe sighed, crossed

the room and took a seat beside him. Pointless to get mad now, since the deed was done. Besides, at least now the boy knew that leaving wasn't Gabe's choice.

"All right," he said softly. "What was so important you were running around in the dark to find me?"

Jake shot him a sidelong glance from under a fringe of brown hair. "I saw you and mom kissing at the dance."

Gabe's eyebrows lifted. The kid had had a full night.

"And you didn't like that?" he asked.

"Well, it's kinda disgustin' to be kissin' and such."

Gabe smiled despite the situation. It wouldn't be too many years before Jake changed his mind about kissing. Too damned bad Gabe wouldn't be around to walk him through his first love and first heartbreak.

"But," Jake went on, "I liked seein' it."

"You did?" He smiled and ran one hand over the boy's head.

"Yeah. It felt kinda . . . *right,* you know?"

"Yeah," Gabe admitted sadly. "I know."

"So anyhow," Jake continued after taking a long breath, "I was gonna ask you to marry us. Me and my mom, I mean, so's you could really be my pa and everything. And I wouldn't care if you wanted to kiss her sometimes."

A cold, hard fist squeezed Gabe's heart and wrung it so tightly, tears glimmered at the backs of his eyes and his throat closed up with emotion. "Ah, Jake," he said on a sigh, "there's nothing I'd like better, but—"

"But that ol' Devil won't let you, huh?"

"That's right." Man, Hell couldn't be much worse than this, he told himself.

Then Jake grinned and surprised him again. "Well, don't you worry none, 'cause I fixed it."

A flicker of worry stirred inside him. "Is that right?"

"Yep." A proud smile split his features.

"Well, how'd you do that?"

"I prayed."

Gabe smiled at the boy. He looked so sure of himself. So positive that now the trouble was fixed. Idly, Gabe wondered if he'd ever had that kind of faith. He couldn't even remember a time when he'd believed that a prayer would turn things around. And it was a damn shame to shatter Jake's illusions and disappoint him again.

But it was better than having the child sitting around waiting for a miracle that wasn't going to happen.

"Thank you, Jake," he said and meant every word. "I don't think anybody's ever prayed for me before. But—"

"You'll see," the boy interrupted him and patted Gabe's knee. "God can beat up some old Devil easy. This'll fix everything and you won't have to go no-where."

"Anywhere."

"Anywhere," Jake repeated with a nod.

Draping one arm around the kid's shoulders, Gabe pulled him closer and gave him a hard hug. When the boy's thin arms came around his middle and squeezed back, Gabe's heart twisted just a bit tighter and he actually found himself wishing he could believe in miracles himself.

An hour later, Gabe and Jake sat in the restaurant's empty dining room, sharing a wedge of chocolate cake that had enough frosting on it to almost completely disguise the slight charred flavor.

The front door flew open and crashed against the wall.

They both turned in time to see Maggie rush into the room and slam the door closed behind her. A high flush of color stained her cheeks and, even though her lips looked a little blue from the cold, her eyes were wide and bright with hope.

"Good, you're both here," she said and hurried across the room. Picking up Gabe's cup of coffee, she cradled it between her hands and sighed at the warmth drifting into her bones. "Oh, that feels good."

"Not surprising," Gabe said. "It's freezing outside."

"Yes." She grinned at him, then reached out to ruffle Jake's hair. "Gorgeous, isn't it?"

"Are you feeling all right?" he asked and stood up to take a closer look at her.

She grabbed his hand and set the coffee cup down. Gabe instantly took both of her hands in his and rubbed them, trying to ease away some of the iciness.

"I feel wonderful," she said and gave him a quick, hard kiss.

Not that he minded, but, "Maggie, what's going on?"

"I have a plan," she said proudly.

"A plan?" Jake asked.

"And it'll work too," she said, nodding at her son before turning back to look into Gabe's eyes.

"To beat that Devil?" Jake prompted.

Gabe looked at the two of them. "You knew he knew?"

Maggie nodded, sparing her son a quick glance. Naturally, she hadn't been pleased that he'd followed them out into the night. But she could understand why he'd done it. He'd wanted to keep Gabe with them as much as she did. "He told me."

"Well, I wish somebody had told me," Gabe said.

"That's not the point now," she told him and launched into her story. "I went to see the reverend Thorndyke."

"Yeah?" Gabe looked at her warily.

"And though it took me a while to convince him I was serious . . ." She paused and asked, "Why is it, do you think, that a man who spends his whole life preaching against sin and Hell doesn't want to accept that you've actually seen a devil?"

"I don't know," Gabe muttered. "Maggie, what did you do?"

"I enlisted his help in the fight," she said proudly.

He let her go, stepped back and shook his head. "There is no fight," he said tightly. "I already told you that. The deal is done. There's no getting out of it."

She wouldn't accept that. "If there's a way in, there's a way out," she said flatly.

"Maggie, stop trying. Accept what is and try to live with it. I am."

She stepped in close to him and tilted her head back to look up into his eyes. "You're going to give up that easily?"

A spark of anger lit his eyes and she was pleased to see it.

"It's not easy, believe me," he snapped, then shot a look at Jake and lowered his voice. "Nothing about this is easy. But it's the way it is. And your preacher can't change it."

"It's worth trying," she told him just as hotly.

"Damn it, Maggie . . ."

The front door opened again suddenly, and in a rush

of cold air, a man walked in, dropped his carpetbag, and
yelled, "Hello, everybody!" Then he spotted the other
man and, clearly surprised, asked, "Gabe?"

"Grandpa!" Jake shouted and scurried across the
room.

"Henry?" Gabe asked.

"Daddy!" Maggie exclaimed.

"Daddy?" Gabe echoed in a hollow voice.

The oil lamps Maggie had lit before taking Jake upstairs
to his room flickered crazily in the gloom. Left to themselves, the two men stared at each other. Silence
stretched uncomfortably between them for several
minutes before Gabe finally spoke up.

"You never told me you had a family," he said, staring hard at the portly older man.

"Well . . ." He waved one hand absently. "You know
how it is. A man don't want too many people knowing
his business. Makes for too much trouble."

"Uh-huh." Meaning, someone might know where to
come looking for you if they needed to find you for some
reason, like serving a warrant.

"Ah," Henry said, spotting the leftover dessert. "Cake.
Looks good. Someone else must've made it." He took a
bite, savored it, then wrinkled his brow as he tasted the
tinge of scorched flour. "Nope. I guess my girl's still
burning things, eh?" He chuckled and shook his head
indulgently.

"She's getting better," Gabe muttered, offended for
Maggie's sake. Besides, how could the old coot just
stand there talking pleasantly when he knew damn well

he'd left Gabe to face an angry mob just a few weeks ago?

As if he could read minds as easily as that devil, Henry set the cake down, dusted his palms together, and gave Gabe an apologetic smile. "I'm, uh, sorry about that little ruckus a while back."

"Ruckus?" Gabe repeated incredulously.

"I wanted to get word to you, boy." He paused and shrugged. "Those folks weren't very trusting at all. Started making noises about checking my background, can you believe it?" He shook his head. "It's a sad thing this world is coming to. No trust anymore. Anyway, I had to hightail it out of there quick. Wasn't a way to reach you to warn you off. But anyhow, I'm glad to see you came to no harm."

"No harm, Henry?" All right, there was the anger he thought had gone. Rushing him, filling him like water pouring from a jug.

Henry winced, shot a look at the open doorway behind him, and lifted one finger to his lips. "Ssh. This here's between you and me."

"No harm?" Gabe asked again, ignoring Henry's plea for quiet. "You damned fool, those people *hanged* me!"

Shocked, Henry took a step back and snapped his gaze up and down Gabe before saying, "Well, it looks as though they did a mighty poor job of it."

"Don't you believe it." Gabe tugged at his shirt collar and pulled it down far enough to show the old man the rope scar around his neck.

"Oh my," the other man said, shaking his head. "That looks quite painful."

"Yeah, Henry. It *was*." And suddenly it all came rushing back. The noose tightening. The slow loss of air.

The pain exploding in his head, and then waking up to find himself in a darker version of the real world talking to the demon who wanted to claim his soul.

He fought down the urge to grab Henry Whittaker by the lapels and shake him like a dog would a bone.

"My dear boy," Henry said solemnly, "I can't tell you how sorry I am."

Gabe threw his hands wide and let them fall to his sides again. Shaking his head, he snapped, "Well, Henry, you're going to be a helluvalot sorrier soon."

"Whatever do you mean?"

So Gabe told him. Told him about the Devil and the deal he'd made. And told him that very shortly, the two of them would be sharing a companionable bench in the fires of Hell.

To give him his due, the older man only blanched slightly, swallowed hard, and then sighed. "Well, I can't say as it's a surprise to discover where I'll be spending eternity. Although I had hoped for a few more years, yet."

"Me too," Gabe admitted dryly.

"If it's any comfort," Henry added, clapping Gabe on the shoulder, "I don't blame you a bit for taking that deal. Two more months of life would have been worth just about anything." He eased himself down into a chair. "Have you enjoyed them?"

Sighing, Gabe sat down opposite him. No matter what, it seemed to be impossible to stay mad at Henry. They'd known each other too long. Been through too many scrapes together. Besides, the old thief, despite his . . . *profession*, had a good heart and a friendly nature. And he was Maggie's father.

Bracing his elbows on his knees, Gabe cupped his

head in his hands briefly, then looked up and said, "Yeah. I surely have."

The older man stared at him for a long minute as realization dawned on his features. "Ah," he said on a sigh. "That's how it is, then."

No point in lying about this. "I love her, Henry."

"I can see that, boy." His voice was kind, tinged with sorrow.

"And I'm going to lose her."

"As am I," Henry said.

Gabe looked at him. "I didn't know," he said, "that you were her father when I made that deal."

"I know that."

He didn't get it. He didn't understand. "Henry, don't you see what this means?"

The older man just looked at him blankly.

"Not only am I leaving her, when she might even now be carrying my child, but I'm taking *you* with me." Disgusted, Gabe shook his head again and rubbed the back of his neck. "She'll be alone. Just her and Jake."

"Your *child*?" Henry echoed and even his voice sounded strained.

Gabe glanced at him and saw flames flickering in the old coot's eyes. Maybe he'd said too much. "Now, Henry—"

"You son of a bitch!" Jumping to his feet, he glared down at the younger man and said, "It wasn't enough to haul me off to Hell, you had to dishonor my *daughter*?"

"I told you—" Gabe started to say.

"You're hauling *who* off to Hell?" A woman's outraged voice asked.

Both men turned to stare at Maggie, silhouetted in the open doorway. Not for the first time recently, Gabe didn't have a clue what to say next. But then, apparently, Maggie wasn't going to give him a chance to say anything.

"You're here for my *father*?" she demanded.

"Now, Maggie—"

"Maggie honey," Henry tried to cut in, "this here is between Gabe and me."

She turned on him like a snake.

"As for *you*!"

As any wise man would, he backed up a step.

"*You're* the thief Gabe was sent to collect?"

"Now, 'thief's' a harsh word, Maggie sweetheart."

"That's what your 'business' is? All these years you've been stealing from people?" Maggie marched closer, her gaze locked on the father she felt as though she was seeing clearly for the first time. "Is that how you bought this restaurant for me? With stolen money?"

At that, Henry straightened up and huffed out an indignant breath. "I do not *steal*. I'm not some common hoodlum waving a gun at innocent people and tearing their money from their pockets."

"No," Gabe agreed, crossing his arms over his chest and watching Henry's discomfort with the first real pleasure he'd felt in a week. "You smooth 'em out of it. Before the poor rubes know it, they're broke and you're gone."

Henry shot him a withering glance. "Is it my responsibility to protect people from their greedy natures? Is it my fault that people are willing to put their hard-earned money into foolish schemes in the hopes of becoming wealthy overnight?"

Maggie stared at her parent. "How long has this been going on?" Then she answered her own question before

Henry could open his mouth. "All my life, hasn't it? Did Mother know?"

The old thief cleared his throat. "Of course she knew. We had no secrets."

"I can't believe she never told me," she muttered. "I can't believe I never guessed."

"You're overreacting, my dear," her father soothed.

"Overreacting?" She shook her head. "I don't think so."

"I'm not a bad man, Maggie," he said, holding his hands out, palms up in supplication.

"Then why is there a spot in Hell with your name on it?"

He cringed slightly. "Alas, it seems the requirements for eternal damnation are a tad more stringent than I had supposed."

Gabe snorted a laugh. He had to give it to the old coot. Unrepentant to the last.

Maggie shifted her gaze to him. "And you."

Now it was his turn to back up. God help him, but she was magnificent when she was angry.

"You come into my life, make love to me, make me love you, make my *son* love you, and all the while you're planning on taking my father to Hell?"

"Good point!" Henry crowed, obviously delighted to have Maggie's emotional gun barrel pointing at someone else.

"I told you," Gabe said tightly, "I didn't know he was your father."

"But you knew she wasn't your wife when you bedded her, you dog," Henry accused.

"Yes, but I proposed," Gabe told him.

Henry visibly relaxed. "Ah, that's a relief."

"And I refused," Maggie snapped.

"You *what*?" her father screeched.

Sighing, Maggie said, "Father, why don't you go upstairs and keep Jake company? Gabe and I have to talk."

She looked at him and could see that he was quite obviously torn between remaining and having his say or getting out of harm's way. His sense of self-preservation won out in the end though.

"Fine," he snapped then faced Gabe. "But this isn't finished."

When he was gone, Maggie looked at the man standing just beyond her reach and wondered how she could still love him, knowing that not only was he going to leave her, but take her father with him? She should be furious. She should be outraged. But instead, all she felt was a profound sorrow that seemed to open up a wide, dark hole inside her.

Love apparently was something that defied reason. It simply *was*. And there was nothing she could do to change it . . . even if she wanted to. Which she didn't. Still, there was one question she had to ask.

"Is there anything else I should know?"

"About Henry?" he asked, then shook his head. "No. That's it."

"Not just about my father," she told him quietly. "I meant, is there anything else you have to tell me? Anything at all?"

"Only one thing," he said softly, "no matter what else you believe, believe this. I love you, Maggie. More than I ever thought a man could love anyone."

She sighed and gave him a tired, watery smile before

stepping into his arms and winding her own around his middle. Laying her head on his chest, she listened to the reassuring beat of his heart and whispered, "That's all I need to know."

CHAPTER TWENTY

Gabe stepped back out of her embrace, even though it felt as though he was tearing his own heart out. But he couldn't think with her so close and he had to think. Now more than ever.

He couldn't leave her alone. He simply couldn't. If she was pregnant, she would need her father, at least. And Jake. Jake had to have a man in his life to count on. To depend on. Although the idea of *anyone* depending on Henry was laughable, he was the only one available. Gabe had to find a way out of this mess. A way to save Henry's miserable soul so he'd be around to look after the little family Gabe loved more than life itself.

"Gabe?"

His gaze met hers.

"I can't let you take my father." She sighed and wrapped her arms around her waist. "He might not be perfect, but—"

He smiled sadly. "I'm not going to."

"But your deal—"

Shaking his head, he shoved both hands through his hair, then let them fall to his sides again. "Hell, Maggie. I made that deal out of desperation. I made it before I learned how precious life is." He chuckled to himself. "All life. Even Henry's. I made that deal before I learned how to love. Before I found you." He rubbed the back of his neck, then said quietly, "When it's time, I'll go alone."

She smiled at him then and it broke his heart to realize that he'd go a long, lonely eternity never seeing anything more lovely.

"No you won't," she said.

Frowning, he said, "Maggie, I told you. I won't take Henry."

"I'm not talking about my father. I'm talking about me. When you go to that meeting, I'm going too."

"Like hell you are," he ground out.

"You can't stop me, Gabe," she warned him. "Besides, like I said earlier. I have a plan."

He wasn't sure if that glint in her eyes was a good sign or not. "What kind of plan?"

She stepped up close, wrapped her arms around his neck, and smiled up at him. "Kiss me and maybe I'll tell you."

Hell. Even if the plan stunk, it was worth the price. He bent his head and took her mouth with his, losing himself again in the wonder that was Maggie.

Hours later, Gabe left Maggie sleeping soundly in his bed and walked into the kitchen to find Henry seated at the table, his gaze locked on the bedroom door.

Frowning, he asked the older man, "What is it?"

Henry scowled right back. "What are you doing with my daughter?" he demanded.

"That's none of your business, Henry." Gabe slowly walked to the table, pulled out a chair and dropped into it. Although, if the truth be known, he hadn't been doing a damned thing. Oh, he'd wanted to and Maggie had sure tried to convince him, but in the end, all he'd done was hold her until she fell asleep.

"Damn it all, boy," Henry sputtered, "this isn't right."

"I agree." The only thing right was loving Maggie.

The fight seemed to drain out of the older man and he folded his hands on the table in front of him. Sighing wearily, he shot Gabe a look and asked, "So. This deal you made. How much time do we have?"

"Not much." He grimaced tightly and slumped down lower in the chair, stretching his legs out and crossing his feet at the ankles. Funny how when you knew your life was coming to an end, you noticed the little things about life. Like the curious sensation of goose pimples running along your arms or the way hot air from a still-warm stove felt against the soles of your feet.

"When do we leave?" the other man asked.

Gabe glanced at him and frowned thoughtfully. Strange. It was the only time he'd seen Henry actually *look* his age. Shadows lay beneath his eyes and even his posture bespoke weariness. He was getting too old for the con man game. It was time he settled down here in Regret.

"*We're* not going," Gabe told him. "*I* leave Wednesday night."

Henry's eyes widened. "But the deal was—"

Gabe sat up and shook his head. "Don't worry about that. I'll find a way to talk him out of taking you."

"I don't know," Henry muttered. "Not fair, somehow."

"No," Gabe corrected him flatly. "What's not fair is Maggie losing both of us. So . . ." He braced his elbows on the table. "The deal is, I talk the Devil into waiting for your soul and you stay here. In Regret."

The other man wiped one hand across his mouth, but before he could speak, Gabe continued.

"You take care of them for me, Henry. You be the kind of father she needs. You be *here*." He swallowed hard and kept the words coming despite the fact that he had to squeeze them past the knot in his throat. "You make sure Jake grows up right. Not like you and me."

He nodded solemnly.

"And," Gabe went on, though this was the hardest part of all, "you help Maggie find another man." God, that hurt. Like knives twisting in his guts. "Someone who can love her like she should be loved."

"What about you, Gabe?" he asked. "Do you love my little girl?"

He pushed up from the table and looked down at his old friend. "So much, Henry," he said softly. "So damn much. If I wasn't already dead, this'd be killing me."

And in the shadows, Maggie bit down hard on her bottom lip and leaned against the wall for support. It didn't help, though, and when her legs buckled, she sank to the floor, buried her face against her updrawn knees, and cried as quietly as she could.

The last few days flew past, and before he knew it, Gabe was leaving the restaurant behind and walking slowly toward the meadow and his destiny.

Hands in his pockets, he attempted to enjoy these final moments, concentrating on the feel of the wind in his hair and the sight of a million stars overhead. But no matter how he tried, he couldn't wipe away the images of those he was leaving behind forever.

Dolly, whose warm smile had welcomed him from

the start. The little reverend who'd somehow gotten him into a church again. Even Sugar Harmon, who had, the last few days, been downright . . . friendly. Bass, the deaf barber, Deke Conroy, Woods Harper . . . all the people he'd come to know and care for.

But especially three in particular.

Maggie, who'd refused to say goodbye because she was still furious that he'd dismissed her plan. She'd run off into the night without so much as a farewell glance. Henry, shamefacedly ducking his head and mumbling, "Good luck." And Jake, bravely trying to stem back tears.

Damn. Gabe kicked at a rock in the road and heard it rattle off into the bushes. How could one man find so much to love in a few short weeks only to lose it all in one night?

Tilting his head back, he shot a long look at the stars and whatever lay beyond. "Take care of her, all right?" he whispered and realized that he was actually *praying*. Again. He only hoped someone was listening.

Maggie flapped her arms and walked in circles, trying to keep warm. But the coat she wore protected her only from the chilling wind. It was a deeper cold that had her trembling.

The rustling thud of running footsteps sounded out from behind her and she turned to watch her father hurry across the meadow. When he reached her side, Henry stopped, bent over, and braced his hands on his knees. Gulping in air like a beached trout. Finally, though, he looked up and asked, "Is he here yet?"

"I don't know," Maggie said, sweeping her gaze

across the open ground surrounding her, looking for the Devil dressed like a gunfighter. "Maybe he won't be visible until Gabe gets here."

Still out of breath, Henry puffed, "Well, that won't be long. Only reason I beat him here is he took the road and I came across the fields." He stopped and frowned. "Did you know Mick Samson had a new bull?"

"Yes," she murmured, still looking for that elusive Devil.

"Well, you might have told *me*." Henry clapped one hand to his chest. "Like to stop my heart seeing that snorting monster comin' out of the dark pasture after me."

Any other time she might have smiled at the image of her round-bellied father outrunning a young bull, but not tonight.

"I told him, Mom," Jake called out as he, too, entered the meadow and ran straight at his mother. "He said he'd be right along."

"He who? Who the hell else is coming?" Henry demanded.

"That's what I'd like to know," Gabe said and all three of them spun around to face him. "What's goin' on here?"

"My plan," Maggie said and lifted her chin defiantly, prepared to fight whoever she had to, even Gabe, if need must, to win this battle.

"Damn it, Maggie," he shouted.

"Don't you curse at my girl," Henry yelled.

"Hello, Gabe," Jake called, "are you surprised?"

"Yes," he said and, despite the situation, spared the boy a smile.

"Jake," Maggie said, keeping a wary eye on Gabe, "you'd better go on home now."

"Aw, Mom . . ."

"And take your mother with you," Gabe told him.

She opened her mouth to argue, but was distracted by a sudden twist of shadow that leaped into life between them. The full moon shone brightly down on the meadow, bathing even this splotch of unearthly darkness in a strange silvery light. As she watched, openmouthed, those shadows writhed and shifted until, at last, the man in black stood before them, just as she remembered him.

A spiral of fear unwound in the pit of her stomach, but she fought it into submission. She wouldn't let her own fears defeat her before she'd had a chance to fight for the man she loved.

The gunfighter's gaze swept the little group before landing squarely on Gabe. "What is going on here?"

He flashed a look at Maggie and she saw he was determined to quash her attempts at rescue. "Doesn't matter. Let's be on our way, huh?"

"Oh no," she said quickly and stepped up beside Gabe to glare at the Devil. "I won't let you have him."

"She's right," Henry said. "You take me, but you leave him be."

"You stay out of this, old man," Gabe warned him.

"Old?" Outraged, Henry snarled, "Who're you callin' old?"

Gabe sighed. "You're her father. She needs you."

"You have to marry her," Henry said. "You owe her that, by thunder."

"He doesn't owe me anything, Daddy." Maggie spoke up in her own defense.

"You stay out of this," Gabe warned her. "This is between me and your father."

"Don't you tell me what to do," she snapped.

The gunfighter looked from one to the other of them, opening and closing his mouth as he fought to get a word out. Then Maggie turned on him and she thought she saw him back up a little. But she must have been wrong about that.

"You leave both of them alone," Maggie told him, "you can take me . . . well, after I get Jake raised. I'll go with you then if you leave Gabe here with me now."

Michael sighed.

"Oh, no you don't," Gabe said, stepping in between the gunfighter and Maggie. "You try to take her off to Hell, and I swear to you I'll find some way to make you regret it."

"I already regret it," the gunfighter mumbled, but no one was listening. Forget about getting his wings. He'd be lucky if someone didn't put a new lock on the Heavenly Gates specifically designed to keep him out.

Closing his eyes briefly, he realized that if he could get a headache, he'd be getting one now. Looking from one person to the next, he saw that they were all so busy trying to sacrifice themselves for the others' sake, no one was listening to *him*. Though that should make him happy, at the moment, he only wanted to conclude their business and get back to Heaven, where things made sense. Knowing there was only one sure way to capture their attention, the gunfighter spun himself in a tight, spiraling circle. In a swirl of bright color and glorious sound, he transformed himself into his actual appearance.

And all of them blessedly shut up.

But before Michael could take advantage of the silence, a short blast of hot air rushed at them all from every direction at once. As though the flames of an invisible fire had been stoked, heat filled the meadow as completely as though it were the hottest of summer days rather than a moonlit autumn night.

The small hairs at the back of Gabe's neck lifted as a deep, reddish glow pulsed weirdly directly in front of him.

"Gabe?" Maggie whispered.

"Shh . . ." he coaxed, every nerve alert to the sense of impending danger growing within him.

"Oh dear," Michael muttered.

The pulse quickened, the red light brightened, and the air around them became almost too hot to breathe. Gabe tossed a quick look at the gunfighter, who looked as worried as Gabe felt.

In the next instant, the light faded and a tall, dark man stepped from its center. His night-black gaze swept across the small knot of people.

"Who are you?" Gabe demanded.

Those black eyes settled on him. "I am who that one," he said, jerking a nod at the gunfighter, "pretends to be."

Michael groaned.

Shifting his gaze between the two otherworldly beings, Gabe asked, "Just what the hell is going on here?"

"This is not Hell's business," Michael said with a shake of his haloed head, "but Heaven's."

"So you're not from . . ." Gabe pointed at the ground.

"No," Michael told him.

"But I am," the new man said, stepping in closer to Gabe. "And I've come for what's mine."

"What's happening?" Maggie asked and heard the fear quivering in her voice.

"I wish I knew," Gabe muttered.

"It's very simple really," the dark man said, fixing his gaze on Gabe. "When a man agrees to give his soul to me, I take it."

"You can't," Michael said.

"A deal was made," the Devil told him. "A bargain struck."

"With Heaven, not Hell."

Confusion outpacing any fear he was feeling, Gabe shot Michael a look. "So if you're an angel, why didn't you say so when I died?"

Michael spared him a brief smile, but never actually took his eyes off the enemy. "You all see what you expect to see when you die, Gabriel. You never believed in God, but you certainly believed in Hell."

"With good reason," the Devil added.

"This was all a trick, then?" Gabe asked and his voice was laced with a growing fury.

"Not a trick," Michael said, "a lesson. A learning time for you."

Anger sputtered in his gut. "What the hell does *that* mean?"

"You were a man on the edge of life, Gabriel. You might have gone either way—eternal reward or damnation."

Disgusted, Gabe clenched his jaw. "Then you never meant to take me anywhere?"

"You mean he can stay?" Maggie asked.

"Of course he can stay," Michael said, sparing Gabe a quick look. "If you had been selfless enough to turn down the 'Devil's' offer in the first place, none of this would have been necessary."

"But he didn't turn it down." The Devil·spoke up and moved in closer to Gabe. "He accepted the deal and promised his soul to me. And I'm here to collect it."

Michael moved in, too, and neither of them noticed Gabe shoving Maggie back and out of the way. Literally trapped between Heaven and Hell, he didn't want to take a chance on her being caught in the crossfire.

The night air shimmered with an almost electrical force. Gabe stood at the edge of eternity, waiting for one last, final push into oblivion. Hard to believe that if the true Devil hadn't shown up, then all would be well now. He'd be going home. With Maggie. Instead, he hadn't even been able to enjoy that one bright moment of hope.

Now, he was right back where he'd started. Heart aching, throat tight, he mentally said goodbye to all that he'd come to love and cherish. There was no way out of this that he could see. In another minute or two, he'd be nothing more than a memory.

"Do something," Maggie cried, and he wasn't sure who she was yelling at.

"Step aside, angel," the Devil warned and narrowed his black gaze. "You know you're not powerful enough to test me."

"Perhaps not," Michael admitted.

"You're giving up?" Maggie said, clearly astonished that good would so easily surrender to evil.

"Maggie," Gabe said softly, his gaze locked on the Devil. "Stay back. I don't want you hurt when he takes me."

"He's not taking you," Michael assured him, then shouted "Raphael!" and lifted his gaze Heavenward.

Instantly, light blossomed in the darkness. The full moon's pale glow was lost in the brilliant splash of golden illumination that had the Devil covering his eyes and hunching as if in pain.

Michael gave a relieved sigh and smiled.

Gabe shielded his eyes with his right hand and curved his left arm around Maggie's waist as she stepped up beside him. He wasn't sure who was behind this light, but anything that had the Devil tucking his tail in was all right by him.

"What's happening now?" she asked.

"Damned if I know," he answered. Jake came up behind him. He felt the boy's weight lean against his leg and he dropped one hand to his shoulder. As if from a great distance, Gabe heard Henry muttering something about mending his ways.

A deep voice filtered through the light and warned the Devil sternly, "There is no place for you here."

The dark man, still cowering from the light, protested, "I was promised a soul."

"You were promised nothing," that voice said, disgust evident in its tone. "Leave this place. Go back where you belong."

"A deal's a deal," the Devil argued.

Gabe sucked in a breath as he realized how often he'd said those very same words himself over the years. So maybe the angel had had a point after all, he thought. He *had* been a man on the edge. But as he saw it, he still was.

The demon's howl of outrage rose up, sending a chill along Gabe's spine. He tightened his hold on Maggie and Jake, and when the screeching abruptly ended, he felt their relief as completely as his own.

The Devil was gone as if he'd never been.

And as the brilliant splash of light slowly faded, the voice said softly, "Finish this, Michael, we'll speak about it later."

"Yes, Raphael," Michael said, nodding his head glumly. "I understand."

Gabe looked at the angel. "Who was that?"

"My superior."

"In trouble, are you?" Maggie asked.

"Apparently."

"Good," she snapped and Gabe smothered a smile. "You should be ashamed, an angel pretending to be a devil."

Michael straightened up and lifted his chin bravely. Dismissing Maggie with a single glance, he shifted his gaze to Gabe. "Your lesson has ended, Gabriel. It's obvious to us that you've finally learned the most important lesson in life."

Maggie took hold of Gabe's arm tightly, just in case this was another trick. Jake moved out from behind Gabe to stand in front of him protectively. "You leave my pa alone," he demanded.

"I intend to," the angel assured the boy and Jake looked over his shoulder to flash Gabe a grin.

Michael smiled at the three of them. "You had to find out, Gabriel, that giving to others, being more concerned for someone else's welfare than your own, is what makes life worth living. When all is said and done, love is the greatest gift. You had to learn that."

Gabe's throat tightened as he glanced at Jake's defensive posture, then pulled Maggie in closer. Whatever misery he'd experienced, thinking himself damned, it had been worth it to find her and what they'd discovered together.

"Now what?" he managed to ask.

"Now," the angel said with feeling, "you should all go back to your lives and leave me in peace." Lowering his voice, he muttered, "It's going to take at least a hundred years to recover from this experience."

"Out Satan!" a man yelled and everyone turned to watch Reverend Thorndyke charging the meadow, waving his Bible high over his head.

"Oh damnation," Maggie murmured. "I'd forgotten I sent Jake to fetch him."

"Good heavens," Michael said, horrified.

"Tempt not the Godly. Return to the darkness from which you came," the preacher kept shouting in a tone designed to terrify any self-respecting demon.

"He's got quite a voice on him, hasn't he?" Henry mused as he strolled up to stand beside his family.

"What's under your dress?" Jake asked the angel as he stared at the flowing, silvery robe.

Michael twitched the folds of his robe. "It's not a dress!"

"Lord," the preacher bellowed, "I call on you to smite Thine enemies . . ."

Michael cringed at the humiliation of being expelled by a minister. And grumbling, "Oh, for heaven's sake!," he disappeared.

Reverend Thorndyke kept up his preaching for several minutes on the off chance some other demon was lurking nearby. Henry and Jake sat down to enjoy the sermon and Gabe and Maggie moved off into the shadows.

"I can't believe it's over," she said, staring up into

his eyes and knowing that she'd never tire of the view.

"Me either," he said and lifted one hand to smooth her hair back from her face. "I never wanted to leave you, Maggie."

"I know," she said and caught his hand with hers, planting a quick kiss on his palm before letting him go only long enough to wrap her arms around his neck.

"That angel was right, you know," he said as he pulled her in tightly against him. "I never believed in Heaven." Looking down into her eyes, he added, "Until I met you."

Maggie smiled through her tears. "I love you so much."

"I love you too, Maggie," he said, awed by the rush of feeling surging through him. He'd never expected to find such a treasure, and now that he'd been given the chance to enjoy it, he didn't want to waste a minute of it. Gabe wanted to spend the next forty or fifty years basking in the love he'd found with this woman. In the family they would build together.

"Marry me, Maggie," he whispered.

"Is tomorrow soon enough?" she asked, going up on her toes and tilting her head back to look up at him.

He shook his head and shot a quick look at the reverend Thorndyke. "Not nearly soon enough. What do you say we ask the preacher to do the deed as soon as he's finished banishing demons?"

She smiled at him and nodded. "That sounds perfect," she said. "What better place to start our lives together than in the meadow where we were given a second chance?"

His arms came around her even tighter. Bending his head, he looked his fill of her, still hardly daring to believe she was his. "I swear to you, I will love you forever."

"It's a deal," she said softly.

In the lush silver light of the full moon, Gabe kissed her, sealing this new bargain with the promise of an eternity's worth of love.

And somewhere behind the clouds, Michael received not only his wings, but a new assignment. Guardian angel to one of the twins Sugar Harmon would be giving birth to next spring. And even having to go back to Regret didn't take the pleasure out of those hard-won wings.

Besides, he told himself, it might have been worse. He could have been put in charge of Gabe and Maggie's new daughter. By all reports, she was going to be as difficult as her mother.

KATHLEEN KANE

"[HAS] REMARKABLE TALENT FOR UNUSUAL,
POIGNANT PLOTS AND CAPTIVATING
CHARACTERS."

—Publishers Weekly

The Soul Collector
A spirit whose job it was to usher souls into the afterlife, Zach had angered the powers that be. Sent to Earth to live as a human for a month, Zach never expected the beautiful Rebecca to ignite in him such earthly emotions.

This Time for Keeps
After eight disastrous lives, Tracy Hill is determined to get it right. But Heaven's "Resettlement Committee" has other plans—to send her to a 19th century cattle ranch, where a rugged cowboy makes her wonder if the ninth time is finally the charm.

Still Close to Heaven
No man stood a ghost of a chance in Rachel Morgan's heart, for the man she loved was an angel who she hadn't seen in fifteen years. Jackson Tate has one more chance at heaven—if he finds a good husband for Rachel...and makes her forget a love that he himself still holds dear.

AVAILABLE WHEREVER BOOKS ARE SOLD
FROM ST. MARTIN'S PAPERBACKS